"You know why I'm here."

Tilly gulped and stood, watching the duke with a mixture of defiance and a wholly feminine appreciation.

"You advised my secretary to fix herself up, then told her to divulge certain tender feelings she's harbored for me—"

"Feelings that I'm at a complete loss to understand!" Tilly said.

"Feelings that I could not return—"

"Big surprise!"

"Distressing Miss Darling so much she chose to resign—"

"More power to her!"

Tilly realized they were both shouting. They were nearly nose-to-nose, breathing hard and flushed in the face.

"You will take her place as my secretary." The duke smiled devilishly.

"No way. Forget it. I don't have to do it."

The duke shrugged. "But you do have to. You must replace her in every way." He smiled again. "With the exception of falling in love with me." He tilted her chin with his forefinger and ended in a husky drawl, "Unless you can't help yourself..."

Dear Reader,

The first romance I fell in love with was
Pride and Prejudice, a novel chosen from a list of
required reading in my high school sophomore
English class. The elegant, honorable Mr. Darcy
became thereafter my ideal of manhood. It took a
little bit of work by the feisty heroine to get to the
heart of the hero—hidden under a veneer of pride
and a lifetime of traditional thinking—but it was well
worth the effort.

In *Sign Me, Speechless in Seattle*, I offer just such
another hero and heroine, each from vastly different
worlds and engaged in a battle of wits and wills, but
made for each other. I hope you'll enjoy this playful
mating of opposites as Tilly and Julian, the Duke of
Chesterfield, find themselves accidentally falling
in love.

Warm wishes,

Emily Dalton

Sign Me, Speechless In Seattle

EMILY DALTON

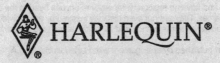

HARLEQUIN®

TORONTO • NEW YORK • LONDON
AMSTERDAM • PARIS • SYDNEY • HAMBURG
STOCKHOLM • ATHENS • TOKYO • MILAN • MADRID
PRAGUE • WARSAW • BUDAPEST • AUCKLAND

To Danilyn,
Lisa's miracle, a heaven-sent cuddly bundle
to pass around at Critique Session.
Thank you for letting me be your honorary aunt,
and for giving this mother of boys an excuse
to buy pink ribbons and lace petticoats.

ISBN 0-373-16750-4

SIGN ME, SPEECHLESS IN SEATTLE

Copyright © 1998 by Danice Jo Allen.

Chapter One

Tilly leaned back in her chair and stared at the computer screen, rubbing the back of her neck. After crafting an inspired sentence advising Mr. Phelps, a diesel mechanic in Fargo, to "quit foolin' around with the butcher's wife before he found himself sliced, diced, wrapped in white paper and sold over the counter as Tuesday's special," her mind had gone completely blank. She knew she had more to say; she just couldn't remember it. She'd been hard at work in front of her computer screen since six that morning and she was running out of steam.

"I need caffeine," she muttered, peering through the blinds that covered the glass walls of her office into the maze of cubicles belonging to junior reporters, secretaries and the various staff necessary to the running of the *Seattle Globe*. "And I need it bad. Where the heck is Amy?"

Tilly stood up and stretched, glad it was dress-down Friday so she could wear jeans and an oversize sweater. She wouldn't even have to change when she got home, just sack out on the couch with her cat, Rebound, and watch the Sonics play the Jazz. But not until she got this "Ask Aunt Tilly" column finished, and for that she needed what Seattle was most famous for—coffee, and plenty of it.

Hitting the key to save her document, Tilly headed for the door. Amy had left her office twenty minutes ago, promising to return pronto with a double mocha latte and a sesame bagel with honey-walnut cream cheese. But somewhere along the way she'd apparently been waylaid. Amy, serving as office gofer till she could work her way into a layout job, was much in demand.

Tilly had started out at the newspaper in much the same humble position as the one Amy held, so she understood and sympathized when the poor girl couldn't always meet everyone's demands in a timely manner. Sometimes, like now, Tilly had to search her out and save her from some other "urgent" errand she'd been coerced into before she finished the errand she'd already undertaken.

"John, have you seen Amy?" she asked, sticking her head into the first cubicle she came to.

John stopped typing and looked up briefly from his computer. "Check Harrison's office. There's a gaggle of women around the TV set."

Tilly raised her brows. "Late-breaking story?"

John's fingers were already flying over the keyboard. He spared her one more rueful glance. "Judging by the subject, I'd say it was more like a heartbreaking story...as in *female* hearts."

Observing John's totally engrossed expression as he turned back to the computer, Tilly knew that an attempt at further questioning would be futile. She sighed and headed for the office of the editor in chief. Harrison Gray had left early for the day—which must account for the confiscation of his office for TV viewing. Since most Fridays everyone simply wanted to get out of there as early as possible to beat the weekend traffic, and it was already four-thirty, Tilly couldn't imagine what could account for this mass female draw to the boob tube. Brad Pitt on *Oprah?*

Sure enough, when Tilly entered Harrison's spacious office, she found it packed with female employees, all of them gazing raptly at the large television set that hung from the ceiling. Clutching Tilly's cooling latte and bagel, Amy was smack-dab in the middle of them.

"What's going on?" Tilly inquired, only to be immediately and collectively shushed.

Amused and somewhat intrigued, she crept to the back of the room, taking care not to block anyone's view for more than a second. Leaning against the wall next to Kate, the *Globe*'s veteran society columnist, she looked at the TV screen to see what was so engrossing. She saw nothing more promising than a local reporter outside the downtown library, standing under a fir tree that still dripped from Seattle's latest May storm.

"What's the deal?" Tilly whispered in Kate's ear. "Another White House scandal?"

"Nothing so mundane," Kate whispered back in her characteristic wry tone. "The duke of Chesterfield is about to make a postlecture appearance."

"The duke of *who?*"

Kate chuckled. "Where have you been, Tilly? Julian Rothwell, the duke of Chesterfield, is the talk of the town."

Tilly wrinkled her nose. "An English duke the talk of Seattle during the NBA playoffs? I don't believe it."

"Believe it."

"Since when?"

"He arrived Wednesday—along with a collection of Roman artifacts that were dug up on his estate in Dorset. You know, marble heads, coins, pottery and such. Seattle's the last stop on his stateside tour. He lectures on ancient Roman history and—"

"Look! There he is! There he is! And he's going to *speak!*" Amy exclaimed.

Along with everyone else, Tilly looked. Suddenly she understood the fascinated stares of the entire office. This duke was no balding potentate with big ears and an odd twitch when he spoke. No, indeed. This duke actually *looked* like royalty.

The kind of royalty a little girl dreamed about.

The kind of tall, handsome hero who twirled his chosen one around the candlelit ballroom as she swooned with delight, even while her glass slippers pinched her toes.

"Isn't he gorgeous?" one of the ladies sighed.

Gorgeous was an understatement, Tilly admitted. Dressed in a classic trench coat, a white shirt and a tie in muted tones showing between the lapels, he towered over the obviously agog reporter. He had to be at least six-three or -four. His hair was blond and swept back from a high and noble brow. His eyebrows had an aristocratic arch, and his perfectly molded lips had just the slightest curl of superiority.

And his eyes...they were as blue as an English lake.

Tilly narrowed her eyes, studying him. Were English lakes as cold as they were blue? she wondered. Because there was a certain glimmer in the duke's startling cerulean gaze that made her want to reach for the thermostat dial and crank it up a notch or two.

As soon as the duke of Chesterfield started speaking, Tilly's suspicions seemed to be confirmed. Although his voice was cultured and attractively deep timbred, his words intelligent and informed, the duke's tone and manner were reserved, aloof... haughty. Yeah, *haughty* described him best. In other words—in the plain and simple words Aunt Tilly would use in her advice column—the duke was "too big for his britches."

"Well, I'd better get back to my office," Tilly said finally. "I have work to do."

"Not your cup of tea?" Kate teased.

Tilly shook her head. "Oh, he's handsome, all right, and I can see why everyone's drooling over him. But he looks to me like he's got about as much genuine warmth in him as one of those marble heads dug up on his estate."

"He does come across rather stiff and dignified," Kate admitted, then flashed a saucy grin. "But, an icy facade sometimes hides a sizzling center."

"Or just more ice," Tilly countered playfully. "See ya, Kate."

Tilly made her way through the crowd to Amy, gently plucked the latte and bagel out of the girl's unresisting hands as she continued to stare adoringly at the TV screen, then went back to her office, shutting the door firmly behind her. She had a column to finish and no time for gawking at dukes, no matter how outrageously handsome this particular peer of the realm happened to be.

Just the thought of those striking blue eyes made Tilly shiver again.... She quickly drank half her cooling latte, then turned her attention back to Mr. Phelps in Fargo and his ill-fated infatuation with the butcher's wife.

An hour later, as Tilly was critically reading over a hard copy of her finished column, someone knocked on her door. Since only the skeleton evening crew was around by then, the interruption surprised her and she dropped her pen. She immediately ducked under her desk to retrieve it. After all, the pen was her favorite...a souvenir from her last trip to Disneyland.

"Damn," she grumbled, down on her hands and knees and still searching for the treasured item when the knock on her door was repeated. "Come in!" she called over her shoulder. She heard the door open. "Whoever you are, you can help me find my Goofy pen," she groused, only half teasing. "It's your fault I lost it in the first place."

"Is it, indeed?"

With her fanny facing the open door, Tilly froze. The voice she'd heard was not Amy's, as she'd expected, and not one of her other co-workers', either. But it was familiar. *Chillingly* familiar.

Slowly she turned to look over her shoulder. Her worst fears were realized. Blinking with astonishment, she stared up into the icy blue eyes of Julian Rothwell, the duke of Chesterfield. He filled the doorway, towering over her like Big Ben over the Thames.

"You," she muttered wonderingly.

His lips turned up slightly at the corners. "You know me, then?"

"I know *of* you. You're a duke."

Again his lips performed that little twist—amusement with just the smallest touch of contempt. "Indeed. But I'm not here to discuss my peerage. I'm here to see Aunt...er...*Tilly.*" He thrust a folded newspaper under her nose. "But perhaps I've been misdirected?"

Still on her hands and knees, Tilly looked down at the newspaper and saw her own column staring back at her, complete with the photo of an elderly female at the top that Harrison had insisted on using when Tilly first started writing the column for the *Globe.* He didn't believe the general population would buy advice from a twenty-something kid fresh out of college like Tilly, so they'd duped the readership with a phony photo.

Tilly had never felt comfortable about representing herself as older than she was, but Harrison wouldn't budge. In fact, despite owning very definite opinions that she obligingly shared with friends when asked to, she wasn't that comfortable with dishing out advice to scores of strangers. But Harrison and her co-workers had insisted that she was good at seeing situations objectively and basically "telling it like it is," and that she was the best choice among the staff for launching another advice column after their former columnist, Aunt Nan, retired.

Tilly finally realized that this was an opportunity she couldn't pass up. She also discovered that she enjoyed responding to the many letters she received. The folksy, almost persnickety tone had been her idea, and one that actually came quite easily to her since she had an excellent model in her own late Grandma Josephine, who offered advice in the same no-sugarcoating manner. Eventually, after receiving a lot of positive feedback from readers, she began to hope she was actually doing some good.

Wonder of wonders, the column caught on like wildfire and went nationwide, so Tilly opted to keep the photo for fear of alienating loyal readers. However, when circumstances dictated, she always owned up to her true identity. Rising to her feet, Tilly realized this was one of those circumstances.

Standing directly in front of the duke, Tilly was dismayed to discover that he still looked just as tall as he had from her vantage point on the floor. She hated to admit it—and she was determined not to show it—but she was awed. He was even more drop-dead gorgeous in person and exuded an aura of power and decisiveness Tilly had never noticed in any other man. And that included all the high-powered politicians and rich business tycoons who showed up at the *Globe*'s annual charity ball.

"Well?" he said at last. "Have I been misdirected? Or are you this Tilly person's—" he eyed her jeans and shapeless sweater "—clerk?"

He pronounced it the British way, the way she'd only heard on reruns of *Upstairs, Downstairs*, "clark." Tilly thrust out her hand. "No…sir." What the heck was she supposed to call a duke, anyway? "I'm not Aunt Tilly's…er…clark. I'm Aunt Tilly herself."

The duke stared at her with an expression Tilly could only describe as horrified. Feeling sheepish, she dropped her hand to her side and fought the urge to bow like a serf before a rankled lord.

"Good God," he finally muttered under his breath. "*You're* Aunt Tilly? *You* write an advice column and influence the lives of thousands of readers? But you're hardly more than a schoolgirl!''

Tilly ignored a niggling of self-doubt and got mad instead. She'd fought all her life to be taken seriously. At a mere five foot three, with red hair cut in a short pixie do, she'd never looked her age. And now this high-and-mighty duke was challenging her right and ability to give advice. To do her *job!*

''I'm twenty-eight years old,'' Tilly informed him, her voice as frosty as his. ''I've written an advice column for five years—which, by the way, has *millions* of readers, not just thousands—and I'm *very* good at it.'' And if he didn't believe her, he could read the tons of letters that testified to that fact!

His eyes narrowed to ice blue slits. ''Are you? Are you, indeed? Well, young lady, I beg to differ.'' He turned, and for the first time, Tilly noticed a slender, thirtyish woman standing behind the duke. And behind her were four men in plain black suits and bowlers, standing at attention like a line of tin soldiers. If they'd been wearing sunglasses, she'd have thought they were the British equivalent of the FBI.

''May we come in?'' the duke inquired stiffly.

''Of...of course,'' Tilly stammered, mimicking his own strained politeness, but wondering who all those people were. Surely he hadn't brought his entire hall of servants with him from England? The duke was intimidating enough without the support of a bunch of poker-faced lackeys.

But Tilly stuck out her chin and tried to look unfazed as the woman and the four men filed into her tiny office and formed a semicircle around her desk. The men remained standing, their hands clasped behind them, their expressions neutral. The woman sat down in a chair the duke indicated with a careless wave of his hand, but she sat on the very edge, her back ramrod straight, her hands gripping a small black briefcase she held in her lap.

Tilly wondered who the woman was, then decided she was probably the duke's personal assistant or secretary. She seemed a marvel of unobtrusive efficiency, dressed in a navy blue suit and low-heeled matching pumps. She wore silver-rimmed glasses, and her hair was dark, short and very neat…just like the rest of her. Tilly felt immediate sympathy for the woman. She would have liked to have smiled at her, made her feel more comfortable, but the woman determinedly stared at the floor.

Her timid manner fueled Tilly's anger at the duke. The poor thing was probably scared to death of her boss and had been cowed into behaving like a mouse. Well, Tilly told herself, no matter how much he towered and scowled and stared, he wasn't going to cow *her* into behaving like a mouse!

Tilly crossed her arms and leaned against her desk, facing the duke with a smirk on her face she hoped was half as irritating as his. "Now, Your Dukeship, or whatever the heck you're called—" Tilly heard the woman make a small sound, like a gasp "—why don't you tell me exactly why you're here."

"I prefer to be called by my family name, which is Rothwell," the duke growled.

"Fine," Tilly snapped back. "And I prefer to be called by *my* family name, which is McKinney."

The duke's brows shot up. "Ah, so you're from Scottish stock. I might have known."

"Your business, Rothwell?" Tilly prompted. She

couldn't believe she was being so rude, but the man brought out the worst in her.

The duke nodded curtly. "Right. My business." He turned to the woman. "Miss Darling, the article, please."

Miss Darling opened the briefcase and pulled out a laminated copy of one of Tilly's columns. She handed it to the duke, and he began to read, his tone businesslike and hurried.

"Dear Aunt Tilly,
I've been dating a man for ten years. We work together and live together, and I've always been faithful to him. Unfortunately he hasn't always been faithful to me. I've forgiven him every dalliance in the hopes that he'll marry me at last, as he's promised to do over and over again since the day we first slept together. I love my *Pooky*—"

He stopped to wince.

"—but I'm getting tired of waiting and forgiving, only to be made a fool of once more. What do I do, Aunt Tilly?
                                    Melancholy in Minnesota."

The duke looked up. "Do you remember this letter, Miss McKinney?"

"It's *Ms.* McKinney," she corrected.

"All right, *Ms.* McKinney," he growled. "Now about the letter...do you remember it?"

"Vaguely," Tilly acknowledged with a shrug. "I

get a lot of letters about unfaithful partners. Especially unfaithful *men.*"

The duke ever so slightly inclined his head, then icily inquired, "And do you always dispense the same advice?" Without waiting for an answer, he resumed reading.

"Dear Melancholy,
Kick Pooky out of your bed till he comes to you on bended knee and with a shiny rock for your left ring finger. Remember the old adage 'Why buy the cow if the milk is free'? Listen, sweetie, quit giving Pooky free milk or you'll never get pelted with rice on your way to a bona fide honeymoon."

The duke looked up again and drawled. "Such quaint phraseology."

Tilly gave a defiant nod. "But no truer words were ever spoken. I stand by my advice one hundred percent. What I told her to do is the only way to deal with a man who won't commit."

"*Every* man?" The duke took a step closer to Tilly and stared down his aristocratic nose at her. "Do you think it's wise to generalize like that, Miss McKinney?"

He'd hit on one of her sore points. Tilly had often grappled with the problem of generalization in her column, but she had no choice. She couldn't know every letter writer intimately. But she wouldn't admit this little bit of a doubt to the duke. He'd probably take such a minor point and use it to his advantage.

"How many times do I have to tell you? It's 'Ms.'"

"What if your advice doesn't apply in this particular case? Do you realize you may be ruining some man's life with your interfering advice?"

A startling thought occurred to Tilly. "Oh, good heavens... You're...*you're* not Pooky, are you?"

A smudge of color appeared on each of the duke's chiseled cheekbones. "No, I am *not* Pooky," he muttered in a tone of disgust. "Pooky is the nickname my cook, Mrs. Peevey, has given my chauffeur, Mr. Dunbar. It is *he* who suffers from your meddling."

Tilly crossed her arms over her chest. "*I* didn't meddle. Your cook wrote to *me* for advice."

"And little good it's done her. It was while I was lecturing in Minneapolis. I came down with the flu for three days, and Dunbar had too much time on his hands. His behavior was...well..." The duke gestured ineffectually. "In short, Mrs. Peevey has been miserable ever since. As have I!"

Tilly's eyebrows rose. "You're that involved in your staff's personal lives?"

"Only to the extent that it affects me," he replied hastily. "Ever since Mrs. Peevey...er...cut off Dunbar, I haven't had a decent meal. She burns the roast and weeps into the gravy. My custard is invariably runny, my tea cold and my scones as hard as bricks."

"You poor man," Tilly murmured, trying to hide the beginnings of a smile.

"And as for Dunbar—" a muscle ticked in the duke's jaw "—he's so edgy and distracted, he's been in five—count them, *five*—minor accidents since Mrs. Peevey quit...er...enjoying his company during the off-hours. All avoidable accidents, mind you. The limousine will never be the same."

"You're really making my heart bleed, Your

Lordship,'' Tilly said dryly. "I don't know what I'd do if *my* cook started messing up in the kitchen. I might have to resort to something as unconventional as ordering pizza or Chinese. Or frying myself an egg.''

The duke drew up stiffly. "You don't understand. I run an orderly household. Everyone is important. That is, everyone has a job to do and—''

"As for Mr. Dunbar, you have my complete sympathy,'' Tilly continued wryly. "*My* chauffeur is always in a snit.'' She leaned close and whispered, "But I think it's because he wants a *long* car like all the other chauffeurs.''

Tilly's last comment was followed by a deathly silence. No one in the room so much as twitched. Every unblinking eye was fixed on the duke, who stood as rigid as a lamppost, his expression haughty and displeased, his gaze as cold as steel. Tilly inwardly trembled at her own audacity.

When the duke finally spoke, his voice was surprisingly cool and controlled. "Considering the misery Mrs. Peevey and Dunbar are suffering, I am surprised at your levity, Miss McKinney.''

"You're not worried about them,'' Tilly answered hotly. "You're only worried about yourself.''

"You are mistaken.''

Tilly opened her mouth to argue, but changed her mind. He didn't look like the sort of man to tolerate having his word second-guessed. She gave a huff of exasperation. "What is it you want from me? An apology?''

"No, I want a retraction.''

"A *what?*''

"I've talked myself blue in the face. Mrs. Peevey

won't listen to me. She is determined to abide by your advice no matter what. You will have to tell her yourself that you were wrong. I've taken a suite of rooms at the Royal Covington.''

"The Royal Covington?" Tilly repeated. But of course. It was the swankiest hotel in town. A suite of rooms there was more like a large, luxurious condominium.

"Yes. The Royal Covington." He glanced at his watch. "When can you be ready to go?"

Tilly was torn between amusement and indignation. It was obvious that the duke expected her instant obedience. No doubt he was used to being constantly kowtowed to. And as for her being *wrong*…

"As I said before, Rothwell, I stand by my advice. And everything you've said only confirms my opinion. I will not admit to being wrong when I feel strongly that I'm right. Eventually things will work out for Mrs. Peevey, but it may mean that she and Dunbar never get back together."

"But she's miserable!"

"She was miserable before."

"But only intermittently. At least she wasn't crying *all* the time!"

Tilly wasn't sure if she imagined it or if she really detected a note of compassion in the duke's tone, as if he was actually as concerned about Mrs. Peevey's happiness as he was about the weight and texture of the scones she created.

The duke bowed his head and pinched the bridge of his nose with his thumb and forefinger. Again silence reigned, but this time the duke's minions were looking anywhere else but directly at him. They seemed to have been made uncomfortable by the duke's apparent frustration in dealing with such an upstart as herself.

Tilly felt her chest ever so slightly swell. After all, this was America, where everyone was created equal and the only kind of dukes were the kind you "put up" in order to settle an argument. As these patriotic thoughts filled her, Tilly could almost hear the pipes and drums in the background playing "Yankee Doodle Dandy." Freedom of speech was her right, and she could advise anyone she chose to advise, thank you very much. She would stand by her decision and not give in to this English nobleman no matter how demanding and haughty he became.

"Miss McKinney, I apologize for my brusque tone," the duke said, breaking into Tilly's ruminations and taking her completely by surprise. "I'm afraid I'm rather used to having my way, or saying 'do this, do that,' and it is done. I hope you'll forgive me. I really do have Mrs. Peevey's best interests at heart."

Tilly stared at the duke. His lips were curved in a beguiling sort of chagrined smile. Since ordering her around hadn't worked, she figured he was trying to charm her. The damnedest thing was, it seemed to be working. Her anger was dissipating like air out of a punctured balloon.

"If she's that unhappy, I'm sorry for Mrs. Peevey, too," Tilly grudgingly admitted.

"Then will you talk to her?"

Tilly shook her head. "I won't—"

"You don't have to say you were wrong," the duke hurriedly inserted. "Just talk to her. If she is determined to stick to her decision about Dunbar, she must come to terms with it in some way. She will make herself sick with all that dreadful crying." The duke sighed. "Or poison us with her cooking."

Despite the sudden appearance of his compassionate side, Tilly still had no sympathy for the duke, but she felt a great deal for Mrs. Peevey. She was probably under a lot of pressure from the duke and Dunbar and could use a little moral support.

"Okay, I'll do it."

The duke's eyes blinked shut for a brief moment. "Thank you, Miss McKinney," he said solemnly.

"But I need to finish editing this column. Do you think you and your...er...entourage could wait outside for about ten minutes?"

The duke smiled again and gave a courtly little nod. "Of course, Miss McKinney," he said, and with a flick of his hand the entourage filed out in an orderly fashion, with Miss Darling taking up the rear and the duke walking out backward. "See you in the foyer."

Tilly watched as he pulled the door gently shut behind him, the very model of patience and good manners. Her brows drew together. He'd gone from haughty to almost human in a heartbeat. What was behind this sudden turnabout in the duke's behavior?

JULIAN LEANED against the wall and folded his arms. He let his head fall back against the hard surface and closed his eyes. He wasn't used to waiting and he wasn't sure what to do with himself. And his staff wasn't sure what to do, either. He could sense their nervous shifting as they, too, stood about like idiots in the drafty foyer of a newspaper office.

He'd made it known that he wasn't available for interviews at the moment, and the staff of the *Globe* that remained in the building were keeping a respectful distance.

He had a knack for that—for keeping people at a distance. But he was also usually able to tell people what he wanted them to do and get instant acquiescence. This was not the case with Miss McKinney...or rather, *Ms.* McKinney. It was hard to remember to use "Ms." when Miss Darling preferred "Miss."

Ms. McKinney. Julian could hardly believe that that redheaded little baggage was the reason his household was in such disarray. Who would have thought that a mere chit of a girl would be allowed to take on the persona of wise old Aunt Tilly and dispense advice as freely as the Queen doled out knighthoods these days!

But for all Ms. McKinney's determination to stick by her advice to Mrs. Peevey, Julian still felt he'd won the day. After all, as soon as Mrs. Peevey met Ms. McKinney and realized that Aunt Tilly was nothing but a fictitious front for an untrained dimestore therapist—albeit an attractive and spirited dime-store therapist—she'd value her so-called homespun advice about as much as she valued packaged pie crust and powdered orange juice.

Yes, it was just a matter of time before Dunbar was back in bed with Mrs. Peevey where he belonged. After all, even though Dunbar was a bit of a philanderer, his heart was all for Mrs. Peevey. And wasn't that the most important thing?

Julian frowned and tried to dismiss his own misgivings about Dunbar's behavior. He didn't approve of it, but he didn't think Dunbar was capable of changing. He felt that the only way to restore peace between the two employees he relied on the most, and for whom he had the most affection, was to downplay the differences between them and hope for the best. Surely Ms. McKinney's advice was too radical and caused too much pain.

Julian again forced away troubling doubts and concerns and tried to convince himself that all he really cared about was Mrs. Peevey's deft hand at making light, flaky scones—that is, before Aunt Tilly wreaked havoc on the household. But a return to the cheerful way she sang her Irish ditties—with a beaming eye and rosy cheeks—while she rolled out the dough would be most welcome, too.

Chapter Two

Tilly slipped on her bright blue, hooded vinyl jacket and flipped off the light switch in her office, then just stood in the dark and frowned at the door. She jiggled the keys in her coat pocket and wished she were going straight home to Rebound and the NBA playoffs instead of taking a detour with a duke.

"If this were happening to anyone but myself, I'd think it was hilarious," she muttered. But it was happening to *her,* and so far, she wasn't laughing. She knew that the sooner she walked through that door and faced the dour duke, however, the sooner this whole fiasco would be over.

Tilly took a deep breath, grasped the knob, threw the door open and took a big step...only to find her nose flattened against the ducal chest. And quite a *hard* ducal chest it was....

"I beg your pardon," he murmured, stepping quickly back. "I was about to knock. It's been—"

She felt the blood rush to her cheeks as she stepped back, too. "It...it took me a little longer than I thought." She stared at the front of his oxford cloth shirt, still amazed by the solidity of the body behind the buttons. "But I'm done now," she added brightly. "Where are you parked, Your...er... Dukeship?"

"I asked you to call me Rothwell," he reminded her impatiently. "You Americans can never seem to grasp the intricacies of title etiquette, so it will save us both a lot of bother if we keep it simple. Just *Rothwell*...okay?"

Tilly felt her cheeks flush hotter than ever, but this time with annoyance. The duke's ingratiating manners seemed to have flown the coop. She had probably kept him waiting too long. "Fine," she retorted. "And you can call *me* just McKinney. You sexists can never seem to grasp the difference between Miss and Ms."

He made no reply but sent her a withering glance from under a raised brow, then turned on his heel and walked briskly toward the elevator.

Touché, Tilly thought gleefully to herself as she fell in step behind him, then was followed onto the elevator by Miss Darling and the men in black bowlers. Facing forward, she saw several co-workers peeking at her around cubicle walls with their mouths open. Maybe they thought the duke was whisking her away for a romantic tryst at his posh premises....

Tilly gave them a Cheshire-cat grin and let them think what they wanted to. She didn't mind using the duke to lend her tomboy image a little glamour. But she knew her office cronies wouldn't look so awestruck if they knew she was headed for the regal kitchen to counsel the cook.

It all seemed so ridiculous Tilly wanted to laugh out loud. But since everyone else in the elevator was keeping a somber and dignified silence, a burst of hilarity might be considered ill-mannered. With an effort she kept her giggles inside, but at least now she was finding humor in the situation.

Tilly found less to laugh about when they reached the lobby and walked outside onto the sidewalks, still wet and shiny from the recent rainfall and glowing golden in the late-afternoon sun. Waiting at the curb was a long black limousine, and standing beside it, looking as grim as the grim reaper himself, was a uniformed chauffeur.

Oh, dear. She'd forgotten that Dunbar would be driving the car!

He was older than she expected, probably in his early sixties. He had a small gray mustache and was slightly built, but looked quite spiffy in his uniform. She imagined he'd been quite a ladies' man in his heyday, and probably had run into trouble with Mrs. Peevey by trying to perpetuate his rakish youth.

"Thank you, Dunbar," the duke murmured as the chauffeur opened the car door. Then he turned to Tilly and said, "After you, Miss...er...that is, *just* McKinney."

Tilly wrinkled her nose at the duke and ducked into the car, all the while acutely aware of Dunbar's gaze boring into her. There was a fervid whisper from the chauffeur and a repressive, monosyllabic reply from the duke, but Tilly pretended not to hear and slid across the lush leather seat to the far side of the car. She crossed her legs and tried to appear nonchalant, but she felt as though she were being carted off in supreme luxury to her execution. And the henchman was driving.

Miss Darling sat across from her, the duke slid in beside her and one of the duke's men sat in the front passenger's seat. She noticed that of the four men in bowlers, this one was the youngest and handsomest. He had dark hair and eyes, and shoulders almost as impressive as the duke's.

Then, quick as a wink, Dunbar was behind the wheel and pulling away from the curb. Tilly immediately felt his beady little eyes peering at her from the rearview mirror and she tried to squirm out of view. That appeared to be an impossible feat, however, and the duke was looking at her as if she were harboring fleas.

"Are you uncomfortable, McKinney?" he drawled.

"Of course not," she said lamely, then made a vague gesture that encompassed her surroundings. "I mean, how could I be? This is *posh*. I mean, this limo is twice as nice as the one my boyfriend, Tommy, rented for the prom."

"And when *was* your prom, McKinney? Last week?" the duke inquired sardonically.

"Very funny," Tilly sniffed. Then, desperate for conversation to take her mind off the accusing glare in the mirror—even if it ended up being a shouting match between her and the duke—she inquired, "Say, how are the rest of the guys getting back to the hotel?"

"The 'rest of the guys' have their own car...or, rather, a van," the duke informed her, staring straight ahead. "They will follow behind."

"Why do you need so many people hanging around all the time?" Tilly blurted out. "I mean, what do you do when you get a hankering for a lime Slurpee? Dragging all these people down to the 7-Eleven hardly seems worth the hassle."

The duke eyed her. "I've never hankered for a

lime Slurpee in my life. I don't even know what they are. Do you know what they are, Miss Darling?''

Miss Darling nodded primly. "Yes, Your Grace, I believe I do. They're icy confections of a rather robust taste and consistency. They are very popular in the States.''

The duke nodded soberly. "I see. Well, not every popular thing is worth investigating, is it? And for your first question, McKinney, as to why I need so many people hanging around all the time, the answer is, I don't need them all the time and the only reason I have them with me now is because I came directly from a lecture at the library to your office. They might have gone ahead to the hotel, but Mendenhall, my chief of staff—'' he motioned toward the good-looking guy in the front seat "—likes, whenever possible and feasible, to keep the entourage intact.''

Tilly nodded. "But what do your men do at the lectures?'' She smiled knowingly. "Intimidate people?''

His blue eyes glimmered. She'd have almost thought she found her comment humorous, but his lips didn't crack a smile. "Partly,'' he admitted dryly. "The artifacts are on display before and after the lecture, which poses a security concern. You'd be surprised how many people suddenly get a hankering to walk off with a strigil.''

Tilly couldn't resist. "I know I'm going to sound ignorant, but what's a strigil?''

The duke's lips quirked at the corners. Tilly suspected his smile was condescending, but she wasn't sure. "It is a curved blade with an oiled edge, used by the Romans during a Turkish bath or sauna to scrape away the dirt when they sweat.''

Tilly made a face. "Gross."

"But better than nothing. Soap was unknown at the time."

Tilly was fascinated, but a little shy about asking more questions. "I don't know much about Roman history," she ventured.

"Really?"

Now she was sure he was being condescending, and she couldn't help but immediately feel defensive. "But I don't see much point in studying ancient civilizations, anyway," she informed him, purposely sounding bored. "I prefer to stay up on *current* events."

"We can learn wisdom from the history of civilization, McKinney," the duke said. "Wisdom that could be applied to modern uses. For example, some of our greatest psychological theories can be traced back to the Greeks and Romans. You've heard of the Oedipus complex, I'm sure." He paused, then turned to look her straight in the eye. "You *did* study psychology to prepare you for your present occupation, did you not?"

Tilly blinked several times, forcing herself to tear her mesmerized gaze away from the duke's baby blues. She had the distinct feeling she'd been set up. As they waited for her answer, the duke's, Miss Darling's, and Dunbar's mirror-reflected eyes were fixed intently on her. She might have shriveled up and died then and there if she hadn't detected just the tiniest bit of compassion and encouragement in Miss Darling's usually passive expression.

Tilly's chin lifted an inch. "I majored in English. I minored in journalism. The only psychology classes I took were in my freshman year to fulfill graduation requirements. I found them a mind-numbing bore and I barely passed them with Cs. Is that what you wanted to hear?''

Before the duke could answer, the limousine swerved suddenly to the left, throwing Tilly across the duke's lap. Then the car swerved to the right, braked violently, lurched, then braked again. A man in a passing car—whom they'd barely missed hitting head-on—blared his horn and sped away in a huff.

During this alarming activity, Miss Darling gave out a high-pitched squeak like a stepped-on mouse and Dunbar swore a blue streak in a thick Cockney accent. By the time the car came to a complete stop, the duke had wrapped his long arms around Tilly's hips and was clutching her to his midsection.

Tilly gazed up at the duke through her tousled bangs, and he gazed down at her. He appeared distracted for a moment, even discomposed. Then he gravely inquired, ''Are you all right?''

''Yes,'' Tilly answered in a small voice. ''You…you can let go of me now.''

The duke looked as though he was surprised to discover he was actually holding on to her and released her so suddenly she tumbled to the floor.

''Good God, we'll have you black and blue before we get to the hotel,'' he grumbled as he and Miss Darling assisted Tilly to her seat again.

Trying to restore some semblance of dignity, Tilly straightened her clothes and forced a devil-may-care smile. ''Oh, I'm all right. I've fallen much harder out of the hayloft back home on the farm. I'm surprised, though, that Miss Darling didn't fly across the car, too.''

"Why *didn't* you fly across the car, Miss Darling?" the duke inquired.

"I braced myself, Your Grace. You see, I've grown quite used to Dunbar's unpredictable driving of late," she explained timidly.

"No one should be expected to get used to that sort of driving," the duke growled, then climbed out of the car, apparently to have a word with his chauffeur. Dunbar had gotten out of the car already and was leaning over the hood, his elbows locked, his head bent, as if he was trying to compose himself. And although the duke looked mad enough to spit nails, Tilly noticed that he still laid a comforting hand on the chauffeur's shoulder.

Mendenhall, after solemnly inquiring if "the ladies" were quite well, and receiving a satisfactory reply, got out to talk to the driver of the van that carried the other three men. Tilly was just thankful they'd avoided an accident and were safely pulled over out of the traffic.

"You mustn't judge him too harshly, Ms. McKinney."

Tilly had been staring out the window at the duke's somber profile and was shocked to be directly addressed by Miss Darling.

"Are you speaking of the duke or Dunbar?" she inquired.

"The duke," Miss Darling said hastily. "I think *Dunbar* deserves everything he's getting!" She covered her mouth with a hand and giggled. "Or maybe I should say, *not* getting."

Tilly laughed. "Why, Miss Darling, I do believe you've got a sense of humor. What in the world are you doing working for an old sourpuss like the duke?''

Miss Darling leaned forward and touched Tilly lightly on the knee. ''Oh, you don't know him, Ms. McKinney.''

''Don't be so formal. Call me Tilly.''

Miss Darling smiled shyly. ''And you must call me Emma.''

''What a beautiful name! Just like Jane Austen's spirited heroine.''

Emma blushed. ''I'm sure you don't think *I'm* very spirited. You probably think I'm too quiet and timid and allow the duke to order me about much too—''

''Emma, it's really none of my business how you and—''

''But, you see, I really *love* working for him, and he's always treated me with the utmost respect. He's really very kind, you know.'' She got a dreamy look on her face, as if recalling some fond memory, then turned back to Tilly with a pleading expression. ''As I said, you mustn't judge him by his present behavior.''

''What am I supposed to judge him by?''

''Right now he's very upset about Mrs. Peevey and Dunbar. He hates to see them suffer.''

''I thought he hated tepid tea, hard scones and dents in his fender,'' Tilly murmured dryly.

''Well, *that,* too… But he has a very tender heart and—''

Emma's sentimental description of the duke was abruptly interrupted when he and Dunbar and Mendenhall all got back in the limo. Tilly was astonished by how quickly Emma changed from an earnest confidante to just another silent passenger in the car. And she had no idea what to make of Emma's defense of such a stuck-up, selfish man. Maybe he *paid* his employees to be loyal. Or maybe if they weren't loyal, it was "off with their heads!"

As the limo pulled away from the curb and into traffic, the duke bent near Tilly's ear. "Now do you see what I mean?" he said in a low, urgent voice. "The man is a menace. You must be convinced now that something has to be done to restore peace between Dunbar and Mrs. Peevey."

Tilly did not reply. She wouldn't be bullied or shamed into retracting good advice. She would see Mrs. Peevey and talk to her before she made a single comment on the subject. Taking the hint, the duke remained silent for the remainder of the short trip to the Royal Covington.

When they arrived at the hotel, the van passed them and went directly to the parking garage, but Dunbar pulled up to the curb right in front of the canopied entrance. When he opened the door for them, Tilly carefully avoided eye contact, but she thought she could actually feel the tension in the air as she moved past him to step out of the limo. She was relieved when he got back in the car to drive it into the parking garage.

Observing her watching the limo pull away from the curb, the duke said, "He won't let the valets touch it. He's afraid they'll wreck it. Ironic, wouldn't you say?"

Tilly chuckled and nodded, too relieved for words. She hoped that that was the last she'd see of Dunbar.

A great fuss was made by several members of the hotel staff as the duke and his remaining entourage filed into the lobby. Tilly wondered if Mendenhall had called ahead to alert the hotel to their arrival; she had observed him using a cellular phone just moments before.

"Gee, I guess they didn't have time to roll out the red carpet," Tilly muttered dryly as they were escorted to the elevator.

"Apparently not," the duke replied, deadpan.

Tilly turned quickly and stared at him. "Oh, don't tell me they *really* do roll out a red carpet for you!"

The duke's lips curved in a superior smirk, his eyes twinkling with humor. "Of course not, McKinney."

Tilly laughed self-consciously. "You got me, Rothwell."

"It was easy," the duke informed her. "I knew I could count on you to think the worst of me."

Tilly's mouth fell open. "I never said—"

"You didn't have to. I know you consider me a pompous ass."

Tilly was silenced. She was suddenly faced with two hard truths: one, the duke had a sense of humor and wasn't afraid to employ it at his own expense, and two, she had ably conveyed her unflattering opinion of the duke and had perhaps been ruder than was conducive to the betterment of international relations. If only for God and country, she would try to be nicer.

When they reached the top floor of the building, the hotel attendant used a special key to open the elevator doors. It was then that Tilly realized the duke must have reserved more than a single, luxurious suite. He'd rented the entire top floor! No wonder they gave him the super-duper VIP treatment!

Calculating the expense of renting out an entire floor of the Royal Covington, and traveling with several employees on an extended tour of the United States, Tilly, who was mathematically challenged, could only come up with a sum that rivaled the national debt.

Upon exiting the elevator, Mendenhall made a courtly bow to the duke and murmured, "Good evening, Your Grace," then nodded politely to her and Emma before going left down a long hall, plushly carpeted in a deep jade green. The duke and Tilly and Emma turned right and walked down the hall toward a large, ornate double door at the end.

Her head still dancing with dollar signs, Tilly suddenly inquired, "How much do you charge for a ticket to one of your lectures, Rothwell?"

The duke turned to her, a brow raised. "Why? Are you thinking of attending?"

Tilly blushed. "Well, no. That is…I *guess* I could. How much is it?"

The duke chuckled. "It's free, McKinney. Does that help you make up your mind?"

"Free?"

"Donations are encouraged to the various libraries and museums for whom I lecture, but no admission fee is required."

Tilly was astounded. The duke was doing all this for *free?* He must be as rich as Donald Trump! But far more philanthropic…

"Mrs. Peevey will be in the kitchen, McKinney," the duke told her as he reached for the gilded handle on one of the doors. "I suppose you prefer to talk to her alone?"

Tilly was suddenly reminded of why she was there

and tried to refocus her attention to the problem at hand instead of marveling at all the new things she was continually discovering about the duke of Chesterfield.

"Yes, that is exactly what I would prefer," Tilly replied.

The duke nodded. "All right. But you *will* let me introduce you?"

"Sure." Tilly wondered why the duke was being so cooperative.

The duke nodded again, a strange little smile flitting across his patrician features. "Good. Now, shall we go inside and—*good God!*"

The duke had opened the door to a room hazy with smoke and pungent with the aroma of burned meat. He took one quick look around the main room, then headed down a hall, yelling, "Mrs. Peevey? Are you all right? Mrs. Peevey, answer me!"

Her heart pounding in her throat, Tilly followed, with Emma close behind. As they rounded a corner and entered a small kitchen, she saw the source of the smoke and smell on top of the stove, still hissing with heat and covered with a thick blanket of fire-extinguisher foam.

The apparent perpetrator of the burned offering was sitting in a chair by a butcher-block worktable, her legs sprawled under a modest calf-length skirt and her white apron tossed over her head and being used as a handkerchief as she sobbed her heart out.

The duke heaved a relieved sigh, paused, then inquired in a surprisingly gentle tone, "Mrs. Peevey, are you all right? You aren't burned, are you?"

Mrs. Peevey pulled the apron down to reveal her red and swollen eyes. She paid no attention to Tilly or Emma, but looked straight at the duke as she wailed in an Irish lilt, "The only thing that's burned is your dinner, Your Grace! I've done it again, only this time I might've burned down the hotel and half of Seattle. Oh, you'll be shippin' me to Australia t' cook for the rough hands on your sheep ranch in the outback, you will! *They* won't care if I burn the kangaroo stew!"

Following this outburst, Mrs. Peevey threw her apron over her head again and resumed her torrent of tears. Emma "tsk-tsked" and moved to stand beside Mrs. Peevey, rubbing her back and murmuring consoling words. The duke watched grimly, his hands clenching and unclenching at his side, then turned to Tilly with an expression rife with accusation.

"I...I wonder why the fire alarm didn't go off," Tilly stuttered, trying to divert the duke's fierce gaze.

"I knocked the dotty thing off the wall and threw it in the dishwater," Mrs. Peevey burbled wetly from behind the apron. "The one in the parlor, too! I wasn't about t' have 'em start screechin' and half the hotel up here with axes and fire hoses. I learned how nerve-rackin' such a commotion is when I burned that lovely Yorkshire pudding in Phoenix and set the oven ablaze."

Tilly's eyes widened. She turned to the duke. "You said she was preparing subpar meals. You didn't say she'd turned into a fire hazard."

"They've *both* become hazards to the safety and well-being of others," the duke said soberly. "Now, having seen the effects of your advice firsthand, perhaps you'll want to edit yourself?"

Mrs. Peevey's apron lowered abruptly. "Advice?

What advice?'' She squinted at Tilly from under her
swollen eyelids. ''And who might you be, miss?''

Tilly opened her mouth, but nothing came out.
Suddenly she wasn't so sure she wanted to own up
to who she was. She still believed her advice to Mrs.
Peevey was sound, but she'd had no idea how traumatic the repercussions of following her advice
would be. And she wasn't sure why it hadn't occurred to her before now, but what would Mrs.
Peevey—a plump matron in the autumn of her life—
think of a twenty-something like herself dispensing
advice?

Feeling tongue-tied and helpless, Tilly turned to
the duke. From the self-satisfied look she saw on his
face, which he quickly tried to disguise, she realized
that he had actually been counting on Mrs. Peevey
being disillusioned by Tilly's age and appearance…that he had brought her here with just that
outcome in mind!

Of course, this only appealed to Tilly's stubborn
streak. Somehow she'd make sure the duke's plan
backfired!

''You said you wanted the privilege of introducing
me, Rothwell,'' she reminded him in a level tone.
''*Go ahead.*''

JULIAN PEERED suspiciously at Tilly. Those last two
words—''Go ahead''—sounded more like a threat
than a civil invitation to speak. Her voice was low
and controlled…only perhaps it was *too* controlled.
And the look in those smoldering green eyes of hers!
As a child she was probably the terror of the play-
ground, the sort of pint-sized banshee whose lunch
money you never stole, or whose little brother you

never dared pick on as long as you valued your life...or the ability to sire children as an adult.

But what harm could she do him now? All he had to do was tell Mrs. Peevey that this snippet of a female was the wise old Aunt Tilly who had advised her to quit being so generous with her "milk." She'd immediately see the folly of listening to such a babe in arms and go running back to Dunbar.

Julian smiled and performed a courtly bow. He'd show Tilly that one could still be a gentleman while ruthlessly pulling the rug out from under his opponent's sneaker-clad feet. "Thank you. I will be happy to introduce you." He then turned to Mrs. Peevey. "Mrs. Peevey, I would like you to meet...Aunt Tilly."

"Aunt Tilly?" Mrs. Peevey repeated dully. "*Your* aunt Tilly?"

The duke scowled. "Of course not. As you ought to know, Mrs. Peevey, I don't have an aunt Tilly. This is the Aunt Tilly who advised you to...er...toss Dunbar from your boudoir."

Mrs. Peevey's head jerked, and her gaze fixed wonderingly on Tilly. "*You're* Aunt Tilly?"

Tilly smiled and nodded, looking far more composed than Julian expected. "Yes, Mrs. Peevey. I'm a bit younger than you probably expected, but I'm the person who writes the advice column."

Julian watched with satisfaction as Mrs. Peevey slowly shook her head. "But what...what are you doing here?"

To Julian's horror, Tilly's smile lit up the room. She beamed with self-confidence; she glowed with a trustworthy aura any Girl Guide peddling cookies would envy. "I have come, Mrs. Peevey, to support your decision in tossing out Dunbar."

"*What?*" Julian exclaimed.

"And furthermore," Tilly continued in an authoritative voice, "I have come to give you *additional* advice."

Chapter Three

"What sort of advice, miss?" Mrs. Peevey inquired, dabbing at her nose.

"Good God, Mrs. Peevey," Julian expostulated, "you're not going to listen to her *again*, are you? What could a girl like her know about love, about relationships, about *life?*"

Mrs. Peevey listened attentively to the duke's outburst, then turned back to Tilly. "He has a point, my dear. What sort of background have you got that makes you suitable to give advice? Perhaps you studied psychology in university?"

Julian snorted. "Hardly. She barely passed her psychology courses with Cs!"

Mrs. Peevey looked alarmed. "Is that true, my dear?"

Julian expected Tilly to be a bit rattled, but nothing in her calm voice or demeanor indicated a single jangled nerve. She smiled and moved a few steps closer to Mrs. Peevey, then looked her steadfastly in the eye.

"To begin with, Mrs. Peevey, I'm older than I look. I'm nearly thirty years old."

Mrs. Peevey chuckled. "My, but you're ancient, aren't you?"

Tilly chuckled, too. "No, but I've been around long enough to experience and observe many things. And along with my own experiences, I bring the expertise of my parents to my job as an advice columnist. Both of them are very wise."

"Are *they* psychologists, then?"

"No. They didn't learn their wisdom from a university, either. My father is a farmer in Washougal, a small town by the Oregon border. My mother is a homemaker. They've learned about life by living it...and, of course, they learned from their parents, too. You may have noticed, Mrs. Peevey, that my advice is simple, practical and to the point. I don't use a lot of complicated words. My theories about human behavior have been passed down through generations, from common folk to common folk. And, as they say—" she smiled again "—'the proof is in the pudding.' My advice works."

Julian didn't know whether to applaud or beat his head against the wall. "What a moving speech, McKinney," he muttered. "What will you do as an encore to such an homage to simple, homespun values? Produce your fiddle and perform 'Turkey in the Straw'?"

"Oh, Your Grace, please don't mock her," Mrs. Peevey protested mildly. "She's made her point, and I do believe I want to hear what else she's got to say." She sniffled, her eyes starting to tear again. "I've been miserable since I kicked Pooky out of bed, you know. And so has he!"

"We've all been miserable, Mrs. Peevey," Julian

grimly reminded her. "And the solution seems simple to me."

"It *is* simple," Tilly agreed, taking Julian completely by surprise. She stood next to Mrs. Peevey and put a hand on her shoulder. "But I'm pretty sure *I* have a different solution in mind than you do, Rothwell."

Julian sighed. "You would, of course."

Miss Darling still stood on the other side of Mrs. Peevey, and Julian hoped his secretary was paying close attention; he might need her as a witness to testify in court as to the precise moment he went temporarily insane and put an end to Tilly's reign of terror by tossing her out the window!

"I suppose you don't think I should take Pooky back?" Mrs. Peevey asked, her voice ever so slightly tinged with hope.

"Do *you* think that's the best solution, Mrs. Peevey?" Tilly asked in a quiet, earnest voice.

Mrs. Peevey sniffled again and bowed her head. "No, I don't, truth to tell. It'd be bliss at first, but he'd still cheat on me, he would. He won't feel like he's beholden to be faithful to me till we're married good and proper in the church. And he won't marry me if I don't stick to my guns." She clenched her fist and gave her knee a sound thump. "I've *got* to stick to my guns!"

Julian watched as Tilly smiled with satisfaction at Mrs. Peevey...and the brazen little chit couldn't resist sliding *him* a smug look, too! He was beginning to think he'd been crazy to bring her back to the hotel. What would the little busybody do next?

"Sticking to her guns won't solve Mrs. Peevey's ineptness in the kitchen and her general state of misery," Julian forcefully argued. "Isn't that why you're here, McKinney? To help Mrs. Peevey come to terms with her decision, not just reinforce it?"

"Yes, Rothwell, that's why I'm here," she agreed with a toss of her short hair and a gleam in her eyes. "And what I advise Mrs. Peevey to do now is get on with her life. Find things to do that have nothing to do with Dunbar. Go out with girlfriends." She shrugged. "Go bowling."

"But I don't have girlfriends," Mrs. Peevey protested weakly. "And I've never bowled in my life." She leaned forward and inquired, "Can you bowl in a dress, Ms. McKinney?"

"Mrs. Peevey, I'm going to systematically destroy all your doubts," Tilly announced. "First of all, you're a lovely lady and will have no trouble making friends, but if you want someone right away to share your fun, what's wrong with Emma here?"

Miss Darling looked stunned, but said nothing. Julian had no idea Tilly was on first-name terms with his secretary. Was she trying to pollute Miss Darling's mind, too, with her advice? Over his dead body!

"And so what if you've never bowled before? There's a first time for everything." She grinned. "As for bowling in a dress, it's been done, but I wouldn't recommend it. Buy yourself some slacks, Mrs. Peevey."

Mrs. Peevey pressed her hand to her chest. "You mean *me* wearin' trousers. What an idea!" She tittered and flicked Julian a nervous look.

He'd known Mrs. Peevey since he was a child—she'd cooked for his father—and he'd never seen her in anything but a skirt or a dress, with usually an apron on top. It was rather mind-boggling picturing her any other way. In fact all the female employees at Chesterfield Hall in Dorset wore skirts while on duty. It was simply the way things were done.

"Oh, I've got lots more ideas where that came from," Tilly assured her. "The point is, you need to get out. I'm sure the duke here gives you time off. What do you do during your off hours?"

"I read, or darn Dunbar's socks. Or lately I just cry."

"That's not healthy. And it won't bring Dunbar to his senses any faster. Let him darn his own socks. You need to get out, enjoy yourself. Go dancing."

Mrs. Peevey blushed. "With other men?"

"Can you think of a better way to rattle Pooky's cage?"

"I beg your pardon?"

"You know...make him jealous. I'll bet you used to cut a mean rug."

"If you mean I used to dance a nice jig...it's true, I did. But that was before I took myself off the market. Even Pooky and I, when we were first courtin', used to go down to the King's Arms every Saturday night and dance till the wee hours."

"But he quit taking you, didn't he?"

Mrs. Peevey nodded sadly.

"But he still came home to you at night? To his neatly darned socks and you keeping his bed warm?"

Mrs. Peevey nodded again.

"He's been taking advantage of you, Mrs. Peevey, and it's time you stood up for your rights." Tilly paused consideringly, then added, "In fact I'm wondering if Dunbar is really worth your time and trouble. Maybe you ought to look elsewhere for companionship."

"Oh, no, I could never do that," Mrs. Peevey answered quickly, saving Julian from throttling Tilly then and there for putting such an idea into her head in the first place. "You don't know him as I do, Ms. McKinney. He's got the roving eye, I'll admit, but he's got a kind heart. He's good to me when we're together. Generous and sweet, he is. I could never love another."

To Julian's relief Tilly did not argue the point. "Then you must teach him to respect you. As you've learned the hard way, love's no good without respect. You've kicked him out of bed, but now you've got to take the next step. You have to actually *enjoy* yourself without him."

To Julian's horror he noted a gleam in Mrs. Peevey's eyes that looked suspiciously like the gleam in Tilly's. "This is madness, Mrs. Peevey," he exclaimed. "Dunbar loves you. As you said, he's miserable without you. Gadding about town, trying to 'rattle his cage,' will just make matters worse."

Mrs. Peevey's chin inched up. "Beggin' your pardon, Your Grace, but if Dunbar's so miserable without me, he can marry me...after he's promised never to play 'slap and tickle' with another barmaid, mind you. But in the meantime I'll not be sittin' around weepin' over darned socks. Ms. McKinney's right. I need to get out. And I'll start tomorrow." She turned to Miss Darling. "Emma, dear, would you like to go bowlin' with me tomorrow night?"

At first Miss Darling looked slightly aghast at the suggestion, then her eyes lit up like he'd never seen them do before. She looked at him, then at Tilly, then turned back to Mrs. Peevey. "Why, yes I *would*, Mrs. Peevey. Thank you for asking. I mean, why not? Tomorrow is my day off." She turned back to Julian. "You don't mind, do you, Your Grace?"

"What you do on your day off, Miss Darling, is entirely your own business," he replied stiffly. "And the same applies to you, Mrs. Peevey, however ill-advised I think your activities might be. Now, if you'll excuse us, McKinney and I must retire to the living room for a private word. In the meantime I'd appreciate being served some sort of dinner before the stroke of midnight."

Mrs. Peevey was already up and bustling around the kitchen, and Miss Darling had exited in the direction of her own room by the time Julian had caught Tilly's elbow and firmly propelled her into the adjacent living room. In the middle of the room she spun around and faced him.

"What's the matter, Rothwell? Don't you like the advice I gave Mrs. Peevey? Remember, you asked me here. This was not my idea." She poked her chest with a dainty finger, her heart-shaped face flushed with defiance. If she wasn't such a termagant, he might have thought she looked rather appealing in that moment.

"Yes, I know I invited you here—"

"Actually you *ordered* me here," she corrected.

"Please don't remind me," he answered morosely. "I can see now that it was sheer folly to expect you to fix things."

"Don't you see that this is much too complicated for a quick fix? I mean, honestly, can you condone Dunbar's behavior? Would you want Mrs. Peevey to take him back and be treated like a doormat?"

He turned away. Of course he didn't condone Dunbar's conduct, but in his experience, people rarely changed just because you wanted them to. "It's not my place, or any of my business, to have any sort of opinion about Dunbar's behavior in relation to his private life," he gruffly informed her.

"But you *made* it your business," she argued. "You brought me here to fix things, remember?"

"I was desperate, and desperation breeds stupidity. All I really want is order and tranquility restored to my household. This lovers' tiff has shattered all our nerves and disrupted our usual peaceful, rational activities."

She flung her hands in the air and began to pace the floor. "It sounds like you want to live in a monastery!"

"Hardly," he growled, noticing at that very moment a distinctly unmonklike urge to kiss her.

"Or in a *museum,* for crying out loud! But that would be perfect, wouldn't it? Because you're like one of those *relics* that were dug up on your estate. In case you haven't noticed, Rothwell, women have demanded better than the double standard for decades now. It's obvious Mrs. Peevey's from the old school, but you seem perfectly happy to allow her to remain there, even if it makes her vulnerable to Dunbar's poor treatment. Criminy, she doesn't even wear slacks on her day off! Is that some sort of rule of yours? What kind of place are you running over there in Dorset, or wherever you're from? Come out of the dark ages, Rothwell!"

Julian stared down at Tilly. She had stopped her feverish pacing and was apparently through berating him, as well. Now she simply glared up at him, her feet planted in a defiant pose, her arms akimbo. With her jacket flung back and her chest puffed out like a pigeon on the strut, he saw evidence for the first time that she had breasts under that baggy sweater she wore.

He felt another unmonklike impulse as he continued to return her challenging stare. He wasn't sure whether he wanted to continue to swap insults with her or fling her over his shoulder and cart her off to his bedroom.

Later he would probably be mystified, horrified, by this libidinous urge, but right now it was stronger than anything he'd felt for a female in a long time. Perhaps it was because she was nothing like all the others.... Courted for his title and money ever since he was no taller than the hem of his father's ceremonial kilt, he was used to being pursued, flattered, catered to.

But what was he thinking? He *liked* being pursued, flattered and catered to! It was madness to think otherwise. He was probably only randy at the moment because he'd avoided romantic entanglements while on this lecture tour, and Tilly's apparent dislike of him constituted a sort of primal challenge.

"So?" she finally prompted him, her voice sounding a little edgy...as if their staring contest had shaken her a bit, too.

"I was simply waiting to be quite sure you were done casting aspersions on my life-style and the customs of my country, and trying to come up with a gentlemanly reply."

This reprimand, delivered in a tone of wounded dignity, had its desired effect. Her gaze flickered away, and her arms fell to her side.

"I didn't mean to offend you or your customs," she said in a halting voice. "You just seem so...so...*stodgy*."

He raised a brow. "I call it decorum, McKinney. And I see nothing wrong with it."

"And you appreciate and encourage decorum in your staff, too," she suggested.

He cocked his head to the side. "I suppose I do."

Up came the hands again, firmly planted on her boyish hips. He thought wryly—and with grudging respect—that he hadn't managed to repress her for very long. "Well, I have some advice that could be applied to your whole household."

"*More* advice, McKinney?"

"Yes! I think you *all* could use a night out! Some bowling, some dancing. Maybe even a karaoke bar and Mexican food. Call me any time and I'll give you the names and addresses of the best hangouts in Seattle."

"I'll keep that in mind," he drawled.

"I won't hold my breath," she retorted, a reluctant smile curving her lips. "Lordy, I'm glad I don't work for *you*, Rothwell."

"The feeling is entirely mutual, McKinney," he answered, unable to keep from smiling back. She had quite luscious lips, he decided.

There was a protracted pause as they stared at each other again. He wasn't sure if she was feeling as awkward, and as strangely reluctant, about saying goodbye as he was. She finally broke the spell by thrusting out a hand for a hearty American handshake. He stared down at the small fingers for a moment, then took them into his own, much larger hand in a firm clasp. She returned the pressure, and he found himself inexplicably aroused by such casual contact.

"I'm sorry I've disturbed your peace, Rothwell," she said.

Oh, you have no idea... "No sorrier than I am," he said ruefully. "Goodbye, McKinney." *And good riddance.*

TILLY WAS STANDING outside on the sidewalk in front of the hotel before she realized she had no ride home. The duke had brought her there in his limo, and her car was still parked at the office. Apparently meeting a duke and finding herself embroiled in his domestic affairs had made her absent-minded. But what was *his* excuse?

"Where are your fancy-schmancy manners now, Your Dukeship?" she muttered, looking up and down the street for a taxi.

"Ms. McKinney? Oh, Ms. McKinney!"

Tilly turned around and saw Emma hurrying through the hotel's revolving door. When she reached Tilly, she was obviously out of breath.

"Oh! *Whew!* I'm glad I caught you!" she exclaimed, pressing her palm against her heaving chest. "I...I ran all the way down the stairs and across the...the lobby."

"I told you to call me Tilly," Tilly reminded her with a smile.

"Oh, I'm...I'm sorry...Tilly."

"Don't be sorry. Just catch your breath, then tell me why you ran down the stairs instead of waiting for the elevator."

Emma took one last deep breath, then seemed much more capable of speaking normally. "The duke sent me down to catch you. He...he forgot that Dunbar brought you here in the limo and is simply mortified to think he allowed you to leave without providing for your transportation.''

"Mortified, is he? So his mother *did* teach him a thing or two,'' Tilly observed.

"Oh, yes,'' Emma assured her, taking Tilly's joke seriously. "Until she died when he was five.''

Tilly found herself, once again, the recipient of surprising information about the duke. "That's a tough age to lose your mother...although I'm sure there's no age when it's easy.''

Emma nodded. "Then he went to boarding school.''

Tilly grimaced. "At the age of five? Right after losing his mother?''

Emma nodded again. "I think that's why he's so emotionally aloof.''

Tilly peered curiously at Emma. "Why are you telling me these things about the duke? Are you still trying to make excuses for him?''

Emma clasped Tilly's forearm with both hands, her eyes suddenly aglow with agitated excitement. "Oh, I could tell you a *thousand* things about the duke if you'd only listen! I could talk about him *all* day and *all* night.''

Tilly chuckled uncertainly, a little taken aback by Emma's uncharacteristic enthusiasm. "Well, I don't think it's really necessary to—''

"Because I *love* him, Tilly, from the bottom of my soul!''

Tilly froze. "You love him?''

Emma nodded eagerly and squeezed Tilly's arm till her fingers began to tingle from constricted blood flow. "Yes, I love him, love him, love *him!* I have for years, and it's such a relief to finally tell someone."

Tilly frowned and gently pried Emma's fingers from around her arm. "But why are you telling *me?*"

"Because I need advice, Tilly. Lots and lots of it. I don't know what to do about loving the duke. I can't go on like this without *doing* something! You've done such a marvelous job helping Mrs. Peevey with her problems—I know you'd be smashing at helping me, too."

Tilly started shaking her head and backing away. "I don't think so."

Emma looked crushed. "But why not? Don't you like me?"

"That's precisely why I don't want to advise you, Emma. I like you a lot, but your boss thinks I'm the worst thing that's come along since the American Revolution. If he finds out you're listening to *me*—"

"But I'd never be brave enough to talk to someone else about this, Tilly," she pleaded. "I *trust* you. And I really, *really* need to talk about this. I've kept it bottled up for much too long."

Tilly felt trapped. How could she refuse to listen to Emma? The poor woman had suddenly broken through her timidity and was trying to resolve a long-standing problem. And loving a gorgeous, but marble-hearted, statue like Julian Rothwell was one hell of a problem! If only for pity's sake, Tilly could not refuse Emma's plea for help.

"Call me in about half an hour," Tilly said with a resigned sigh and a smile. "I need to check my calendar. If I don't have a tennis date, maybe we can meet in the morning for coffee and doughnuts." Her smile turned mischievous. "Or tea and crumpets, whatever suits your fancy." She fished in her purse for a business card and handed it to Emma. "Here's my phone number."

Emma pressed the card against her small bosom. "Oh, *thank* you, Tilly. I really appreciate this. I know you'll tell me exactly the right thing to do!"

Tilly wasn't so sure about that, and was about to point out that Emma must make her own final decisions based on facts they hashed out together, but Emma was in no state for reasonable conversation. "Goodbye, Tilly!" she gushed, then turned and walked quickly back toward the revolving door.

"But, Emma, what about my ride home?"

Emma turned pink and laughed like a giddy schoolgirl. "Oh, yes. I'm terribly sorry. I forgot." She walked back to Tilly and handed her a crisp one-hundred-dollar bill.

Tilly looked blankly at the huge sum of money. "What am I supposed to do with this? Buy a moped?"

Emma laughed again. "No, of course not. It's cab fare. The duke didn't think you'd want Dunbar to drive you home."

"He's right about that. If Dunbar got me alone, I'd end up at the bottom of Puget Sound wearing cement shoes. But this is way too much for cab fare." Tilly tried to hand back the cash, but Emma waved it away.

"Nonsense. The duke wanted you to have it. He's very generous, you know. Goodbye, Tilly. I'll ring you up later."

And with that, Emma hurried back through the revolving door and disappeared. Tilly watched her go with a sinking feeling in the pit of her stomach. "No wonder she takes so much guff from the guy. She *loves* him." The *l* word came out in a sort of elongated sneer. "The poor dope."

Sure, he was handsome, rich and had a fancy English title, but what else did he have to recommend him? Well, there was that smoldering sexuality.... When she first saw him on television, his brilliant, icy blue eyes made her shiver. Tilly realized now that the shiver had been a sexual reaction to the man, not an indication of repulsion. She wasn't sure what he did to her, but he definitely didn't repulse her.

Tilly scolded herself for allowing her mind to wander, caught the next cab and went directly home. She was too tired for the trouble of picking up her car at the office and, besides, she had plenty of fare money left to take the cab all weekend if she wanted to! At least she'd avoid parking hassles!

It was dark by the time Tilly climbed the stairs of her brownstone apartment building to the four rooms she shared with only one other breathing creature— Rebound, her cat. She was exhausted and she couldn't wait to kick off her shoes and relax.

The smell of Mrs. Morelli's spaghetti sauce, the sound of Mrs. Peterson lecturing her husband for leaving coffee rings on the table and even the view of the peeling linoleum in the laundry room as she passed it—all were comforting sensations to Tilly.

It's true the apartment building, which was built in the 1930s, could use a bit of work, but it was clean overall and the plumbing and wiring were reliable— and quickly fixed by the super, Mr. Epstein, when it wasn't so reliable.

Tilly had moved to the building when she first got

her job at the *Globe*. Now that her column was so successful, she could afford a much bigger, much nicer place, but she liked the neighborly feel of the building and its close proximity to downtown Seattle.

Coming from a large family and a close-knit farming community, she liked to know the people she lived around and she made sure she welcomed every new tenant to the building. Most of the tenants were of long standing and had become like an extended family to Tilly. She knew she could count on them for help if she found herself in a fix.

In fact sometimes they were *too* helpful. Although she dated frequently, they were always trying to match her up with someone. In Mrs. Morelli's opinion, an unmarried woman of twenty-eight was a precious waste of a perfectly good reproductive system.

Tilly opened the door and flicked on the light. As soon as she stepped over the threshold, she was nearly knocked over by Rebound, who came charging at her and immediately started weaving between her legs and meowing at the top of his lungs.

"Yes, I know I'm late," Tilly apologized, bending to stroke the cat's silky yellow coat. She kicked the door closed behind her. "But I really do have a good excuse. You see, I met this duke—"

Tilly's explanation was interrupted by the phone ringing. She was tempted to let it go to the answering machine, but she thought it might be Emma calling already. She crossed the room and looked down at the caller-ID box connected to her phone. The digital letters spelled out Royal Covington Hotel, so she quickly checked the calendar on the wall where she kept track of her social engagements, saw she was free tomorrow morning and picked up the receiver.

"Hi, Emma. I just barely got here. You must be awfully eager for that advice!"

Tilly's teasing greeting was answered by complete silence.

"Emma? Emma, are you there?"

"This is *not* Emma," replied a cultured, and obviously irritated, masculine voice.

Criminy, it was the duke! Tilly gulped, then answered, "Oh, it's you, Rothwell." She hoped she sounded more self-assured to him than she did to herself.

"Why on earth are you giving *Miss Darling* advice, McKinney?" he demanded.

Tilly bit her lip and twisted the phone cord between agitated fingers. "I don't understand why she told you."

"She didn't tell me. She didn't have to. *You* just told me."

Tilly moved to face the wall, gave her forehead a whack, then rested it there. "I guess I did. But what business is it of yours?"

"If the results of your advice to Miss Darling are half as detrimental to the tranquility of my home as your advice to Mrs. Peevey, I have a right to know what you're up to."

"Don't you have better things to do than call me up to pry into the activities of your staff on their days off?"

He sighed into the phone, then reminded her in a beleaguered tone, "If only you paid attention to the order of events, McKinney, you'd realize that I couldn't have called you to pry information out of you about Miss Darling. I didn't even know about that till you told me."

Tilly felt foolish. "Oh. Yeah. Right. Well…why *did* you call?"

There was another sigh. "I called to apologize about sending you home without providing for your transportation."

She had to give him credit for being a gentleman, so she made an effort to be civil. "Well…thank you. But you already did that. And believe me, the amount of cab fare you gave me could have transported me to Bridgeport, Connecticut." She smiled wryly. "Or was that the idea?"

He ignored her joke and continued with cool politeness, "I would have gone after you myself, but I tend to draw attention when I walk through the lobby of the hotel and might have been detained."

"No harm done," she assured him, plopping into a chair. Rebound immediately jumped onto her lap and started purring loudly. "I'm home safe and sound."

There was a pause. "What's that noise?"

"It's my cat. He's happy to see me." Tilly chuckled. "It's nice to be wanted *somewhere*."

"Well, perhaps you'd be 'wanted' in more places if you didn't cause so much trouble wherever you go," he suggested tartly. "Now, tell me, McKinney, what does Miss Darling need advice about? As far as I know, she doesn't presently have a love interest." There was another pause. "In fact I don't believe in the five years she's worked for me that she's ever been romantically entangled."

Men are as dumb as bricks, Tilly thought. "Let me repeat myself, Rothwell. What Emma needs advice about is not up for discussion."

"When are you going to meet?"

"Not up for discussion."

"Now, see here, McKinney—"

"Oops! Hear that beep, Rothwell? I've got another call coming in. It's probably Emma. See ya!"

"McKinney—!"

Emma hiked Rebound onto her hip, stood up and pushed the button on the phone, disconnecting the duke and connecting the new caller.

"Hello?"

"Tilly? It's me, Emma."

"Hi, Emma." Tilly sat back down, a satisfied smile curving her lips as she pictured the duke fuming and fussing at his posh digs at the Royal Covington. "I'm free tomorrow morning. Want to meet about nine for breakfast?"

Chapter Four

Saturday's weather started out bright and sunny and was forecasted to remain that way clear through the next day. So much fair weather on an early-May weekend was an unlikely scenario for Seattle, and Tilly took it as a good omen. She needed something to give her confidence because she'd had a bad feeling about this meeting with Emma ever since she got up that morning. But now that she was on her way—by cab—to a favorite coffee shop, she knew there was no turning back.

Last night she wasn't worried at all. Last night she'd gloated to herself because advising another one of Rothwell's employees was bound to make the duke madder than a wet hen...or, in this case, a wet rooster. By the sober light of day, however, Tilly reminded herself that this matter was very important, very personal and very emotional to Emma. Irritating the duke was not the main objective here. Although—Emma felt her lips curve in a rueful smile—it *was* a nice bonus.

When she entered the Cuppa Joe, she saw Emma waiting for her at a table in the far corner of the shop. She must have had her eyes glued to the door, because she shot to her feet and raised her arm stiffly in the air, looking as uncomfortable as some kid in a classroom who'd waited till the last minute to ask permission to go to the rest room.

As Tilly smiled and hurried over to her, she noted Emma's day-off attire and felt an immediate justification for interfering again in the duke's domestic affairs. Emma's outfit was no different than the day before, except that her tailored jacket, straight skirt and matching pumps were gray instead of navy blue.

For Tilly there was no question that she'd be wearing jeans all day. And since it was too warm for a sweater, she'd slipped on a short-sleeved, sage green knit top and tucked it into her belt. She was so glad *she* didn't work for the duke!

"Hi, Emma. Have you ordered yet?"

"Oh, no," Emma said with a nervous smile. "That would be rude."

Tilly pulled out a chair and sat down while simultaneously motioning to a waitress. "Hey, coffee doesn't count. When someone needs their morning cuppa, they shouldn't have to wait."

Emma sat down, too. "Oh. Well, I don't *drink* coffee as a rule."

Tilly smiled and scooted her chair forward. "This is the time to break that rule, Emma. Seattle has the best coffee in the States. We wean our babies on it here."

Emma's eyes got very big. "You do?"

Tilly laughed. "I was only kidding."

Emma gave an embarrassed chuckle. "Of course you were."

The waitress showed up just then, thumped a large brown mug in front of Tilly and filled it to the brim with steaming black coffee. "Hi, Tilly," she said with a friendly grin. "What'll it be?"

"Today I want a treat, Karen. Instead of a bagel, I'll have a cheese danish."

Karen nodded, then looked at Emma with raised brows. "And how about you?"

"I usually have tea in the morning...." She turned to Tilly. "But you think I ought to try the coffee here?"

"You don't have to drink it like mine...black and strong enough to strip paint. That's how I like it in the morning, but in the afternoon I usually have a latte."

"That's with steamed milk added to it, right?"

Tilly nodded. "Right. And if you just have a single shot of espresso in it, it won't be too strong."

Emma looked up at the waitress. "I'll have a *single* latte and a cheese danish, too, please."

"Be back in a jiff," the waitress assured them, then turned and left.

Tilly smiled encouragingly at Emma. "Do you want to wade in the baby pool for a while, or do you want to jump right into the deep end and start swimming?"

Emma laughed. "If I decipher that correctly, you're wondering if I want to chitchat first, or if I want to immediately lay out my problems for your expert perusal."

"Exactly. But please don't think of me as an expert—think of me as a friend you feel comfortable talking to, okay?"

Emma nodded and her smile died away. She fidgeted with the end of the paper napkin on the table in front of her. "Well, then, friend, let's just chitchat for a while...at least till the waitress has come and gone.''

"Okay." Tilly folded her arms in front of her and rested them on the edge of the table. "So...is tea still the hot beverage of choice in England, or is coffee catching on?"

"Coffee's becoming very popular in England," Emma told her. "Particularly among the younger people. Traditionalists, however, still prefer tea. The duke, although only thirty-two, is a tea drinker. He's very traditional, you know, but he says his preference for tea is for practical reasons. He says coffee makes you hyper, while tea refreshes and relaxes you. He says that's why Americans are always shooting one another." She bent forward to make her point. "*Coffee nerves,* he says."

At this point Karen returned with their sweet rolls and Emma's latte, giving Emma a chance to catch her breath. When Karen left again, Tilly said wryly, "Well, now that the waitress has come and gone, I guess we can talk about *the duke.*"

Emma caught her meaning and blushed. "He does sort of creep into my conversation even when I'm trying not to talk about him, doesn't he?"

Tilly chuckled. "Well, yeah. 'The duke' says this. 'The duke' says that."

"Oh, but I can't help myself, Tilly!" Emma confessed. "I've been working for him for five years. While he resides at Chesterfield Hall in Dorset, I live on the estate. When he spends time in London, I have a room in his town house. I'm expected to be available whenever he needs me, which sometimes includes late-night projects."

"I hope he pays you well for being so available," Tilly observed.

"Oh, yes. Very well. But I hardly ever need to spend any of it, so I've got pounds and pounds saved away." She sighed. "We've traveled all over the world together, eaten hundreds of meals together." She spread her hands in a helpless gesture. "Is it any wonder I'm in love with him?"

It's a wonder you haven't killed him, Tilly thought, but said instead, "That's a lot of time to spend with someone. Why haven't you told him your feelings after all these years?"

Emma took a cautious sip of her latte. "I was hoping to get some indication of his feelings before I blurted out my own."

"Has he given you any reason to think he returns your…er…affection?"

"No, but I don't believe he'd show it even if he *did* care for me."

Tilly made a puzzled grimace. "Why not?"

"Because I work for him," Emma explained. "He wouldn't think it was proper to make advances. And he wouldn't want me to think he was taking advantage of me." Emma poked at her danish with a fork. "Besides, Lord Rothwell hides his feelings most of the time."

Tilly shrugged and picked up her mug, took a sip. "Maybe he isn't hiding anything. Maybe he doesn't *have* feelings."

"You mean for me?"

"No, I mean for anybody. He appears rather cold to me."

"You're so wrong, Tilly. If you only knew how

generous he is, how—'' She cut herself off. ''But I mustn't tell you everything. He'd be angry.''

Tilly patted her hand. ''I'll take your word for it. You wouldn't like him if he wasn't a nice guy…I suppose. But as I see it, Emma, there's only one thing to do.''

Emma's eyes widened. ''What?''

''You have to tell him how you feel. You can't go on like this forever. If he cares about you, he's not going to let a job get in the way of a relationship.''

''And if he doesn't care for me?''

''Then you're wasting your time. You need to find another less demanding job and start enjoying your life. You've got a nest egg in the bank, so it's not like you won't be provided for while you figure out what you want. There's lots of men out there, lots of things to see and do. Right now the duke is your whole life. If there's no future in it, what's the point?''

Emma clutched her mug and stared into her latte. She looked very glum.

''Have I been too blunt?'' Tilly inquired gently. ''Remember, you make the final decisions about your life. I'm only telling you what I think.''

Emma looked up and smiled wanly. ''I expected you to be blunt. And you've only said what I've been telling myself for the past two years. But hearing it from you gives me the courage to do something about it, Tilly. Thank you.''

Tilly sat back. ''You mean…that's it? We're done?''

Emma bit her lip. ''Well, we're done with *that*

part. But I was hoping you'd also advise me on how to tell him...well...that I love him.''

Tilly shook her head. ''That's where I bow out completely, Emma. You're going to have to use your own words for that. Words that come straight from your heart. Besides, I've never confessed my undying love to *any* man, so I wouldn't know the first place to start.''

''You've never been in love?''

Tilly gave a firm shake of her head. ''No. Never. So, you see, I'm no help there. But my instincts tell me you gotta just say what you feel.''

''Of course, you're right,'' Emma said seriously. ''I'll do exactly as you suggest. I'll just say what I feel.''

Tilly studied Emma's sober, earnest expression, her slim white hands wrapped tightly around the coffee mug. Her heart went out to the lovelorn girl. She had a pretty good idea how her interview would end with the duke and she knew Emma would initially be heartbroken. But finding a life away from the duke—especially if he didn't care for her—was in her best interests. And the sooner the better. But just so it was no more traumatic than necessary, Tilly couldn't resist the urge to give Emma just a little more advice, especially if there was the tiniest possibility that the duke *did* care for her.

''Emma...what are you going to wear when you tell the duke?''

Emma looked struck. ''I don't know. I haven't really thought about it.''

''Has he ever seen you in anything but a tailored suit?''

''Only once or twice, I suppose.''

"I suggest you buy something very feminine, very unbusinesslike."

"Okay."

"And about your hair—"

Emma reached up and stroked her smooth cap of hair. "My hair?"

"Maybe you should fluff it up a little." She peered closely at Emma's face. "And wear a little makeup."

"But I *am* wearing makeup."

"Not enough. You've got great bone structure and beautiful skin, Emma. Play them up. And your eyes are so darned blue…have you ever considered wearing contact lenses?"

"But the duke likes my tailored appearance," Emma said uncertainly. "He said it was one of the reasons he hired me."

"That's the point, Emma. He hired you to be his secretary, not his lover. I'm sure you've seen some of the duke's dates. Are they tailored looking, or are they feminine and glamorous?"

Emma thought for half a minute, then got a determined look on her face. "Tilly, have you got time to go shopping with me this morning…and maybe go to the hairdresser's, too?"

Tilly smiled. "You bet. But drink the rest of your latte and eat your danish, 'cause you're gonna need your strength."

FOUR HOURS LATER, Tilly and Emma climbed out of a taxi in front of the Royal Covington. "Wait for me," Tilly instructed the driver as he opened the trunk and handed packages and shopping bags to the bellboy.

Emma and Tilly faced each other on the sidewalk,

both women clearly reluctant to end their companionable day.

"It's been fun," Emma said with a shy smile. "Thank you, Tilly. Thank you for everything."

Tilly smiled back. "Hey, it was a treat. I love to help other people spend their money." And she couldn't believe the incredible results of spending a few hundred dollars. Emma's transformation from a nondescript employee of the duke of Chesterfield to a stunning young woman in a pale pink sundress was incredible. Her hair framed her tastefully made-up face in a new, softer style, and her blue eyes, spiked with long, dark lashes, glittered like jewels.

"The contacts were a *very* good idea of mine," Tilly said with satisfaction. "You look gorgeous."

Emma blushed. "Thank you. I just hope the duke thinks so."

"Oh, he'll think so. He's got eyes, hasn't he?" Tilly hesitated, then added, "But you realize that while the duke might think you're the prettiest little gal in town, that doesn't mean—"

"Oh, I know," Emma interrupted her. "I'm being very realistic about this. If the duke doesn't have feelings for me, and doesn't expect to develop any, I'm handing in my resignation." She smiled bravely. "It will be difficult to leave, but now, thanks to you, I have a better self-image. I'm very optimistic about the future."

"I'm glad, Emma." Tilly grabbed Emma's hands and squeezed them. "Remember…whatever happens today with the duke is what was meant to be. Go forward and conquer, girlfriend."

Emma laughed and impulsively hugged Tilly.

Then, after one more affectionate smile between the two women, Emma turned and walked into the hotel.

TILLY SPENT the rest of the afternoon cleaning her apartment and returning phone calls. There were several messages on her answering machine when she got home—some from fellow employees of the *Globe* wondering what she'd been doing with the "duke dude" the day before, and some from friends who wanted to go out that night.

But Tilly was in no mood to go out. She couldn't quit thinking about Emma and wondering how her interview with the duke had gone. She just hoped that if the duke had no feelings for Emma, he'd let her down gently. And if he did have feelings for her, that he'd treated her with the respect and affection she deserved.

What Tilly was really hoping for was Emma's emancipation from such an overpowering employer and a future filled with lots of dates and parties and an exciting job that didn't require her to take on the personality of a drone. After spending the day with Emma, Tilly felt like she'd made a friend of the shy woman, and she had an earnest interest in her happiness.

By dusk Emma was done with her cleaning and was making popcorn for dinner, which she intended to consume in front of the TV as she watched Jimmy Stewart charm Katharine Hepburn in *The Philadelphia Story*. Stewart was her kind of guy. Earnest, unassuming, incorruptible, tall—

"Tilly! Tilly, open the door!"

Tilly hurried to open the door for Mrs. Morelli.

"What's the matter, Mrs. Morelli? Not another

grease fire?'' Tilly had had enough kitchen disasters to last her for a while.

"No! No fire! Something better!" Mrs. Morelli exclaimed, her large dark eyes bright with excitement.

"Gee, Mrs. Morelli," Tilly joked, "what can be better than a grease fire?"

Instead of answering, Mrs. Morelli grabbed Tilly's arm and dragged her toward the living-room window that faced the front of the building. "Come and see. There's a long dark car out front and—"

Tilly stopped in her tracks, her heart suddenly beating out of control. Mrs. Morelli, a first-generation American from Italy, had a somewhat limited vocabulary and a charming accent. "You mean...a limousine?"

She nodded her head vigorously. "Yes! Yes! A *lee*mousine. What the movie stars go to the Oscars in, you know?" She leaned forward and whispered, "It's *him*. That duke everyone is talking about. He's here."

"Are you sure?" Tilly asked feebly.

Mrs. Morelli gave an elaborate shrug and threw her hands in the air. "I saw him on television yesterday, and today, plain as the nose on my face, he's standing outside by that *lee*mousine with a bunch of guys dressed in black and wearing funny hats."

"That sounds like the duke, all right," Tilly muttered.

"Well, come and see for yourself!" Mrs. Morelli urged, tugging Tilly to the window.

Tilly went, peeked out just far enough to see the duke scowling up at the building, then plastered herself out of sight against the wall. There was no doubt in her mind why he was there.

"Who do you think he's come to see?" Mrs. Morelli wondered aloud. "Or maybe he's just lost and needs directions. I got lost all the time when I first moved here."

"He knows exactly where he is," Tilly said grimly. "He's here to see me."

Mrs. Morelli twirled around and gazed at Tilly with astonishment. But just as Tilly expected, her expression eventually turned speculative. "He's picking you up for a date, yes? Lucky girl. *Smart* girl." Mrs. Morelli's eyes flitted over Tilly's jeans and casual top, then narrowed with consternation. "But you're not ready!"

Tilly pushed off from the wall and moved to the middle of the room. She turned around and crossed her arms over her chest. "He's not my date," she said firmly. "And he's the last man on earth I'd ever go out with."

Mrs. Morelli shook her head in confusion. "But why is he here?"

"To wring my neck, probably."

Mrs. Morelli's eyebrows shot up. "He's mad at you? But that's good, too. You can make up after."

"It's not like that, Mrs. Morelli. The duke—"

But Tilly was interrupted by the sound of several pairs of footsteps coming up the stairs.

"You'd better leave, Mrs. Morelli," Tilly told her, opening the door and gently guiding her in the direction of her own apartment across the hall. "You don't want to see this."

"Yes, I do. But I'll settle for hearing all about it when he leaves," she bargained.

Tilly nodded distractedly, glanced furtively in the direction of the stairwell, then quickly shut the door and leaned against it. She jumped when, less than ten seconds later, there was a sharp rap against the wood. She took a deep breath, blew it out slowly, then opened the door.

Tilly looked up into the stern face and the brilliant, hooded eyes of the duke of Chesterfield. His tall form filled the doorway. With his broad shoulders, lean hips and ever so long legs, his figure was as imposing in a blue knit pullover and gray slacks as it had been in a trench coat. Or perhaps more so... The toned musculature of his chest and shoulders was obvious under the soft, slightly clingy fabric of his shirt.

"Rothwell," she croaked.

"McKinney," he answered mockingly. "May I come in?"

She licked her lips. "Okay...but only you this time. Your men can stay outside." She wasn't going to be intimidated again by numbers.

The duke nodded curtly, then turned and conveyed his wishes with a single look directed at Mendenhall. The men stepped back, the duke stepped inside and Tilly shut the door.

He stood with his back to her, surveying the room. Tilly immediately felt defensive, as if he was comparing his palatial home in Dorset with her much, *much* humbler surroundings. She walked around and stood in front of him, forcing him to look down at her.

"Would you like to sit down?" she asked, her tone polite but stilted. She motioned with an elegant wave of her arm toward her comfortable fifteen-year-old sofa, which was in dire need of reupholstering or replacing. But if she got a new couch, she couldn't eat buttered popcorn while she watched TV, and there was no way she was giving up her popcorn.

"I'd rather stand, thank you," he answered coolly.

"Because you don't like my couch, or because you're so much taller than me and want to intimidate me?"

His blue eyes glittered. "I wish I *could* intimidate you," he murmured dryly. "I brought along all four of my so-called minions to try to intimidate you, and you ordered them to stay outside. Is there no limit to your—what is that homely term? Ah, yes. Your *gumption?*"

Tilly was a little taken off guard by the duke's question. If she'd felt it was at all possible, she might have thought he'd slipped her a backhanded compliment. In her neck of the woods, gumption was considered a good thing.

"I'm not sure what you're getting at, Rothwell," Tilly hedged, inwardly squirming under the duke's continued scrutiny. "So, why don't you get to the point? To what do I owe this lovely, but unexpected, visit?"

He sat down, crossing his long legs ankle to knee, and leaned back against the old cushions as if he were there to watch basketball and down a few brews. He smiled at her lazily...and she felt that shivery sexual awareness again.

"I hardly think my visit unexpected. You know exactly why I'm here, McKinney. It's about Miss Darling."

Tilly nervously licked her lips and sat down on the edge of a chair opposite the sofa. "Yes. What about her?"

His lips pursed for a second, then his sexy smile came back full force. She felt like a quivering, mesmerized field rabbit being stalked by a beautiful, devious golden fox. "You're determined to make me work for a confession, aren't you?"

Tilly shrugged and nonchalantly flicked away a tiny piece of popcorn hull that had stuck to her knee. "I haven't got anything to confess."

The smile disappeared. "Haven't you? Well, perhaps you've forgotten." He sat forward on the couch, his hands loosely clasped together, his elbows resting on his knees. "Let me jog your memory."

Tilly gulped and sat very still, watching him with a mixture of fear, defiance and…yes…a wholly female appreciation for such an awesome combination of brains and brawn.

"You advised my secretary to tart herself up—"

Instantly incensed, Tilly rose to her feet. "'Tart herself up' is a completely incorrect and insulting description of what Emma did today."

The duke stood, too, hovering over her like a menacing thundercloud. "Then told her to divulge certain tender feelings she's harbored for me—"

"Feelings that I'm at a complete loss to understand!"

"Feelings that I could not return—"

"Big surprise."

"Which distressed Miss Darling to such an extent that it has effectively ruined our former extremely satisfying working relationship—"

"Bondage, you mean."

"Prompting her to tender her resignation!"

"More power to her!"

By the end of this exchange, Tilly realized they

were both shouting and probably engaging the interest of the entire building. The duke was bent forward at the waist, and Tilly's chin was thrust up as high as it could go. They were nearly nose to nose, breathing hard and flushed in the face.

Tilly was the first to turn away. She walked to the window and forced herself to calm down. As she focused on an antique shop across the street, the duke drew near. His footsteps were almost soundless on the carpeted floor, but his presence announced itself by the sheer pull of his magnetism.

Tilly was afraid to turn around. She felt like a coward, but his nearness confused her. She wasn't sure how it was possible, but he angered her and attracted her at the same time, and both with the same intensity.

"I apologize for raising my voice," he said. "As a rule, I never do...."

Tilly turned around. Meeting his eyes was difficult, but she was ashamed of being cowardly and wasn't going to allow herself to wimp out. His brows were knit, his mouth serious, but his eyes held a hint of puzzlement...as if, like her, he was trying to sort out jumbled feelings.

"If you didn't come here to read me the riot act, why did you come?" she asked him. "If you expect me to try to talk Emma out of her decision, you're barking up the wrong tree, Rothwell. She did what she had to do, and I'm proud of her for doing it."

He continued to stare at her with that bemused expression, then nearly bowled her over when he said quietly, "I didn't like hurting her, you know. I never had the slightest idea she had those sorts of feelings for me."

Could the duke actually have a heart after all? Tilly wondered.

In a softened tone she asked, "Did she take it okay?"

He nodded, still with that furrowed brow, that troubled, slightly distracted expression. "Yes, of course she did. She's a trouper...and very lovely. And it didn't take makeup and contact lenses to point that out to me. Yes, I admit 'tarted up' was an inexcusable term to use, but I was angry. I'm going to miss her. She was an excellent secretary and a very pleasant person to have around. She never caused me a moment of grief."

The furrow disappeared. "You, on the other hand..." His eyes grew brilliant once more as they focused on Tilly. "This is all your fault, of course."

Tilly gave a huff of exasperation. "No, it isn't. This would have happened eventually. It was just a matter of time."

The duke drew himself up quite tall. "A matter of time, you say? But timing can be so crucial. I'm left without a secretary for the final days of my lecture tour."

"She won't finish out the week?"

"It would be extremely awkward for us both. Of course, I left it to her to decide, but she lost no time in booking a late flight to London tonight, directly after she is through...er...bowling with Mrs. Peevey."

Tilly couldn't hold back a chuckle, which helped her to feel a little less tense. "I'm glad she didn't stand up Mrs. Peevey."

"But you couldn't care less that she left *me* in the lurch?"

"You can call temporary services and hire another secretary for the week...or even two or three secretaries, if you want."

"Well, I *don't* want. I want *you* to be my secretary, McKinney."

Tilly laughed nervously. "Very funny, Rothwell. Tell me another."

"I'm not making a joke. I'm perfectly serious."

Tilly sobered. "But you don't like me, and I don't like you."

"That doesn't matter. In fact, perhaps it's preferable. There'll be no chance of you developing amorous feelings for me."

"You can count on that," Tilly assured him, with perhaps too much force. "But I have no intention of—"

"I need someone clever who'll catch on quickly," he interrupted, then gave a devilish smile. "You're as clever as they come, McKinney. In a matter of hours you've managed to completely disrupt my peaceful, organized household. The least you can do is fill in for Miss Darling for the remainder of my lecture tour."

Tilly propped her fists on her hips. "You're a real pill, Rothwell. In case you hadn't noticed, I've already got a job."

He flicked his wrist in an elegant dismissal. "You have the next week off."

"I do not." She *had* scheduled Thursday and Friday off to spend a long weekend with her family in Washougal, but not the whole week.

"You do, too. I know about your plans to visit your family, and your boss, Harrison Gray, has graciously granted you Monday through Wednesday off, as well, in order to make amends to me for the loss of Miss Darling. I'll only need your help through Wednesday morning.''

''Harrison would never do such a thing!''

''But he already has.''

Tilly was nearly at the end of her rope. Was everyone conspiring against her? ''He can't *make* me work for you.''

''No, he can't.'' The duke paused, observed her for a moment, then quirked his lips in a small, irritating smile. ''But I think you will, because if you don't, I'll sue the newspaper for the loss of time and money and the mental anguish occasioned by the resignation of Miss Darling...which was, of course, instigated by your advice.''

Tilly threw her hands in the air and took a quick pace around the room, thinking furiously. Facing him again, she challenged, ''You'd never win such a flimsy case, and Harrison knows it.''

He conceded this point with a token nod of the head. ''Perhaps...but Mr. Gray does not want the bother of finding out. He seems perfectly happy to settle this matter out of court.'' At her stunned and disbelieving silence, he saw the portable phone by the sofa, lifted the receiver and suggested, ''If you don't believe me, why don't you call him?''

''Oh, I'll call him, all right,'' Tilly muttered, at her wit's end. How could this possibly be happening? ''But later, when I'm alone and no one will be shocked by my language.''

The duke shrugged and replaced the receiver. ''Very well. Although I'm quite certain nothing you could say would shock me, McKinney.'' He rubbed his hands together. ''Now...how soon can you be packed and ready to go?''

Chapter Five

Julian smiled down at Tilly's flushed and angry countenance. Her green eyes flashed like warning signals on an about-to-explode bomb. She was really quite lovely when she was mad...which, in his experience with her, was most of the time.

He couldn't remember the last time he'd had so much fun. But then, successful retaliation was always enjoyable, and Tilly was such a satisfactory foil. Indeed, she was a worthy opponent, but he had outmaneuvered her at last.

Perhaps with her constantly with him for the few days, kept busy and under his watchful eye, he could curtail any further meddling among his staff till he had a chance to get them all out of the country. What was left of his staff, he wished to remain intact.

"What did you just say about...about *packing?*"

"A little slow on the uptake, aren't you, McKinney?"

She shook her head disbelievingly. "You can't mean it. You don't really expect me to move into the hotel with you?"

Julian examined his fingernails. "In my very suite. I'm sure you'll find Miss Darling's room comfortable and convenient." He gave her a devilish smile. "It's just down the hall from mine."

Tilly vigorously shook her head and backed off. "No way. Forget it, Rothwell. If I have to fill in for Emma—which I'm still not convinced is going to happen—I can do it while maintaining my sleeping premises right here. I'll come early and stay late, but I won't sleep under your regal roof, Rothwell."

Julian shrugged. "But you have to. That's what Miss Darling did, and that's what I expect you to do. You must, in essence, replace her in every way." He smiled again. "With the exception of falling in love with me." At her stricken expression, he couldn't resist sauntering up to her, tilting her chin with his forefinger and saying in a husky drawl, "Unless you can't help yourself, of course."

To Julian's delight Tilly jerked her head away, turned on her heel, grabbed the portable telephone and stomped into what he presumed to be her bedroom. Standing in the doorway, she shook the phone at him and said, "If you won't leave me alone to talk to Harrison, I'll call him from in here. And I expect you to respect my privacy, Rothwell."

"Don't worry, McKinney," he assured her. "I don't follow women into their sleeping quarters unless I'm invited. And even then—" he gave an elaborate shrug "—sometimes I refuse."

She narrowed her eyes and sent him a seething glare that scorched across the distance between them like the sizzling fuse on a lighted stick of dynamite. Without another word she threw the door shut and locked it from the other side.

Julian chuckled to himself. Despite the fact that he was still smarting over the loss of his excellent secretary, he was having a delightful time. And he might as well make the best of things because Miss Darling's decision was final. She was never coming back.

Sobered by the memory of that painful interview with Miss Darling, Julian strolled to the window and looked out at the darkening street below. He would miss her, but she was entirely correct about the necessity to leave now that she'd bared her soul to him.

If only Tilly had kept her damnable advice to herself... But Julian had to admit that she was right about it being only a matter of time before Miss Darling handed in her walking papers. It was not conducive to one's peace of mind to be smitten with one's boss, and Julian truly cared about Miss Darling's peace of mind.

Just as he cared about his entire staff. They were like family to him, which he supposed was something Tilly would never understand. She apparently had a large and loving family, and had enjoyed a carefree childhood on a farm in...what was the name of that town?

He, on the other hand, had been an only child raised by a strict, undemonstrative father, whom he saw only on holidays from Eton and Oxford. Even when his father died ten years ago, leaving Julian the title, acres of valuable property and enormous sums of money, he had had no final words of tenderness for his son. He'd simply gritted his teeth and succumbed to a painful disease without a single word of complaint...or of love. It was the old soldier in him, Julian supposed. Or the famous British "stiff upper lip."

Julian turned away from the window, impatient

with his somber reflections. He could hear the agitated murmur of Tilly's voice behind the closed door and could imagine her consternation when she realized that Harrison Gray entirely supported Julian's demand to use her in the capacity of secretary for the next few days.

Julian had no intention of suing the newspaper, and Gray knew it. He suspected that the intrepid editor of the *Globe* was looking to get a story out of Tilly's little adventure.

Julian smiled. Just thinking about having her around for a while to torture at will was a cheering thought. And he admitted to himself that he would enjoy having her around for other reasons, too. He was attracted to her. A light flirtation with the chit would be diverting.

She was certainly nothing like the usual female he was attracted to, the leggy, languid beauties he squired around London and Paris and occasionally took for Greek-island holidays on his yacht. But they inevitably bored him. His title and his riches were daunting to most women, and they never talked back. Tilly couldn't help but talk back, and he liked her for it.

Julian snooped around her apartment, taking in the old, comfortable furniture, the bits of antique china interspersed with stuffed Disney figures, and inspected the piles of old movie videos. Her apartment was homey and lived-in, just the sort of place he liked. It reminded him of his holiday cottage in Cornwall. The one he'd loved to visit as a small child during the summer months with his mother before she died...

He turned when he heard a door creak open. When

he saw Tilly standing there with a fierce scowl on her pretty face, he knew the conversation with her boss had gone just as he'd anticipated.

"You don't expect me to come tonight, do you?" she said at last. "Emma won't even be gone yet."

Julian strolled to the middle of the room and slid his hands into his pant pockets. "No, I don't expect you to come tonight. Tomorrow night will be soon enough."

He saw her stiffen. "Why not Monday morning? What's the point of coming the night before I actually start working for you?"

"I start work very early in the morning. And sometimes I require assistance during the night."

She glared at him. "What sort of assistance?"

He shrugged, smiled. "You know...in case I have an inspiring thought."

Up came the small chin, jutting out like the prow of a ship. "A lot of men have inspiring thoughts in the middle of the night. Get this straight, Rothwell— I'll have nothing to do with your nocturnal inspirations."

He raised a brow. "You misunderstand, McKinney. I'm writing a children's book, an instructional anthology of stories based on the Roman artifacts I've collected. Sometimes I get ideas for it in the middle of the night."

The chin lowered. "Oh."

"Heavens, what did you think I meant?"

He watched her turn a delicious shade of pink. "I wasn't thinking anything."

"What a marvelous achievement. How do you do that?"

"How do I do what?"

"How do you think about nothing? It sounds relaxing."

Her eyes fluttered shut, and she heaved an enormous sigh. "Shouldn't you be going, Rothwell? I've got things to do, like figuring out what to do with my cat for the next few days."

Julian looked around. "You have a cat? Unlike you, he must be shy and retiring. I haven't seen a glimpse of him."

"He's a tomcat. He's out doing his thing," she explained.

"I see," Julian said gravely. "Well, what about asking the lady in apartment 3C to take care of him so he can continue to do 'his thing' on his own prowling grounds?"

Her eyes narrowed. "How do you know about Mrs. Morelli?"

"Is that her name? I noticed her peeking at me through her door as I finished climbing the stairs. She looks very...er...friendly."

"She's that, all right," Tilly said with a sigh. "And I'm sure she wouldn't mind taking care of Rebound for me." Her brows furrowed. "But I'll have to come by and see him now and then, or he might freak out and run away."

"You have my permission to do so."

Her head reared up. "I didn't ask permission."

"No, you didn't," he answered with dry amusement. "But I gave it to you anyway."

"Now, see here, Rothwell, I don't need your—"

"I'll send Dunbar with the limousine tomorrow evening at six," he interrupted, moving toward the door.

This stopped her cold. "Dunbar?"

"Don't worry. I'll threaten to dock his salary if he so much as harms a single titian hair on your head. Besides, I'll send my man, Mendenhall, with him. Mendenhall's thoroughly reliable—thank God one of my staff is! We'll start off the evening by having dinner."

"Dinner? With you?" She followed him to the door, her brows furrowed again. She sounded nervous, and he found that highly satisfactory.

He turned, his hand on the doorknob. "You needn't be afraid of eating with me. My friends tell me my manners are impeccable. Besides, this will be a *business* dinner, McKinney. I'll go over your job requirements at that time."

The worried furrow in her brow only slightly relaxed. "Oh. Okay."

He skimmed her from head to toe. "And about your clothes—"

"What about my clothes?" she challenged. "I won't buy an entire new wardrobe of suits with coordinating shoes and handbags, Rothwell."

"Of course not, but you do have a few skirts, don't you?" He opened the door and stepped out into the hall. "It is customary in my household for female employees to wear skirts or dresses. It's more businesslike, too. Besides, I've always preferred looking at women whose attire distinguishes them somewhat from the male staff."

"You don't have to look at me at all, Rothwell," Tilly retorted.

"But we'll be together almost constantly, McKinney. I won't be able to help occasionally glancing your way, now, will I?"

"Is this skirt-wearing fetish of yours written into

some kind of policy contract? In other words, do I *have* to wear skirts, or are you just demanding it in that lordlike way of yours?"

He lowered his brows in mock reprimand. "What's the matter, McKinney? Got knobby knees?"

He watched her jaw tighten and her color rise. "I'll ignore that comment. And as for what I wear to work, Rothwell, you're just going to have to trust me to decide for myself what's comfortable and appropriate. In other words I'll wear what I please, and you can like it or lump it."

Her voice was a catlike growl that he found most alluring. He'd have to make sure he kept her angry most of the time.

"All right," he conceded cheerfully. "Wear what you please. Till tomorrow, then, McKinney. Goodbye." He smiled and bowed, then closed the door and started down the hall. Halfway down the stairs he heard what he was quite sure was someone kicking a door, followed by a muffled exclamation of pain. His smile broadened.

AT 5:55 P.M. ON SUNDAY, Tilly stood at the door to apartment 3C and handed Rebound to Mrs. Morelli.

"Please don't let him stay out all night, Mrs. Morelli. I'm afraid he'll run away."

Mrs. Morelli took Rebound and held him against her large bosom. "What if he doesn't come when I call?"

"Just crack a window and open a can of something with the electric opener. He'll come."

Mrs. Morelli dipped her head and looked into Tilly's downcast face. "You are sad, Tilly. You should be excited. You'll be living with a duke for four days."

"Not all English noblemen have Charming as their last name, Mrs. Morelli," Tilly said with a sigh.

"Give him a chance," Mrs. Morelli urged. "Don't judge too quickly." She leaned forward and whispered, "He's handsome and rich. Give the guy a little slack."

Tilly laughed at the sound of American slang coming out of Mrs. Morelli's mouth. Then she gave Rebound a last scratch behind the ears and headed back to her apartment. "See you, Mrs. Morelli," she called over her shoulder. "And thank you."

"You said you'd tell me all about it when you get back," Mrs. Morelli reminded her.

"Of course," Tilly answered with a final smile as she opened her door, then quickly closed it behind her. "Of course," Tilly repeated to herself as she leaned momentarily against the door. "I'll give you all the details, and believe me they'll be gory."

Tilly pushed off from the door and moved around her apartment, turning out lights and closing drapes. She fully expected the duke's chauffeur and main man to be punctual. By the single light she'd left on, she stood in front of the narrow full-length mirror by the door and examined her appearance one last time.

"I know that comment about knobby knees was just a cheap trick to get me to wear a skirt, Rothwell," she mumbled aloud as she surveyed her black tailored pants, shiny gray-and-white-striped vest and white long-sleeved shirt with an open collar. "And I'm not taking the bait."

She felt sleek and sophisticated in the outfit she was wearing for her so-called orientation dinner at

the Royal Covington; it even made her look taller.
And she felt she looked perfectly professional without wearing the skirt that also went with the vest and
blouse.

"Knobby knees," she repeated disdainfully. "No
way, Rothwell." She smoothed the vest over her hips
and turned slowly to get a good view from all sides.
While she'd always appreciated the slim proportions
she'd inherited from her mother, she'd never thought
much about her knees. She felt a moment's doubt.
The duke *was* just taunting her, wasn't he?

Her inspection was interrupted by the doorbell
ringing. She glanced at the wall clock and saw that
it was precisely six, just as she'd anticipated. She
grabbed her black blazer off the back of the couch
and slipped into it, then opened the door.

"Good evening, Ms. McKinney," Mendenhall in-
toned soberly. "Are you ready?"

"Ready as I'll ever be," she said wryly.

Mendenhall didn't bat an eye or crack a smile. My,
he was serious for such a young stud!

"May I carry your bags?"

Tilly stepped back and waved toward her single
suitcase and overnight bag. "Be my guest. I packed
light, so don't worry about straining your back packing five hundred pounds down the stairs."

"Thank you," he said, smiling vaguely. Then the
smile abruptly vanished, and he simply stood there,
chewing the inside of his lip and staring at the floor.
Tilly waited uncomfortably, wondering if there was
some kind of protocol she wasn't aware of. Was she
supposed to hurry out the door ahead of him, her
nose in the air, before he could pick up her bags?

"Ms. McKinney, I'd like to say something to you."

Tilly waited again, but he said nothing. She gave an encouraging nod of her head. "Yes, Mendenhall, what did you want to say?"

Finally he lifted his gaze to meet hers. "I wanted to commend you on your advice to Miss Darling."

Tilly choked on a laugh. "Really? You're not just bamming me, are you?"

His brow furrowed. "'Bamming' you, ma'am?"

"You know...pulling my leg. You really think I gave Emma good advice?"

He nodded gravely. "Yes, I do."

"And you don't feel the tiniest bit disloyal to the duke?"

"Actually I do," he admitted. "But Emma...that is, Miss Darling...deserves to be happy. We'll... we'll all miss her, but it's for the best. That's all I wanted to say, ma'am."

And when he said that was all he wanted to say, that's exactly what he meant. He picked up the suitcase and overnight bag and started down the stairs. Tilly locked her door and followed close behind.

Several times on the way to the hotel Tilly tried to get Mendenhall to talk again, if for no other reason than to get her mind off Dunbar's menacing glare in the mirror. She chose safe subjects about ordinary, everyday stuff, but he refused to be drawn into conversation. He kept his replies short, polite and to the point. Tilly finally gave up.

Once they arrived at the hotel, Mendenhall escorted her inside, into the elevator, and right up to the duke's suite without uttering another word. He rapped briskly on the glossy wood paneling of the double doors, then, without waiting for someone to answer, turned one of the gilded handles and ushered Tilly inside. He set down her luggage on the parquet floor of the entry hall.

"Come this way, Ms. McKinney," Mendenhall instructed, then lightly touched her elbow and guided her through the main room—plushly carpeted and elegantly furnished—and down a hallway to another set of closed double doors. "I believe the duke will be waiting for you inside."

"Is...is this his office?" Tilly inquired nervously.

"No, it is the dining room," Mendenhall answered.

"What...what about my bags?" She was stalling and she knew it. But the idea of facing what was on the other side of those doors was either frightening her or exciting her; she wasn't sure which. She was shivering from head to toe.

"I'll see that they get to your room."

Tilly looked up and down the hall. There were a lot of doors. "Which *is* my room?"

Was she imagining it, or did Mendenhall look slightly amused for a moment before his features returned to their usual deadpan expression? "I'm sure the duke will show you later. Good night, Ms. McKinney." He bowed and took off down the hall, disappearing around the corner.

"Hell," Tilly muttered under her breath. She looked at the door, wondering if she was supposed to knock or just barge in. Deciding to show her disdain for the usual protocol—of which she was completely ignorant anyway—she opened the door and nonchalantly strode in.

She was disappointed when she found no duke in

the room to be offended by her conduct. But her disappointment was quickly forgotten as she gazed with admiration at the scene before her.

The room was only of moderate proportions, which reinforced the intimate mood that had been created already by candles and the delicate scent of a small, tasteful floral arrangement in the middle of a linen-draped table. Crystal and china gleamed in the candlelight. And beyond the table was a floor-to-ceiling view of Puget Sound. Irresistibly drawn to it, Tilly crossed the room to stand in front of the window.

The sun was just setting, and flamingo pink and mango orange shimmered on the water, gilded the sails of drifting boats, and tinted the clouds that dotted the sky like a herd of fat, fluffy sheep.

Tilly stood with her arms folded tightly over her chest, mesmerized by the view, but with a growing uneasiness building in her gut. "This is how you conduct business, Rothwell?" she murmured to herself.

"What did you say, McKinney?"

Tilly twirled around, feeling as startled as if he'd caught her stuffing the silverware down her pants. The duke was standing just inside the door, holding a bottle of wine. "I wasn't saying anything," she blurted. *Good Lord, he looks gorgeous.*

He smiled, shut the door behind him and sauntered toward her. The candlelight gleamed in his blond hair, picking out amazing highlights of silver and gold. He was wearing a black, banded-collar shirt that looked like silk, tucked into a pair of pleated-front slacks. His waist and hips looked even slimmer than she remembered, his chest broader....

''Incredible, isn't it?''

Her mouth fell open briefly before she realized he was referring to the view, not his chest.

She gulped and turned toward the window again. ''Yes. Yes, it is incredible.'' They were both incredible. The view *and* his chest.

She felt his nearness as he stood just to the side and behind her. Heat crept up her neck, making her scalp tingle. Her heart was beating like Thumper on speed. She was impatient with herself for such a knee-jerk physical reaction to a man she didn't even like, but who had been blessed with more than his fair share of attractiveness.

''I've quite liked this hotel,'' he said presently. ''The accommodations have been delightful.''

''But nothing like the ducal stronghold, right?'' she quipped, moving to stand behind one of the dining chairs, her hands gripping the carved finials at the top till her knuckles turned white. She felt safer with furniture between them.

He looked at her with a sort of tolerant amusement, a wry smile curving his lips. ''Well, you know what they say, 'There's no place like home.' ''

Tilly was surprised. ''That's what Dorothy says in *The Wizard of Oz*. You haven't really seen the movie, have you?''

He set down the bottle of wine, decanted it, then moved around to her side of the table. Tilly's heart hammered even harder. ''Why not? I know it's an American classic, but you don't mind sharing, do you?''

When Tilly realized that he wanted to pull out her chair for her, she moved quickly out of the way.

"Well, why not share Judy Garland?" she said. "You gave us Benny Hill, didn't you?"

As she sat down, he bent near her ear to whisper "Ouch."

She laughed nervously and hoped he didn't make a habit of whispering things to her. It tickled rather nicely.

"Before I scoot you in, McKinney, would you like to take off your jacket?"

Tilly was feeling rather warm, so she made a small, wincing smile and started to shrug out of her jacket. Of course, he would assist her, and the feel of his fingers brushing against her shoulders was even more unnerving than the whisper had been.

The deed done, he finally scooted her in and returned to his side of the table. Now she could breathe.... Then, in one fluid movement, he sat down, made a steeple with his hands and smiled at her over his manicured fingertips. "Tell me, McKinney, what is 'Tilly' short for? Mathilda?"

"Yes. Mathilda. Named after my great-aunt on my father's side. My full name is Mathilda Jean McKinney. Want my social security number, too?"

He chuckled. "I might if I was planning to pay you for working for me, but as it is…"

"Right," she murmured. "I forgot. This is slave labor."

"Tell me about your home, McKinney."

"What's to tell?" She shrugged. "You've seen almost every square inch of it."

"No. I mean where you were raised. Your home before you came to Seattle to work on the paper."

"Is this part of the official preemployment interview?" she inquired uneasily.

"Does it have to be?"

This confused her. That the duke would be genuinely interested in her humble home had never occurred to her. People who owned estates didn't care about the peons who owned less palatial digs, did they?

While she mulled the matter, the duke poured them each a fluted glass of red wine. "You're really interested?" she asked finally.

He handed her the wine. "Yes, I'm really interested."

Tilly took a substantial sip of the wine, then another. It was delicious, her throat was dry, she was nervous and she hadn't eaten for hours. "I was raised on a farm in a small town near the Oregon border called Washougal," she began.

He nodded. "Ah, that was it. Washougal."

She looked embarrassed. "I've already told you this part."

He lifted an open palm. "Please go on, McKinney."

She took another drink of wine, and the duke refilled her glass. "Well, okay. The house is a large, two-story farmhouse with a wraparound porch and a dozen or so drafty rooms...only one of which is a bathroom. But my mom makes the big old place really homey with lots of flowers and pictures and pillows. It's surrounded by huge trees and lots of barns and other outbuildings for the animals and farm equipment. We've got fields of wheat and hay and corn as far as the eye can see."

The duke sat back in his chair, one elegant hand curved around the stem of his wineglass. "Go on."

Tilly shrugged. "That pretty much sums up the farm. Isn't the farm what you wanted to hear about?"

The duke pursed his lips, his eyelids lowering slowly over his brilliant blue eyes, then lifting again. "Yes, thank you," he said tartly, as if his patience was being tried. "But perhaps I should word my request in more specific terms. McKinney, tell me about yourself."

She laughed. "You've got to be kidding! My life must be deadly dull compared to yours."

He rested his chin on one fist. "I doubt that."

She leaned over the table. "Have you met the Queen?"

"Well...yes."

She sat back in her chair and lifted her hands in the air, palms up. "I rest my case."

At first the duke said nothing, just sat there, his chin on his fist, staring at her. Then, suddenly, he threw back his head and laughed. It was a deep-throated, thoroughly unrestrained laugh that took Tilly completely by surprise. And it was so infectious, she started chuckling, too.

While they enjoyed this unusually pleasant moment, the door opened and Mrs. Peevey stuck her head in. "You called, Your Grace?"

"No, Mrs. Peevey," the duke answered, his eyes still brimming with laughter, "but come in, won't you? As long as you're here, I might as well ask you to bring in the salad and—"

The duke's smile vanished abruptly. All humor disappeared from his eyes. Mrs. Peevey had stepped into the room, but just barely. She seemed to be trying to hide behind the door.

"Mrs. Peevey, are you wearing what I think

you're wearing?'' the duke inquired in a voice dripping with hauteur.

Mrs. Peevey's round cheeks turned red as apples. ''Well, Your Grace, if you think I'm wearin' trousers, then you're absolutely right.''

Chapter Six

Julian couldn't believe it. Mrs. Peevey in trousers? It was tantamount to seeing the Queen in a bustier and army boots!

"And exactly *why* are you wearing trousers, Mrs. Peevey?" Julian inquired with what he thought was admirable calm. He didn't dare look at Tilly; she was probably blatantly brandishing a cheeky grin.

Mrs. Peevey wiped her palms nervously on her apron front. "Well, you see, Your Grace, I bought this pair of trousers on my day off yesterday so I could wear them bowling with Miss Darling—"

"That much I already know, Mrs. Peevey," Julian informed her, perhaps a little more tersely than he intended. "What you do on your day off is certainly your business, but what you do while you're working for me is *my* business, as well. You know my female employees have always worn skirts while on duty."

Mrs. Peevey nodded and snatched a quick glance at Tilly, probably for moral support. Julian looked at Tilly, too, the thought just occurring to him that she was more than likely responsible for Mrs. Peevey wearing trousers to work. Tilly looked back at him with wide, innocent eyes and a quivering mouth. The blasted little busybody was trying not to laugh!

"I know what you're thinkin', Your Grace," Mrs. Peevey quickly put in. "But it wasn't Ms. McKinney's idea for me to wear trousers to work. It was mine."

"Against my wishes, Mrs. Peevey?"

"But I didn't think you'd mind once I explained how—"

"There's nothing to explain, Mrs. Peevey. Female employees in my household, in my father's household and in my grandfather's household, have always worn skirts."

Mrs. Peevey shook her head in puzzlement. "But...but why, Your Grace?"

Julian felt discomposed. "Why? Well, because they always have."

"But times have changed, Your Grace. Trousers are much more practical and modest. If you only knew how many times I've twisted my back trying to bend over to get a pot out of the cupboard without—" she blushed "—well, without showin' my bloomers."

Tilly made a choking sound, and Julian darted a look at her. She was demurely sipping her wine and looking elsewhere.

Julian ignored her and turned back to Mrs. Peevey. Trouble was, he didn't have a clue what to say. He certainly did not want her twisting her back for any reason, much less simply to keep her underwear safely hidden beneath her skirts. He'd never given a thought to skirts versus trousers in the practicality department or the modesty department, and he wished the mention of Mrs. Peevey's bloomers hadn't today forced him into thinking about the matter.

But that he should enforce a policy simply because his father and grandfather had done so, didn't make any sense, either. While he honored tradition, he certainly was not averse to progress. He used an electric shaver, didn't he? He occasionally took long road trips on his Harley and couldn't function without a cellular phone and a fax machine, none of which wonderful inventions his father or grandfather had had access to.

So why was he so reluctant to give in to the trousers issue? But Julian knew why. It was because Tilly supported the idea. And it was Tilly who started this trousers business in the first place by suggesting that Mrs. Peevey go bowling. And lastly perhaps it wasn't the trousers he objected to so much, but what he was afraid it would lead to.

"I know what you're thinking."

Julian's head snapped in Tilly's direction. "I doubt it, or you'd be running from the room, fearful for your life."

She chuckled, not sounding the least bit frightened. "You're thinking, 'First trousers, then anarchy.' It's hard to give an inch when you're worried it will end up being a mile."

"I'm not worried about anything, McKinney," he growled, irritated because she was dead right. "I'm simply trying to run an orderly household."

"And making sure you're the only one who 'wears the pants,' right?"

Tilly had made a joke, but Julian was not amused. He didn't like being teased in front of an employee. A duke was required to maintain a certain amount of dignity, after all, even if the employee in this case had known him since he was knee-high to a cricket mallet.

"Mrs. Peevey, you and I will discuss the matter of trousers at another time. In private. For now you may...er...keep them on."

Mrs. Peevey, who had been looking quite uncomfortable since McKinney made that crack about wearing the pants, nodded and said respectfully, "Oh, thank you, Your Grace."

"Now, if you'll please serve the salad."

"Of course, Your Grace. Comin' right up, as they say," she chirped, apparently trying to break the tension in the room. Then, with one last, worried glance at both him and Tilly, she scooted out of the room.

"You're angry with me, aren't you?"

He took a sip of wine, then eyed Tilly over the rim of the glass. "What do you think?"

She gave an exaggerated sigh. "Of course you are, but I guess I shouldn't be surprised. Ever since we met, you've been angry at me almost constantly."

"You can leave out the modifying 'almost,'" he said caustically. "And I've had plenty of reasons to be angry."

She frowned. "I was just hoping that since I'm going to be virtually under your feet for the next few days..."

"Under my feet, eh?" he repeated grimly. "Now, why does that sound so satisfactory?"

She forged on. "I was just hoping we could try to get along. And when you laughed just now, I thought we might be starting off on the right foot."

"What's with all the feet analogies, McKinney? Do you have a fetish?"

She looked so exasperated by his continued sarcasm, he was tempted to think she was earnest about trying to keep the peace. However, *he* was exasperated, too, and ready to give up on the idea of flirting with a disaster on two legs named Mathilda Jean McKinney. It was too bad, too. She looked damned sexy in that sleek outfit she had on, even if she was wearing pants.

He sighed. "The only way we're going to get through the next couple of days, McKinney, is to keep strictly to business."

"Well, candlelight and all *this*—" she gestured toward the table and the view, which was quickly turning into a magical midnight blue sky and twinkling lights on the water "—was not my idea."

"I frequently eat by candlelight, McKinney," Julian told her repressively. "You didn't think I did all *this*—" he gestured toward the table and the view "—just for you?"

She was silenced. And judging by the high color suddenly scorching her cheeks, mortified. He was immediately sorry. He shouldn't be taking his frustration out on her, even if she was the major cause of it.

"I beg your pardon. That was very rude of me. Will you forgive me?"

She looked surprised, then confused, but only said, "Of course."

Julian nodded. "Thank you. Now, perhaps we should discuss tomorrow's agenda and some of the things I'll need you to look after. Did you bring a notebook?"

Tilly looked at him blankly. Of course she hadn't

brought a notebook. "I didn't think I'd need one at the dinner table."

"I told you it would be a business dinner," he said. "Didn't you believe me?"

If she hadn't believed him before, she did now. He was all business, as brisk and cool as the shady side of the North Pole. What she did have a hard time believing was that he was the same man who had inquired about her home earlier and laughed at her joke.

At her continued silence, the duke finally said, "It doesn't matter. I'll have Mrs. Peevey bring you one." He glanced impatiently toward the door. "Where is she anyway?"

Mrs. Peevey took ten minutes to bring them the salad, but it was worth the wait. When the duke complimented her on the crisp endive, tasty dressing and homemade croutons, she smiled and said, "Yes, I'm back to my old self in the kitchen, I am. Though Dunbar snarled about it, goin' out bowling did me a world of good, and I mean to do it again quite soon. Dancing, too, if I can find a partner. I had ever so much fun." She beamed at Tilly. "And I owe it all to you, miss."

While the duke may have been delighted by the return of Mrs. Peevey's culinary skills, her lighthearted mention of Dunbar's continued surliness, her intention to go dancing with some unnamed partner, and her gratitude toward Tilly seemed to stick in his craw. This was apparent because, despite the deliciousness of the food, the duke ate little, spending most of his time barking instructions to Tilly to write down in the notebook Mrs. Peevey brought her.

Consequently Tilly wasn't able to eat much, either.

But she *was* developing a definite craving for "duke's head on a platter." She already had a task list as long as her arm, and he wasn't through yet.

Besides a lot of letter typing and other miscellaneous boring business, it appeared she would be spending the next morning making or confirming arrangements for an afternoon tea with a history professor from the University of Washington, and an interview with a television reporter directly after the lecture. A *female* reporter.

Tilly was furiously trying to keep up with the duke's rapid-fire dictating and, at the same time, vividly imagining him with an apple stuffed in his mouth, when he inquired, "Did you get everything down, McKinney?"

"I think so."

"You *think* so?"

She glared at him. "Yes, I got it all down."

"Good." He stood up. "Then I'll say good-night and see you bright and early in the morning."

"How bright and early?"

"Six-thirty."

"You've got to be kidding! Why?"

He gestured toward the notebook. "The list of things to do is before you. If we don't start early, it won't all get done."

"Do you always have so much business to conduct while traveling?"

"I like to keep busy. However, since our tour concludes this week, in addition to the two lectures remaining, there are loose ends to tie up before returning to England."

She sighed. "Where do I report for duty, Rothwell?"

"In my office, of course."

"What about breakfast?"

"Mrs. Peevey serves tea and toast in my office, then we sit down for a full English breakfast at nine."

"Okay. So where's your office? I don't exactly know my way around this place, you know."

"It's two doors down from your bedroom."

She grimaced. "Not to sound repetitive, but where's my bedroom?"

He sighed heavily. "I'll show you. Come."

"What? Before my dessert and coffee? This feels like the bum's rush, Rothwell. What happened to those impeccable manners you told me about?"

He frowned. "It is rather early to retire, I suppose, but your room has a television. I told Mrs. Peevey I didn't want any dessert tonight, but I'll have her bring you something to your room if you like. As for coffee, no one in this household drinks it—therefore Mrs. Peevey doesn't make it."

Tilly shook her head wonderingly. "Now you've really got to be kidding. No one in this household drinks coffee?" She stood up, dropped her napkin to the table and was surprised to find herself a little dizzy. She hadn't eaten much, so her starved brain cells must have soaked up the wine like a sponge. She'd been nervous, too, and she couldn't even remember how many glasses of wine she'd downed to try to calm herself.

"Coffee's what gets me started in the morning," she continued to explain fervently. "I can't even function till after my first cup." And she'd need it even more tomorrow because she might have a bit of a hangover. She weaved slightly as she stepped away from the table.

Julian eyed her suspiciously. "You'll have to order room service, then, because Mrs. Peevey had the hotel staff remove the coffeemaker from the kitchen to make room for other, more important items. And order it early, McKinney, because I want you functioning *efficiently* by six-thirty."

Maybe the wine was to blame, but Tilly couldn't resist. She saluted him. "Righto, *sir!*"

He gave her a quelling look. "Very funny, McKinney. Do you want me to show you to your room or not?"

"Please lead the way, Rothwell," she said, mimicking his own lofty manner, then she bowed low and waved an arm toward the door. When she stood up again, her head was spinning, but she managed to steady herself and avoided falling flat on her face.

The duke's brilliant blue eyes narrowed, and he bowed even lower than she. "Oh, no, McKinney, after you."

Tilly suppressed the urge to giggle, then held her head up high and waltzed past the duke through the door. She had to admit he was a very clever and amusing man...that is, when he wasn't being stodgy and overbearing.

Her bedroom was three doors down. He flicked on the light, demonstrated its dimmer switch and gave her a brief tour of the room, complete with private bath, phone and television. Her luggage had been placed by the large closet, her clothes hung up and her bed invitingly turned down.

"Will this do, McKinney?" the duke inquired with that annoying note of sarcasm in his voice that always made her want to come back with something equally annoying.

"I don't know. How's the view?" she quipped as she moved to the window and grabbed hold of the cord for the drapes.

"I'm sure you'll find it satisfactory," he drawled.

She raised her brows. "We'll see." She opened the drapes and was treated to a view of downtown Seattle, complete with Space Needle. "Oh, you're right," she murmured approvingly, forgetting to be difficult. "It *is* beautiful."

He moved closer till he was standing just behind her. "But I have to confess, my bedroom has the best view of all."

The duke's closeness and the deep note in his voice nearly did Tilly in. She was goose bumps from head to toe. But just to prove to herself she was in control, she turned to say something mouthy, but apparently turned too fast. The room tilted and she felt herself falling.

She reached out frantically and caught the duke's upper arms. Despite her embarrassment, she still noticed how nicely developed his biceps were. Did dukes pump iron like ordinary folk, or were they just born muscular as part of their noble birthright?

At the same moment that she grabbed him, he grabbed her by the shoulders and propped her against his chest. She looked up, and his face was just inches away. In the dim room—courtesy of the dimmer switch—his eyes looked more gray than blue. A dark, stormy gray. And boy, did he ever smell good....

He smiled lazily, lifted an elegant hand and lightly traced her cheek with his thumb. "I hadn't meant my comment about the view from my bedroom window as an invitation, McKinney, but...it could be," he said seductively.

Tilly felt the blood rush to her cheeks and her dizziness disappear. It seemed she'd found an alternative to sitting with her head between her legs to get blood flow back to the brain! The combination of embarrassment, arousal and anger was proving to be extremely effective in boosting circulation to her extremities.

Tilly ignored the way her traitorous lips tingled with anticipation and was about to tell Rothwell where to put his invitation, when suddenly he chuckled. "You're so fetching when you're mad, McKinney," he said, gently easing her over to the bed and helping her to sit. "Don't bother to scold me for being lascivious. Save your strength. I was only teasing you."

"I know that," Tilly snapped. "And you don't need to coddle me. I'm not sick."

"Just soused?" he suggested. He straightened up and gazed down at her. Tilly couldn't decide if he looked slightly shocked or just mildly entertained. But at least he didn't look angry anymore, or aloof. "You didn't drink that much wine, McKinney," he stated. "How did you get soused?"

"I'm not 'soused,'" Tilly informed him with an offended sniff. "I'm just a little tipsy."

"Did you have something to drink before you came to dinner?"

Tilly glared at him. "Oh, just a fifth of vodka or two. *Of course* I didn't drink something before dinner! I'm not a drunk. I just haven't eaten enough today to counteract the alcohol in the wine."

"Well, maybe being a bit woozy will help you sleep tonight," he said philosophically. "We've got a busy day tomorrow, and it starts early."

"So you've already told me," she reminded him.

He nodded. "Then I'll say good-night."

"Good night," Tilly answered.

But he didn't go. He just stood there, his arms folded over that bodacious chest of his, and stared at her. She stared back till his gaze dropped to the carpet, skittered around the room, then bounced irresistibly back to her like a Ping-Pong ball on a string.

"Are you quite sure you're all right?"

Tilly was surprised, flattered and downright flustered. "Yes. Yes, of course I'm all right, but thank you for asking."

He nodded a third time, stood restlessly for a couple more minutes, then abruptly left the room without saying another word, closing the door behind him.

Tilly didn't know what to think of such strange behavior. It was almost as though the duke didn't like leaving her alone. Was he really that concerned about her slightly tipsy state? Or had he been hanging around hoping she'd ask again about that view from his bedroom window?

Tilly shook her head to clear it of such nonsense. The duke had no more interest in her romantically than she had in him. And even if he *was* interested, she certainly wasn't the type of female who went to bed with a man she'd only known a couple of days. Especially when she didn't even like the guy. Aunt Tilly would call that sort of behavior "as foolish as fryin' bacon in your birthday suit."

Although it was way too early to go to bed, Tilly figured she might as well change into her nightie, wash and cream her face and brush her teeth before watching some TV. She hoped there was something on that would get her mind off the duke.

Her nightly ritual complete, she climbed into bed, plumped up a couple of pillows behind her back and reached for the remote control. She surfed the channels for a while, then settled on a cable channel that was about to start the movie *The English Patient.* Tilly had wanted to see it when it was in the theaters, but never got around to it. Now seemed like a good time to watch a long artsy movie, and if it put her to sleep, that was okay, too.

But if she'd thought watching TV was going to help her get the duke out of her mind, she'd picked the wrong movie. Ralph Fiennes, a gorgeous hunk of British male with a cultured accent and eyes like sapphires, reminded her of you-know-who. The scenery was gorgeous, the cinematography first-rate, the story compelling and the love scenes...oh, those love scenes! Tilly had to toss off the blanket and press a cold washcloth to her face and neck.

At the end of the movie, Tilly cried. It was beautiful and romantic, but extremely tragic. And instead of going to sleep, she lay awake for hours thinking about it.

Tilly wasn't sure why the movie had affected her so strongly, but she had to admit that Ralph Fiennes's physical resemblance to the duke might have something to do with it.

But the duke was nothing like the character Fiennes portrayed in the movie, Count Almasy. The count turned traitor because of his love for a woman, the lovely Katherine. Tilly just couldn't imagine the duke getting that jazzed over any female. Although there *were* times when she wondered if the duke was trying to hide a tender side.

Tired of thinking about tragic lovers and the passion potential of the duke, and desperate for peaceful slumber, Tilly replayed in her imagination the final scene of her favorite movie of all time, *It's a Wonderful Life.* She saw it all: George Bailey holding ZuZu as he stood by the Christmas tree, Mary snuggled against his side and the whole town singing "Auld Lang Syne" and dumping money in a bowl to save "the richest man in town" from going to jail.

Tilly snuggled under the covers, and as they sometimes do before falling asleep, her thoughts began to drift. Suddenly George Bailey looked like the duke, and Tilly was the devoted wife at his side. She sighed and smiled. She'd always liked happy endings.

JULIAN LOOKED at his watch. It was six forty-five, and no Tilly. He stuck his head out of the office door into the hallway. He caught a glimpse of Mrs. Peevey scurrying toward the kitchen, still wearing trousers. But this time a different color...bright pink.

They hadn't had their little talk about wearing trousers yet, but it was hardly necessary. Trousers in the very traditional Chesterfield household seemed destined for permanence. But perhaps he could suggest a more reserved color choice.

"Mrs. Peevey?"

She stopped in her tracks and turned slowly, like a burglar caught in the act. She had a fretful expression on her face. "Yes, Your Grace?"

"Where's McKinney? Is she up?"

"She's up, Your Grace, but just barely. The poor little thing hardly slept at all last night."

Her, too?

"She's had her shower, but she's just now got her coffee from room service. The poor dear, her eyes are all puffy this morning, like she cried herself to sleep." She hesitated, her brows furrowed, then inquired, "Your Grace, you didn't hurt her feelings last night, did you?"

Julian snorted. "McKinney's too thick-skinned to have her feelings so easily hurt, Mrs. Peevey. If her eyes are puffy, it's not because of any cruelty on my part." Although *thick-skinned* might describe her temperament, it didn't describe her actual skin. He remembered all too vividly how soft her cheek had felt when he'd gently caressed it with his thumb.

"Oh, I didn't mean to imply that you're cruel, Your Grace," Mrs. Peevey hastily explained, then smiled teasingly. "Only the way you two carry on sometimes, you'd think you were two lovers havin' a spat!"

Julian stiffened and frowned. "What nonsense, Mrs. Peevey."

Mrs. Peevey immediately sobered. "Sorry, Your Grace. I must be off to the kitchen now to get your tea and toast. Ms. McKinney will no doubt be along any moment."

"She'd better be," Julian growled, then went back inside his office and closed the door.

"Like two lovers," Julian muttered as he paced the floor, his hands stuffed in the trousers of his heather gray suit. "What a mistake *that* would be."

But mistake or not, it was that very appealing idea that had kept him up half the night. He had left her in her bedroom with the intention of doing some research for his book and taping some dictation to be transcribed later in England, after he'd hired a new secretary. But his thoughts continually returned to the room across the hall and down a couple of doors where Tilly was sleeping...or *not* sleeping.

Did she wear a nightie or pajamas? Or perhaps an oversize T-shirt? He was sure she'd look equally smashing in all three, or nothing at all....

Julian's frantic pacing picked up. His plan to revenge himself by forcing Tilly to take Miss Darling's place, and enjoy a light flirtation in the process, was complicated by an ever growing urge to actually get to know Tilly. To converse with her. To exchange ideas. And afterward, of course, to make passionate love to her.

Why he was so obsessed with the little termagant, he wasn't sure. She was quite attractive, of course, but not in the way that made men swoon as she walked past them. In Tilly's case most men probably thought she was jailbait and noticed her hardly at all. But Julian had had no choice but to notice Tilly, and now he couldn't quit.

What was he going to do?

Ready to jump out of his skin, Julian headed for the door, intending to hurry Tilly along by personal invitation. But when he opened the door, he took one step into the hall and stopped. Mendenhall was already at Tilly's door. And in the next moment he was actually inside her room with the door shut firmly behind him!

Julian was flabbergasted, and in the next moment, furious. What would Mendenhall be doing in Tilly's room? He'd give them five minutes, then find out for himself.

Chapter Seven

"Thank you for seeing me, Ms. McKinney. I know it's dreadfully early, but I thought it would be the best time to catch you."

"Well, you sounded pretty stressed on the phone. I'm supposed to be slaving away for the duke already—"

Mendenhall glanced nervously at the door. "Already?"

Tilly smiled reassuringly. "But he can wait."

Tilly had had just enough time to get dressed in tailored forest green slacks and a tucked-in white silk blouse after Mendenhall's call. And luckily she wore very little makeup, so she got that on, too, before he arrived. Now she sat down in a chair by a small table and indicated the chair opposite her.

"Have a seat and help yourself to coffee, Mendenhall. They sent extra cups." She glanced up quickly. "Oh, but the duke said none of you guys drink coffee."

Mendenhall looked longingly at the steaming coffee carafe and took a deep breath. "It smells delicious, and I'd love some." He sat down and immediately began pouring himself a cup. "Contrary to what the duke believes, I drink coffee every chance I get.''

Tilly chuckled and raised a brow. "How terribly untraditional of you, Mendenhall. By the way, what's your first name?"

Mendenhall took a sip of coffee and sighed with satisfaction. "It's Brian."

Tilly held out her hand. "I'm Tilly. Pleased to meet you, Brian."

He smiled and shook her hand. "Pleased to meet you, too, Tilly."

"I do feel as though we're meeting for the first time, Brian, because as the duke's main man in black you keep a pretty impenetrable wall around you."

Brian gulped more coffee and nodded. "Yes. That's the way the duke wants me to do my job. That's the way he wants us all to do our jobs. Something about the way his father did things. But it's not for me."

This time Tilly raised both brows. "Oh? What *is* for you?"

Brian set down his cup and proclaimed fervently, "I'm an artist, Tilly. A painter!"

"Then what the heck are you doing dressed like an undertaker and escorting a bunch of relics around the country?" she exclaimed.

Brian blushed bright red. "I took the job because of…well…because of—"

It suddenly dawned on Tilly that Brian was clearly in love—either with the duke or with Emma. She took a stab. "Emma?"

Brian looked relieved and nodded his head vigorously. "Yes. I met her at a friend's party, found out about this job and did everything in my power to get the duke to hire me.''

"And you succeeded. How long ago was that?''

"Three years ago.''

Tilly chuckled and shook her head. "And you've felt this way for three whole years? How do you Brits propagate? No one seems to be able to get together!''

Brian looked sheepish. "It's not a universal condition among the English.''

"Just within the duke's domain, eh?'' she suggested.

"I know it seems that way. But I would have told Emma my feelings if I hadn't already figured out she was in love with the duke.''

"You knew?''

"Everyone knew…except the duke.''

"Frequently the object of affection is the last to know.''

"Now she's gone and—''

"There's no point in staying with your job.''

He nodded.

"Why didn't you tell her how you felt before she left?''

"She was upset. She was handling things pretty well, but I could tell she was hurting. I wanted to give her time to recover, time to get settled back in England before I told her my feelings. But now I'm afraid—''

"That she'll get on with her life before you have a chance to try to be part of it?''

He sighed heavily. "Yes. Exactly. What should I do, Tilly?''

Tilly took a sip of coffee, then answered, "I think you already know what to do."

Brian looked anxious. "Well, I know what I *want* to do. I want to go after her right away. I want to take her in my arms and tell her I love her. I truly believe her feelings for the duke were merely infatuation and gratitude—"

Tilly winced. "Gratitude?"

"You'll probably be surprised to hear me say this, Tilly, but the duke truly is a good man. He's treated us all quite well. He keeps up a wall, too, but I think he actually cares about his staff."

"You couldn't exactly say he wears his heart on his sleeve, though," Tilly remarked dryly.

"Nonetheless, I feel loyal to the duke. I don't like leaving him in the lurch, you know, to fly off to London. But that's what my heart's telling me to do. I know it's just a matter of staying in the States a few more days, but still..."

"Brian, aren't the other three men who work for the duke pretty experienced? Couldn't they take over your responsibilities for the remainder of the tour?"

His brows were knitted in worry. "Probably. But he won't like it if I go. He'll draw himself up stiff as a board in that way of his."

"Why do you care? You don't want to continue working for him at all, do you? You want to be a painter."

"Right. But I hate to displease him."

Tilly shook her head in amused exasperation. "You guys worry too much. He *needs* to be displeased now and then. It's good for him. Believe me, Brian, the duke will manage without you. The worse that could happen is the duke will make me take over your job, as well as Emma's! If you really want my advice, I say go after her. I think she's a treasure."

Brian beamed. "Isn't she?"

"And likely to be snapped up pretty fast if you don't stake your claim first. Do you think she's got feelings for you?"

"Yes. Yes, I do. And without the dashing duke around to compare me to, I think she'll appreciate my good points and give me a chance."

Tilly smiled. "I don't know why she didn't immediately appreciate you and give you a chance, despite the 'dashing' duke lurking around. You're quite a handsome and personable man, Brian."

Brian grinned. "Thank you, Tilly."

They smiled at each other over their coffee cups, both pleased with the conversation. When someone knocked on the door, they were still smiling. "Come in," Tilly called.

The door opened and the duke stepped into the room, looking mad enough to wring necks. He narrowly eyed Brian, then Tilly, his blue eyes even more brilliant than usual.

Brian's smile vanished and he sprang to his feet. "Your Grace!"

"Mendenhall," the duke answered coldly. "What are you doing in here?"

"Talking with Ms. McKinney. You know... *prepping* her on the day's activities," he improvised.

The duke looked pointedly at the cup of coffee Brian still clutched. "How kind of you. But why didn't you do the same for Miss Darling? I don't ever recall finding you in *her* room."

"She...she didn't need to be...er...prepped, Your Grace."

The duke nodded curtly. "I see. But did it never

occur to you, Mendenhall, that *I* wanted the job of prepping Ms. McKinney?''

"No, Your Grace, I—"

Tilly couldn't stand it any longer. She had to speak up. "Brian, tell him the truth."

The duke's eyes widened and glimmered like jewels. A muscle ticked in his jaw. "The truth?"

Brian looked panic-stricken at first, but Tilly urged him on with her eyes. He sighed, then faced the duke. "She's right. I need to tell you the truth, Your Grace. I have feelings for— That is, I want to reveal an attachment to—"

The duke cocked his head to the side and took a single step forward. "Yes?" he prompted in a low voice that was almost a hiss. Tilly thought the duke sounded downright menacing. She didn't blame Brian for stuttering and hesitating. She was surprised he could speak at all!

"To...to...Miss Darling," he managed to say at last. "There, I've said it."

The duke appeared stunned. "Miss Darling?"

"Yes. I've loved her for three years. It's the only reason I sought employment in your household in the first place, Your Grace. I really want to be a painter. And now that Emma's gone, there's no point in staying. I have to go after her."

Now that Brian had got started, he couldn't seem to get it all out fast enough. "I'm sorry, Your Grace, but I'm tendering my resignation, effective immediately. As soon as I can, I'm flying home. I'm sorry to leave you at such short notice, but as Tilly pointed out to me, you'll manage without me for the brief time you intend to remain in the States. I hope you understand. And I *do* thank you for everything."

Brian stood very tall and stiff and stuck out his hand to be shaken. He looked worried that the duke might ignore this token of friendship, and Tilly was afraid he was right. She waited and watched nervously.

After looking for some time at Brian with a slightly puzzled expression on his patrician features, the duke shook his hand. "I'm sorry you're leaving, Mendenhall. You're an excellent employee." His gaze strayed to Tilly as he added in a bemused tone, "And have always been so very *reliable*. But if you must go, you must go."

Brian appeared quite pleasantly surprised by the duke's reaction. He pumped his hand happily and said, "Thank you for understanding. Thank you, Your Grace! Now, if you don't mind, I must call the airlines. I hope I can get a seat on the Concorde."

He waved at Tilly as he breezed out of the room on cloud nine. "And thank *you*, Tilly."

Tilly slid a cautious look toward the duke, expecting an outburst of British expletives. But it didn't happen that way. He stared at her for a moment, his gaze wandering distractedly over her features, then her figure, then back to her face. She didn't know how to feel, where to look.

Why wasn't he yelling at her?

"You're late, McKinney," he said finally. His voice was cool, controlled, aloof. "Please finish your coffee and join me in the office as soon as possible." Then he turned and left.

JULIAN RETURNED to the office, closed the door behind him and sat in the chair behind his temporary desk. With his hands resting limply on his knees, he stared into empty space.

My God, he thought. *I was jealous!* He'd wanted to strangle Mendenhall—a man he respected and cared about almost like a brother—because he thought he'd claimed Tilly's affections. Or slept with her. Neither possibility had pleased him.

And now that he knew Mendenhall was in love with Emma and leaving his employ to pursue her and a career as a painter—a *painter?*—that mattered not at all compared to his relief that Tilly was not the object of Mendenhall's affection!

He'd just lost another valuable employee because of Tilly's meddling, but it was a moot point. He was experiencing unprecedented feelings of possessiveness toward a female. Such an unusual state of emotion was extremely surprising and unsettling. He had to decide what to do about it before Tilly—

The door creaked slowly open. She entered, looking chagrined...and adorable, puffy eyes and all.

McKinney.

"I'm here," she announced.

"So I see."

"Are you angry?"

"What do you think?"

Up came the stubborn chin. "I don't have to, but I can explain."

Julian rose abruptly. "I'm sure you can. But there's no time for that." He gestured toward the desk. "There are three tapes to be transcribed, the letters and documents in the mail by noon, if you please. When you're through with those, start at the beginning of the list we composed last night and work your way down it. I'll check in periodically to answer any questions you might have, but I think you'll be able to figure out what to do without my help.''

She looked bewildered. "Where are you going to be?"

"Very busy elsewhere."

She laughed uncertainly. "What if I file my nails on the job? I thought you'd want to stick around and crack the whip."

He raised a brow. "You sound disappointed."

"Fat chance!" she denied quickly. "It'll be a lot easier getting things done without you around to distract me."

"I distract you?"

She blushed. "Maybe *irritate* is a better word."

"The feeling is entirely mutual, McKinney."

Now that they were sparring, she looked more at ease. "What about tea with the professor? Last night you said I was required to go. Have you changed your mind?"

"No. Be ready by three-thirty. As you know, we're to meet Professor Grisswold at four o'clock at Lambs' Tearoom. Of course, you'll be confirming with Professor Grisswold's secretary *and* the tearoom? I want the best table available."

"I'm sure that won't be a problem once I tell them I'm personal secretary to the duke of Chesterfield," she said dryly.

"Good." He turned to go, then turned back. His gaze flickered over her trim figure in pants and a soft white blouse. "You might want to wear a dress to tea."

Her chin climbed the usual inch or two. "Why?"

"Because you'll probably feel more comfortable."

She snorted. "I doubt that."

He smiled. "Do as you please, then." *But don't say I didn't warn you.* "Only do remember to bring a notebook to the restaurant. When things get interesting, I'll expect you to take notes."

"Sure. If things get interesting, I'll start taking notes. Only what *I* think's interesting, you might not, and vice versa. But I expect you'll let me know when things get interesting...right?"

"If you're not sure whether or not things are getting interesting, I'll definitely let you know," he assured her in a rueful tone. "I'll check on you later, McKinney."

"Whatever."

Julian closed the door behind him and moved through the living room to the main doors. He was headed down the hall to speak with Mendenhall and the others to discuss matters related to Mendenhall's resignation and the delegation of his responsibilities, but his mind was full of Tilly. He was thinking about the tea that afternoon and imagining her reaction when she met the University of Washington's preeminent history professor. He wondered if the rumors were true....

Julian smiled. Yes, perhaps the tea would prove to be instrumental in helping him come to terms with his feelings for the meddling Ms. Mathilda McKinney. And maybe things would get so interesting, McKinney would actually forget she was supposed to take notes in the first place.

His smile broadened.

TILLY WAS an efficient typist and she would have had the three tapes transcribed in no time at all if she hadn't replayed certain passages over and over again. There was one particularly interesting letter to the duke's publisher in New York; apparently he'd already sold rights to his anthology of stories.

In the letter he gave short synopses of two of the stories, and Tilly found herself surprised and impressed by the duke's creativity. When he'd first mentioned the anthology, she'd wondered how he was going to come up with something entertaining from such a bone-dry source as Roman artifacts. But he'd taken certain facts and woven them into perfectly delightful fiction.

For example one of the stories revolved around some toys that were buried with the toys' owner, a child whose grave was found on the duke's estate. The story had to do with a day in the life of a six-year-old Roman boy named Marcus. Children reading such a book would be entertained and educated at the same time.

Apparently remains of an entire Roman villa—which was more or less a working farm in those days—were found on the duke's estate, providing him with all kinds of story possibilities.

"But *why's* he doing it?" Tilly murmured as she listened once more to the duke's mellifluous voice detailing the highlights of the story. She glanced over at a picture on the desk, a portrait whose background she assumed was Chesterfield Hall, his seat in Dorset. It was a huge limestone edifice. Elegant and stately. "He sure as heck doesn't need the money."

In the foreground of the picture the duke posed with two Labradors. His hair gleamed golden in the sun and was attractively mussed by the wind. He was dressed in a white shirt—the sleeves rolled up to his elbows, the collar open to show a strong, tanned neck—jodhpurs and long black boots. He had an arm around each dog, all three of them looking as happy and carefree as ants in a sugarcane field.

And sexy... *Hooo, boy.* In this picture the duke had the corner on sexy. She could almost smell the sun in his hair and the slightly sweaty, leathery scent of a man who'd just been horseback riding.

Tilly wondered why he couldn't always look so relaxed and approachable. But then, he was at home in the picture, not on tour in a foreign country.

Tilly wondered who took the picture. Around whom *was* the duke that relaxed? Some English chick with a pedigree as long as Tilly's to-do list?

Impatient with herself for wondering about stupid things, Tilly took the picture and placed it facedown on the desk. Maybe the real duke wasn't there to distract her, but the at-home duke in the picture was turning out to be even more of a distraction.

Tilly wondered when the real duke was going to lower the boom about Mendenhall. When he'd come to her room that morning, she'd never seen him looking more formidable. It was strange that he hadn't read her the riot act over her latest interference in his domestic affairs, but she wasn't going to look a gift horse in the mouth. As long as the duke kept silent on the subject of Mendenhall, she wasn't going to bring it up, either.

By three o'clock Tilly had completed every single item on the list. She'd skipped breakfast and lunch, settling for a bagel sandwich and coffee at her work space, and hadn't seen the duke at all. She was a little miffed that he hadn't checked on her at least once as he'd said he would, but then again, maybe he had confidence in her ability to do the job and wasn't that worried.

Tilly liked that explanation for the duke's nonappearance, and went off to her room at three o'clock to get ready for the tea feeling pretty good about herself. After all, if the duke had been trying to overwhelm her with things to do, he'd failed.

At 3:25 she had just finished styling her freshly washed hair and was putting on her watch. She'd decided to wear a tailored, off-white pantsuit to tea. She thought she looked stylish yet professional. She didn't want to primp too much; after all this wasn't a date and she didn't want the duke to think she was "tarting" herself up for him. Besides her watch, the only jewelry she wore were pearl studs in her ears.

At three-thirty she was about to leave her room and go down to the living room to meet the duke when there was a knock on the door. Surprised, Tilly opened it. There on her threshold stood the duke, managing to look studly and scholarly at the same time. The pin-striped navy blue suit he wore spelled *class* with a capital *C*.

As he straightened a cuff, his gaze flickered over her, revealing no reaction whatsoever to what she was wearing. "I see you're ready, McKinney."

"You look nice, too, Rothwell," she said irritably. She wasn't sure why she was disappointed. She didn't really expect him to compliment her, did she?

"You'll do," he said dryly. "But you'll wish you'd worn a dress."

Tilly slipped past him into the hall, traces of his sandalwood aftershave teasing her and conjuring up sexy images. "I've never been to Lambs' Tearoom, Rothwell," Tilly curtly informed him, "but from what I've heard about it, I'm quite sure a dressy pant-suit like this will be perfectly acceptable.''

"Acceptable, yes. Preferable, no."

"Maybe in your opinion," she retorted. Would he ever give up on this skirt-versus-pants thing?

The duke did not reply, but lightly touched the small of her back as he ushered her through the double doors and again as they got on the elevator. Both times Tilly's temperature shot up and her heartbeat went slightly bonkers. She hated being attracted to a man whose personality she found so abrasive. She'd learned from all the letters she'd received over the years that an attraction based solely on the physical was more than a little dangerous. But tell that to her twitter-pated hormones.

Tilly was used to Dunbar's resentful glares by now, and the trip to Lambs' Tearoom in the limo was achieved without incident or accident. Inside the tearoom, which was located on the top floor of the priciest department store in Seattle, Tilly was immediately struck by the elegance of the place...and by all the women in chiffony dresses and pastel suits with pleated skirts. There were even a few hats. Apparently spring was in the air, when young women's fancies turned to skirts.

This did not, however, discompose Tilly. She was used to attending affairs in pants when the majority of the other women wore dresses. In fact she thought it gave her a certain professional cachet. With her chin up, she walked confidently with the duke toward a table by the windows with a view of Puget Sound.

"I see the professor has not yet arrived," the duke observed as they made their way across the room.

Tilly sat down and placed her handbag on the floor

beside her chair. "In case you're wondering, Rothwell," she announced, "I'm not at all bothered by the fact that I'm one of the few women here in pants."

He sat down, took the menu from the pretty server with a smile, then unfolded it. From behind the large menu, the duke said, "How kind of you to keep me informed of your feelings, McKinney, but you should know that when I suggested you wear a skirt to tea, it wasn't in deference to the usual attire worn at this particular establishment. You are suitably dressed as you are. In fact I'm sure there are other women here in pantsuits—you just haven't seen them yet. I daresay, as this *is* America, there's even bound to be one or two females in jeans."

"Then why did you make me feel like it would be stupid if I wore pants?" Tilly demanded.

He lowered the menu, folded it and set it aside. He rested his elbows on the table, twined his long fingers together and propped his chin. His blue eyes gleamed. "I thought since the professor would be wearing a skirt—"

"The *professor* wears skirts?"

"Yes. In fact, Professor Grisswold is notorious for her skirts."

"*Her?*"

"Yes. Didn't you take into consideration that the professor might be a woman? Tsk, tsk. How terribly sexist of you."

"I just didn't know, that's all." Her eyes narrowed. "But why's it such a big deal that she wears skirts? I mean, beyond *your* strange obsession with it."

"Oh, I'm not obsessed, McKinney. It's just traditional at Chesterfield Hall to wear skirts. I couldn't care less what the rest of the female sex chooses to wear...unless, of course, they happen to be my date. *Then* I have an opinion."

"I'll bet you do."

"But in Professor Jamie Grisswold's case, it's not solely because she wears skirts that's she's notorious—it's how she wears them." He shrugged nonchalantly. "Or so I've heard. I've only seen a publicity photo of her...from the neck up, as it were. I've heard she's forty-something, but she doesn't look a day over thirty to me." His gaze shifted to a place beyond Tilly. His blue eyes lit up like Christmas lights. "Ah, but now you'll see what I mean. Here's Professor Grisswold."

As the duke stood up to greet their guest, Tilly turned and watched the notorious professor walk across the room to their table. Or maybe the better description would be *vamp* across the room to their table. Her hips had more swing in them than Tiger Woods's best drive to the fairway. Every eye was on the striking, statuesque blonde in the jonquil tailored suit with a skirt that ended ten inches above her knees. Her legs looked long enough and shapely enough to propel her over buildings in a single bound. The only question that remained was, was she faster than a speeding bullet and more powerful than a locomotive?

As soon as the professor reached the table, the duke held out his hand and said, "Hello, I'm—"

"I'd know you anywhere," the professor purred in a throaty contralto, placing her hand in his. She had some kind of nebulous accent. German, maybe? Hungarian? Or maybe just plain phony-baloney?

PLAY

RUN
FOR THE
ROSES

and get

THREE FREE GIFTS!

HOW TO PLAY:

1. With a coin, carefully scratch off the silver box at the right. Then check the claim chart to see what we have for you — **FREE BOOKS** and a **FREE GIFT** — **ALL YOURS FREE!**

2. Send back the card and you'll receive two brand-new Harlequin American Romance® novels. These books have a cover price of $3.99 each, but they are yours to keep absolutely free.

3. There's no catch. You're under no obligation to buy anything. We charge nothing — ZERO — for your first shipment. And you don't have to make any minimum number of purchases — not even one!

4. The fact is, thousands of readers enjoy receiving books by mail from the Harlequin Reader Service®. They like the convenience of home delivery...they like getting the best new novels months before they're available in stores...and they love our discount prices!

5. We hope that after receiving your free books you'll want to remain a subscriber. But the choice is yours — to continue or cancel, any time at all! So why not take us up on our invitation, with no risk of any kind. You'll be glad you did!

The Harlequin Reader Service® — Here's how it works:

Accepting free books places you under no obligation to buy anything. You may keep the books and gift and return the shipping statement marked "cancel." If you do not cancel, about a month later we'll send you 4 additional novels and bill you just $3.34 each, plus 25¢ delivery per book and applicable sales tax, if any.* That's the complete price — and compared to cover prices of $3.99 each — quite a bargain! You may cancel at any time, but if you choose to continue, every month we'll send you 4 more books, which you may either purchase at the discount price...or return to us and cancel your subscription.

*Terms and prices subject to change without notice. Sales tax applicable in N.Y.

If offer card is missing write to: Harlequin Reader Service, 3010 Walden Ave., P.O. Box 1867, Buffalo NY 14240-1867

BUSINESS REPLY MAIL
FIRST-CLASS MAIL   PERMIT NO. 717   BUFFALO, NY

POSTAGE WILL BE PAID BY ADDRESSEE

HARLEQUIN READER SERVICE
3010 WALDEN AVE
PO BOX 1867
BUFFALO NY 14240-9952

NO POSTAGE
NECESSARY
IF MAILED
IN THE
UNITED STATES

Whatever it was, it was blatantly sexual. Up close she looked a little more fortyish, but not much. *Damn it.*

"I've seen your picture in the papers and on television often enough, but I must say you're even handsomer in person."

"And you're even more enchanting than I was led to believe," he suavely returned as he lifted her hand to his lips and kissed it.

Tilly thought this was supposed to be a business meeting, not foreplay!

"Professor Grisswold—"

"Call me Jamie."

"Jamie, I'd like you meet my…er…secretary, Ms. McKinney." The duke turned toward Tilly and slightly inclined his head. His eyes twinkled with some sort of emotion. Lust, maybe?

Professor Grisswold turned and stared blankly at Tilly as if she were surprised to discover there was someone else in the room, much less at their table. Irritation flickered in her bedroom eyes, then she forced a wincing smile to her pouty lips and said, "How do you do?"

"Pleased to meet—"

But Professor Grisswold had already turned her attention back to the duke. "Now you must allow me to call you by your first name, too, Your Grace." She gave a husky laugh. "Although 'Your Grace' does have a rather pleasant ring to it."

Julian laughed and held out her chair for her. "If you wish, you may call me Julian. Since we'll be discussing the possibility of setting up a foreign-exchange program between the University of Washington's best history majors and those at Cambridge, we'll be talking frequently by telephone and it would become cumbersome, to say the least, to—''

''You're in charge of setting up a foreign-exchange program for Cambridge?'' Tilly broke in, dumbfounded. ''But you're not—''

''No, I'm not an instructor or an administrator of any sort,'' the duke confirmed with a polite smile. ''But they gave me the responsibility nonetheless. However, as I was saying—''

''Doesn't your secretary know that you're a huge contributor to the history department at Cambridge, Julian?'' Professor Grisswold inquired with a puzzled and derisive look in Tilly's direction. ''And then there's your scholarship program in archaeology, not to mention your support of the dig just started in Derbyshire—''

''She's new,'' the duke interrupted. Tilly was amazed to note that the duke was blushing. *Blushing!* As if he was embarrassed to have his philanthropic activities discussed so openly. ''Now, Jamie—''

The professor was all smiles again, her attention fixed on the duke and his baby blues. Even when the server came and the duke ordered the complete high tea for the three of them, she didn't take her eyes off him for even a nanosecond.

But in a way Tilly couldn't blame her. She'd never seen the duke so charming. He talked, he smiled, he laughed. They discussed in depth ancient Roman history one minute, then compared tennis scores the next. As the British say, they were getting along swimmingly. And Tilly might have been a flea on the neck of a llama in Lapland for all the attention she was getting.

She couldn't really blame the duke, because he

actually tried to include Tilly in the conversation from time to time, but Professor Grisswold had no intention of sharing the limelight. She always managed to monopolize the conversation and force the duke's attention back to her.

So, while Tilly devoured cucumber sandwiches, scones with raspberry jam and clotted cream and drank cup after cup of Earl Grey tea, Professor Grisswold devoured the duke with her eyes. At one point Tilly dropped her napkin and had to duck under the table to retrieve it. What she saw was enough to make her want to toss her crumpets. The professor had slipped off one of her high heels and nudged her foot under the hem of the duke's trousers. The woman was caressing the duke's leg with her toes!

Tilly came up so fast she hit her head on the table. When she finally emerged from under the tablecloth, rubbing her skull, the duke inquired, "Are you all right, McKinney?"

"I think so," Tilly answered in a mortified voice.

"Ah, good," the duke replied dryly. After a brief pause he added with what was at once a perfectly angelic and an absolutely devilish smile, "By the way, McKinney, I think now's the time to start taking notes...don't you?"

Chapter Eight

Despite the fact that they were once again on a perilous journey across town with Dunbar behind the wheel, Julian eased back into the cushy leather of the limo with a satisfied sigh. Things had gone even better at the tea than he'd hoped for.

His eyelids shuttered, he gazed across to the opposite seat, where McKinney stared out the window and slumped like a sulky child, her shoulders hunched, her arms crossed and her knees squeezed together so tightly you couldn't have separated them with a crowbar. Her body language told all. She was seriously miffed.

And if she was just a bit jealous, too, he'd succeeded in paying her back for what he'd endured when he'd thought Mendenhall was in her bedroom for an amorous assignation. What it all meant in the long run, he didn't have the slightest clue. Hopefully it had no deep meaning. For now, it was enough to have successfully retaliated.

He suppressed a chuckle and looked outside through the rain-dappled glass. It was late afternoon, overcast and drizzling, the streets full of rush-hour traffic and people cramming the sidewalks. But it was a cheerful scene, full of activity and bustle. It reminded him of Christmas in London.

"It was too short."

Julian turned to Tilly. She was glaring at him, her green eyes snapping, her complexion radiant.

Excellent.

Julian pretended ignorance. "What was too short, McKinney? The tea? But the lecture starts at seven and I've a great many things to do beforehand—"

"No, her *skirt!* Her skirt was too short. A mature woman like her shouldn't be wearing a skirt that barely covers her...her—"

"Careful," he murmured with a ghost of a smile.

"Her *assets.*"

"You're talking about Jamie, I assume?"

"No, I'm talking about Queen Elizabeth II! Of course I'm talking about Jamie Grisswold. Have you seen another female today wearing such a short skirt?"

Julian shook his head sadly. "Unfortunately no."

Tilly threw up her hands. "You are something else, Rothwell," she exclaimed. "How could you let that woman maul you like she did?"

"Hmm? Oh, you must be referring to the activity under the table."

Tilly's eyes narrowed. "You *are* talking about her playing footsie with you, aren't you?"

Julian widened his eyes, all innocence. "Of course. What else?"

"Coming on a bit strong, wasn't she?"

"Dear Aunt Tilly, what *should* I do?"

Tilly crossed her arms again. "Aunt Tilly would tell you she's got no business fondling what's not for sale. She'd tell you to sue her for sexual harassment," she grumbled.

"If everyone sued Jamie Grisswold for sexual overtures, court dates would be backlogged till the middle of the next century."

Tilly's head jerked around. "What do you mean? Did you know she was like that?"

"I had heard something about her being flirtatious."

"Flirtatious? That woman's come-on was about as subtle as a—"

"Ten-ton lorry?"

"Going ninety miles per hour down the freeway!"

Julian laughed. "You're exaggerating. But don't worry, McKinney. She's not my type."

Tilly turned a delightful shade of fuchsia, like a particular rose he grew in the garden at Dorset. "I'm not worried. Why would I be worried, Rothwell? I was just offended to have to watch another woman flaunt herself like that. But what you do is your business."

"And in this case, it *is* business. While she did come on a bit strong, I couldn't be rude to her because she and I will be working together on the foreign-exchange program."

"So you're just going to put up with her manhandling?"

"She is an attractive woman, you know. *Putting up with* it seems an odd way to describe something so pleasant."

"Humph!"

"But she'll have difficulty manhandling me by long distance. Besides, I tactfully made it clear that

I wasn't interested in a romantic relationship with her.''

"Oh?"

"I didn't burn any bridges, however—''

"Of course not.''

"But when you went to the ladies' room she suggested—'' He broke off, shrugged. "Ah, well. Never mind.''

She leaned forward. "What did she suggest?''

He raised a brow. "McKinney, do you really want to know the details? Suffice it to say, she offered and I politely declined.''

She blushed again and turned away, reverting to the same body language as before: arms crossed, knees pinched together. "As I said before, it's none of my business. I'm just your secretary, and only for a couple more days, thank God.''

A couple more days, Julian mused as he resettled in his comfortable seat and again enjoyed the passing scenery. Long enough, he hoped, to get this little termagant out of his system for good. This sort of delicious thrust and parry couldn't possibly stay fascinating much longer. And once he'd kissed her— which he hoped would be soon—maybe the thrill would diminish sufficiently to ensure peace of mind.

He would never allow it to go beyond kissing, of course. After all, a gentleman shouldn't make passionate love to a woman, then flee the country the day or two after. And once he was back in England, that would be the end of it.

Julian wasn't sure why, but suddenly the cheerful view outside dimmed a little. It must be because the rain was suddenly coming down in buckets.

FOR THE HOUR AND A HALF prior to leaving for the library for the duke's lecture, Tilly fretted alone in her bedroom. She was summoned for dinner, but she begged off. Since this was the third meal Tilly had declined that day, Mrs. Peevey was worried. Tilly reassured her by describing how she'd stuffed herself at tea.

It was true; Tilly had no appetite. When she remembered how she'd behaved on the way home from Lambs' Tearoom, she was mortified. She was sure the duke had gotten entirely the wrong impression and probably thought she was jealous. Of course that was a load of nonsense…

Or was it? As Tilly freshened up for the lecture, she analyzed her feelings. She got nowhere fast. She couldn't deny that she was physically attracted to the duke—heck, who wouldn't be?—but those kinds of skin-deep attractions had never tempted her before. She had always been smart enough to steer clear of an entanglement that was destined to be over with as soon as they'd hit the sack once or twice.

But this time was different, and Tilly wasn't sure why. She was getting a better idea of what kind of man the duke was, and she had to admit he was looking better by the hour. He was obviously a philanthropist and civic minded. He was intelligent and creative. He could be charming, but only when he wanted to be. And when he didn't want to be, he was one stiff-rumped son of a gun for sure.

In Tilly's experience he was usually being dictatorial and sarcastic, mocking her at every turn. But then, *she* was constantly provoking *him*.

This thought cheered Tilly up a bit, and she left her room at precisely six-thirty to meet the duke by the elevator as prearranged. She had suggested meeting at the elevator because she found it unsettling to be continually picked up at the door of her bedroom by a peer of the realm. What if he caught her with her hair in a towel and toothpaste foam oozing from the corners of her mouth?

On her way through the living room, Tilly was stopped in her tracks. Raised voices engaged in loud argument could be heard coming from the kitchen. It was Mrs. Peevey and Dunbar!

"Dancin', my aunt Fanny!" he shouted. "You're only goin' out t' meet men, that's what."

"And what if I am, Tom Dunbar? What do *you* care? We're through with courtin', you and I."

"Don't give me that! You're tryin' t' make me jealous, that's what. But it ain't workin', y' hear? I won't be tricked into marryin' you, Margaret Mary Peevey."

"I wouldn't marry you now, Tom Dunbar, if you swam the channel with a two-hundred-pound anchor tied t' yer ankle t' prove your love. But if'n you want t' try somethin' foolhardy like that, you've got my blessin'!"

Tilly was standing in the middle of the room, wondering what to do, when the duke strode in from the hallway.

"Ah, you're ready," he began, then stopped when he heard the yelling.

"I wasn't eavesdropping," Tilly hastily told him. "I was just surprised to hear them shouting at each other like that."

He stood still for a minute, listening, then gave her a beleaguered look. "Why are you surprised, McKinney? You endorsed this fiasco of a separation. If they were still sharing living quarters, they wouldn't be at each other's throats.''

She propped her fists on her hips. "When are you going to get the big picture, Rothwell? If they were still sharing living quarters, Dunbar would be enjoying a wild bachelor's life while Mrs. Peevey stayed at home, weeping over darned socks. Does that sound fair to you?''

He flung an arm in the direction of the kitchen. "Do you think *that* is an improvement?''

"Of course not. But it takes time to work things out.''

The duke looked at his watch. "At the moment time is something I don't have. I have a lecture to do in twenty-five minutes, and my accident-prone chauffeur is working himself into a tizzy.'' He sighed. "Though I loathe the practice, it seems I must meddle.''

As she followed him to the kitchen, he peered suspiciously at her over his shoulder. "I'm coming along because I'm good at meddling,'' she explained tartly.

By the time they reached the kitchen, it appeared the argument was over. Mrs. Peevey was standing at the sink, scrubbing a pot as if her life depended on it, and Dunbar was staring grimly out the kitchen window at the rain-drenched street below. He turned when they came in, looked respectfully at the duke, then glared openly at Tilly.

"It's time to go, Dunbar,'' the duke said coolly. "Have you brought the limo 'round already?''

"Yes, it's parked out front, Your Grace,'' Dunbar answered peevishly. "Are you ready, then? *Both* of you?''

When he continued to glare at Tilly, the duke repressed him with a raised brow and the stern admonition, "Dunbar, mind your manners or you might find yourself driving a taxi to support yourself."

Dunbar was surprised and chagrined. He probably didn't expect the duke to reprimand him for Tilly's sake. Neither did Tilly.

"Yes, Your Grace," Dunbar murmured, then bobbed his head and scurried out of the kitchen.

Without another word the duke followed. Tilly hesitated, exchanged a commiserating look with a red-eyed Mrs. Peevey, then followed him across the living room to the double doors. This time he didn't touch the small of Tilly's back as she preceded him through the door, but simply stood to the side, looking aloof and unhappy.

The drive to the library was fraught with tension, the only sound the drumming of the rain on the roof of the limo. Tilly was worried about Dunbar driving in the state he was in, but Fox, a new man in black, sat in the front seat to replace Mendenhall, and he kept a sharp eye on the road.

The van containing the other two men in black followed them to the library, then Fox and his assistants dashed in and out through puddles with the various props the duke used during his lecture. Inside they set up tables and brought out the relics for display, which had been locked safely away in a special vault the library used to store valuable documents and books.

Everything came together quickly and efficiently, and in no time at all, the lecture hall on the top floor of the library was filled to overflowing. During this entire time, Tilly had had nothing to do. She wondered if it was because the duke was too angry to speak to her, or if Emma hadn't had anything to do at the lectures, either. But still she was expected to be there in case she was needed.

Tilly had a seat in the front row and was nearly deafened by the applause that greeted the duke as he stepped up to the podium. Although she was prepared at this point to grant the duke a certain amount of charm and intelligence—at least when he was dealing with *other* people—she still couldn't imagine him making a two-hour lecture on Roman artifacts interesting.

Boy, was she ever wrong! At the end of the two hours, Tilly was clapping as enthusiastically as everyone else. Charts, slides and various other visual aids accompanied the duke's narrative, but it was the duke himself that made the lecture such a success.

He told jokes…funny ones. He connected with the audience with appropriate eye contact. He was erudite, charming and witty. Add to that the fact that he was darned easy on the eyes, and his popularity was no mystery.

Afterward the duke was surrounded by audience members and reporters, asking for autographs and quizzing him as much on his personal life as on ancient Roman history. Tilly just stood in the background and watched, a strange sort of queasiness attacking her stomach. As the American press and public so frequently did, they had created yet another celebrity.

"Hey, are you the duke's secretary?" An attractive middle-aged woman motioned toward Fox, who was busy with the others in dismantling the displays. "That guy over there says you are."

"He's right. I'm...I'm the duke's secretary," Tilly admitted haltingly. She was stunned to realize she was proud of the fact...almost possessive. "What can I help you with?"

The woman darted a look around them before slipping something into Tilly's hand. Tilly opened her palm and looked down at...a hotel key! If she was stunned before, now she was horrified.

"Will you give that to the duke?" the woman whispered. "And tell him the cute brunette in the gladiator sandals would love it if he could drop by the Roosevelt Motel sometime tonight." She winked at Tilly. "Tell him I've got a toga he'd just die for."

Tilly wasn't sure what she said, or if she said anything at all, but the woman moved away and rejoined the throng of admirers around the duke.

Tilly looked down at the key again and shook her head. Who would have thought the duke would have groupies? This was the kind of celebrity worship that sometimes turned perfectly nice, ordinary people into egomaniacs. And the duke wasn't "ordinary" to begin with. How did all this affect him?

Tilly shoved the key into her pocket and walked up the aisle to the door. She was in no mood to be a romantic go-between for another groupie. She'd wait in the limo for the duke.

Fifteen minutes later Fox and Dunbar got in the limo. Fox turned to Tilly and said, "The duke instructed me to escort you home, Ms. McKinney. He said he'd call later when he wanted us to pick him up. He's got an interview with some reporter."

Tilly nodded. Yes, now she remembered. She'd confirmed the interview herself. It was with Gretchen Blaisdell, the cute blonde who anchored a Seattle channel's local news at six and ten on the weekends. Tilly's heart sank. Here was yet another female who would probably flirt outrageously with the duke. What man could withstand being idolized and lusted after by so many women and not have a swollen head the size of Delaware?

Tilly stared out the window at the glistening sidewalk, the distorted reflection of a street lamp splashed over its gray surface. As Dunbar started the engine and pulled the limo away from the curb, she asked herself why *she* should care how big the duke's head got. After all, it really had nothing to do with her.

AT MIDNIGHT, Tilly woke up. After much tossing and turning, she'd finally managed to get to sleep, but now she was famished. The cucumber sandwiches and scones at Lambs' Tearoom were just a distant memory. If she called room service, she'd probably wake up Mrs. Peevey or the duke—if he was even home yet—when the server came to the door. She decided to raid the kitchen instead. Surely there would be leftovers from Mrs. Peevey's bounteous meals.

Tilly threw on a short pale apricot robe over her shorter nightie of the same color and tiptoed barefoot down the hall toward the kitchen. One of the lamps in the living room was still on, but turned low. Its light was enough to guide her safely in the direction of the kitchen. She pushed open the swinging door and took a single step onto the cool tile floor when she was stopped by a sight she'd never dreamed she'd see in a million years.

Illuminated by a night-light by the sink, the duke

was leaning against the farthest counter, wearing nothing more than a pair of striped pajama bottoms. His hair was mussed, and he was intently squeezing chocolate syrup onto a mounded tablespoon of peanut butter.

In fact the duke was so intent on what he was doing, Tilly was pretty sure she could back out without being noticed. Ducking her head, she took one careful step, then another—

"McKinney?"

Drat. Foiled again!

Tilly looked up. He held the spoon of chocolate-coated peanut butter in front of him and stared as if he'd seen a ghost. She stared back. Boy, wouldn't the toga chick kill to be in her shoes, with her view, about now!

"Yes, it's me," she finally admitted rather sheepishly, then remembered belatedly to pull her robe together in the front and tie the belt. She noticed that his gaze was immediately riveted to her hands and what they were doing, and she felt her cheeks burn with embarrassment. Then his gaze drifted down to the hem of her robe, where she was showing more leg than even Professor Grisswold had had on display that afternoon at Lambs' Tearoom.

"When did you get home?" she blurted out, desperate to divert his attention, but wished she could kick herself afterward. It was none of her business!

He pulled his gaze away from her legs with what appeared to be a rather flattering amount of reluctance. "Two hours ago," he told her distractedly. "You had just gone to bed."

"Oh," was her short reply.

His eyes seemed drawn to her legs again, then he

quickly looked up as if he was aware that she might consider him rude or lecherous. Tilly would have given anything to have on a pair of baggy pajamas about then!

"The interview went longer than I expected," he told her, still holding the spoon of peanut butter in front of him like a lecture stick...or a gun. Maybe subconsciously he wanted to shoot her!

"Oh," Tilly repeated stupidly.

"Er...yes. Gretchen...that is, Ms. Blaisdell...had a great many questions."

"I'll bet she did," Tilly murmured dryly.

The duke raised a brow. "What does that mean?"

Tilly chuckled nervously. "Just that you've become something of a celebrity around here, especially among the female population. In fact—" Tilly stopped, suddenly shy about bringing up the brunette in the gladiator sandals and the motel key.

"What?" he prompted her, seeming to suddenly notice he was still holding the spoon of peanut butter and placing it on the counter. He moved toward her. "What were you about to say, McKinney?"

Tilly wished he'd stay on his side of the kitchen. As he drew near, she couldn't help looking at his chest. My, but it was fine.... Every muscle was defined, and a thatch of springy, dark blond hair made a V on his chest, then narrowed enticingly to a line that disappeared into the band of his pajama bottoms. His stomach looked as taut and muscled as his chest.

"Now I won't feel so guilty about staring at your legs," he said with a wry and oh so sexy smile.

Tilly blushed hotter than ever. "Well, it's hard not to notice something that's right in front of you."

He laughed. "People do it all the time. I wasn't

aware that Miss Darling was in love with me, and Miss Darling wasn't aware Mendenhall was in love with her.''

"Feelings are different," she muttered, diverting her gaze to the belt on her robe, her fingers clutching the knot as if it might untie and her robe spring open at any moment.

"Oh, and by the way, they're not at all knobby."

"I beg your pardon?"

"Your knees. They're not knobby at all. In fact I can't understand why you continually hide your legs under trousers. They're quite shapely. Quite lovely."

"Th-thank you," she stuttered, still avoiding eye contact. Must he stand so close?

"But you were about to tell me something about my celebrity status among the female population."

Tilly was beside herself. The duke's nearness was playing havoc with her senses. He smelled good, he looked good, and she would bet money that he'd feel and taste good, too. What was the matter with her? She was thinking like one of those stupid groupies!

Panicked, Tilly blurted out, "Well, actually, it's kind of funny what happened." She forced a laugh that sounded about as believable as the latest Elvis sighting.

He ducked his head, trying to catch her eye as she looked anywhere, everywhere, but at him. "Yes?"

She talked fast. "There was this woman who came up to me after the lecture and asked if I was your secretary."

"Go on."

"When I said I was—because I *am* your secretary at least for the moment, although not much longer, I hope—she gave me something to give you. Along with a message.''

The duke placed his thumb and curved forefinger under her chin and gently forced her to look at him. His touch made her heart pound and her nerves sing. And looking into his eyes, which had turned a stormy gray blue, made her light-headed and dizzy.

"If she gave you something for me, why didn't you give it to me at the library?"

"I...I was going to give it to you in the limo," she croaked through a suddenly dry throat. "But you stayed behind to talk to...to that television reporter."

The duke's nod was almost imperceptible. He cupped her face in both hands now and continued to stare down at her, his absorbed gaze roaming at leisure over each blushing feature. Tilly stood perfectly still and allowed it. No, despite every lick of sense she had, she not only allowed it; she *enjoyed* it. She'd been complimented and kissed by lots of men, but no one had ever looked at her quite the way the duke was.

"You said she had a message, McKinney," he whispered throatily, his thumbs skimming her cheekbones in delicate strokes. "Was it important?"

Tilly swallowed. "I...I don't know. It *might* have been."

He smiled and pushed her tumbled bangs away from her temple, then ran his long, elegant fingers through her hair...slowly. Tilly closed her eyes on a gasp. "It might have been? What do you mean?"

Tilly forced her eyes open. She hadn't touched a drop of alcohol since the day before, but she felt drunk. "It...it depends on how you feel about certain things...."

He chuckled and put his hands on her shoulders, then pulled her ever so slowly, ever so gently, ever so securely against that warm, hard chest of his. As if they belonged to some other much more foolish female, Tilly's own hands floated up to rest on the lean muscles of the duke's upper arms. "What things, McKinney?"

"Gladiator sandals, togas, cute brunettes and motel keys!" she blurted out in a breathless whisper. "She gave me a *motel key*, Rothwell!"

This time he threw back his head and laughed outright. "A motel key! Oh, McKinney, that must have infuriated you! To be used as a go-between by a sex-starved anglophile!"

Tilly was not amused. "So, this isn't new to you? I suppose this happens all the time?"

"Not all the time," he replied, his eyes twinkling. He slid his arms around her, twined his fingers together and rested his clasped hands in the small of her back. "But certainly more often than I'd ever thought possible. After all, I lecture on ancient Roman history, which most women would consider a rather dusty subject."

"It all depends on who's lecturing, I guess," Tilly muttered, the feel of his arms around her and his hard chest against hers making her skin tingle in all the wrong places. Or *right* places, depending on how you looked at it. For Tilly, it was wrong. All wrong. So why hadn't she skedaddled out of there already?

"You flatter me, McKinney."

"I wasn't trying to," she snapped.

"Very well. So...where is it?"

Her eyes narrowed. "Where's what?"

"The key, of course."

"Rothwell—" she began angrily, pushing at his chest with her fists.

"McKinney," he growled, pulling her back into his arms. "As usual you're jumping to incorrect conclusions. I have no intention of chasing after some trophy-hunting, toga-wearing groupie who only wants to tell her gal pals at the office that she's bedded a duke. Besides..."

She grew still in his arms and scowled up at him, at the aristocratic planes and chiseled angles of his face, at the thick golden hair and brilliant blue eyes. Hells bells, why was he so damned gorgeous?

"Besides?" she prompted irritably.

He gave a crooked smile. "I much prefer redheads to brunettes." Then he dipped his head, his lips hovering over hers as he gazed into her eyes. That he seemed to be asking permission to kiss her was both surprising and sweet.

This was the point at which Tilly should run out of the building and down the street screaming, like one of those poor Japanese city dwellers in a Godzilla movie. Because everyone knew what happened if you stayed. You were doomed.

But she didn't run. Like an idiot, she stayed.

The duke must have seen the white surrender flags waving, because he no longer hovered, but landed, his lips making contact with Tilly's and sending her senses into a spin. This was no tentative kiss, like so many first kisses were. He kissed her like he meant business.

He kissed her like she imagined Prince Charming must have kissed Cinderella. Like Prince Phillip must have kissed Aurora, alias Sleeping Beauty.

But Tilly was through with comparisons. She was too busy kissing him back.

Chapter Nine

Tilly's lips were soft and responsive, and what Julian had intended as a tentative, experimental kiss quickly escalated into something much more involved and passionate. As he explored the sleek, warm surfaces of her mouth with his tongue, she kissed him back with the same curiosity, the same eagerness. All the pent-up tension of their sparring over the past few days now seemed to be channeled into their kissing.

He drew her close, her slim, soft curves fitting perfectly against him like pieces of a puzzle. His hands roamed up and down her back and into her silky hair, the feel of her as intoxicating as more than a few "wee drams" of Scotland's best Highland whiskey.

Desire thrummed through his veins like warm honey. He wanted her. In a matter of minutes after their first kiss, he wanted her more than he could ever remember wanting anything.

"Tilly," he murmured against her neck, liking the way the consonants in her name clicked off his tongue, gentle and easy. The name fit her as perfectly as her body fit against him.

She chuckled, her voice breathless and uncertain.

"So now that we've kissed, we're friends enough to call each other by our first names?"

"Uh-huh," he said as he nibbled his way down her neck and along her collarbone, pushing her robe and the strap of her nightie to the side for better access to soft, warm skin that smelled like sweet talcum powder. She trembled and gasped most satisfactorily.

"So, I should call you Julian," she said, then whispered in his ear in a wicked imitation of Jamie Grisswold's husky voice, "Or would you prefer 'Your Grace'?"

"Call me whatever you want, my sharp-tongued little meddler," he said, his voice lowering to a rasp, "as long as you don't make me stop kissing you."

Tilly knew that stopping him was exactly what she should do, but she couldn't imagine stopping him from doing anything at this point. In fact she might even collapse and die on the spot if he suddenly stopped kissing her.

How was this aloof, irritating English nobleman making her—a freckled little American tomboy— feel so special, so sensual, so *womanly*? Was she following in the ill-fated footsteps of English governesses and chambermaids over the centuries who had succumbed to the sexual wiles of the master of the house, and then found themselves pregnant and banished by the jealous lady of the house?

Whoa, she was getting way too Victorian in her thinking! She and Julian were two mature adults living in the twentieth century. If they wanted to have sex, no one need get pregnant, and no one need be banished by anyone.

Sex? Who said anything about sex?

After another kiss that rocked Tilly to the soles of her bare feet, she drew back and stared up at him. At the duke. No, at the man...*Julian.* His expression was ardent, and his eyes gleamed like sapphires. She had to face the facts. He wanted to make love, and so did she. If someone was going to stop them, it probably wasn't the two people standing in that room with matching swollen lips and respiration rates that rivaled those of mountain climbers just reaching the summit.

Reaching the summit... Not a good analogy.

Suddenly self-conscious, Tilly allowed her gaze to drift to Julian's chest. She watched the rapid rise and fall of his breathing, then fanned her hands just below his collarbone. She could feel the frantic beating of his heart reverberate against each sensitized fingertip. She was awed by the fact that *she,* Mathilda Jean McKinney from Washougal, Washington, was the reason his breathing was fast and his heartbeat was racing out of control.

She began to caress him. Her fingers explored the smooth contours of his beautiful chest, then slipped into the dip of his sternum, following the sexy line of fine blond hair to the band of his pajama bottoms. He seemed to be holding his breath as she followed that line upward again, then skimmed her thumbs over his nipples. She couldn't resist; she bent her head and took one wine-colored nipple in her mouth, taunting the hard nub with her tongue.

He moaned. He reached down to cup her face and captured her mouth again, his lips hard and insistent and irresistible. As he continued to kiss her, he lifted her at the waist and set her down on the butcher-block table where Mrs. Peevey chopped vegetables.

In one fluid movement he untied her robe and slipped his hands under her hips, bringing her legs up and around his waist.

Tilly almost fainted when she felt his arousal against her. Now there was no denying how much he wanted her...and the feeling was mutual. When his hands slid up the slick cotton fabric of her nightie to cup both breasts at once, she instinctively arched into his palms. He gave an exultant murmur and kissed her again. Deeply.

That was when the phone rang.

Tilly nearly jumped out of her skin, and Julian gave a muffled whelp of pain. She'd bit his tongue!

One of the amenities of the luxurious lodgings Julian had rented at the Royal Covington was a telephone in every room. The din of so many phones ringing at once at twelve-thirty in the morning had instantly jarred Tilly from a state of sensual euphoria to one of guilty terror. The tongue-biting was incidental to the terror.

At first Julian looked dazed, then irritated. Tilly was almost sure he said, "Good God, Tilly, why'd you bite me?" But it sounded more like *Dood Dod, Thilly, why'dth you bite me?*

"I'm sorry," she groaned. "I didn't mean to."

"And who the hell ith calling at thith hour?"

Tilly unlocked her ankles from around Julian's waist and sat up straight. "More importantly, who just answered the phone?"

"Mth. Peevey musth have." He pressed his fingers against his mouth and winced. "I think I hear her thtep in the living room."

Tilly panicked. "She's looking for you. Oh, my gosh, she can't see us like this!" With Julian's assistance, she hurriedly squirmed off the table and was just tying her robe when Mrs. Peevey's head appeared around the kitchen door.

"That you, Your Grace?"

"Yeth, Mth. Peevey," Julian replied with his usual dignity. "The phone ith for me, I gather." Julian winced again and flicked a quick, accusing look at Tilly.

Tilly shrugged and winced back. "I'm sorry," she mouthed.

Mrs. Peevey, her graying hair pulled back in a functional braid and wearing a floor-length flannel nightgown, stumbled into the room. That she was very upset was immediately apparent. She didn't even seem to notice the duke's lisp. "Your Grace, it's Pooky," she whimpered as she wrung her hands in front of her. "He's gone and got hisself in a brawl."

"A brawl?" Tilly couldn't believe it.

Mrs. Peevey looked with some surprise in Tilly's direction. It seemed she hadn't noticed her at all till she'd spoken. But now her eyes widened, and her gaze bounced back and forth between Tilly and the duke with undisguised curiosity.

But Dunbar's troubles were more pressing and more important at the moment, so she quickly confirmed, "Yes, a brawl. At the Dime-a-Dance Bar. The owner's holdin' him and says he won't call the police if we pick 'im up in no less than fifteen minutes."

"Fifteen minutes?" the duke repeated irritably. Tilly was relieved to note that his lisp had disappeared...or was at least under control. She was sure his tongue still hurt. "Just exactly where is this Dime-a-Dance Bar?"

Mrs. Peevey shook her head sadly. "I don't rightly know, Your Grace. The man who called gave me an address, but I was too sick with worry for it to sink into my brain, so t' speak."

Julian ran a hand through his disheveled hair. "We can look up the address in the phone book, but even then it might take us more than fifteen minutes to find the bloody plathe—I mean, *place*."

"I know where it is," Tilly offered. "And I know the fastest way to get there."

Julian gave her a doubtful look. "Are you sure?"

"Just get dressed, Jul—er...Rothwell." She'd used Julian's first name again, something she wasn't sure he wanted her to do in front of the others. She snatched a glance at Mrs. Peevey to see if she'd noticed her slip. Judging by that lady's raised brows, she had indeed. "Should I call a taxi, or do you want to drive the limo? Or did Dunbar take it?"

"Dunbar never takes the limo 'cept for His Grace's business," Mrs. Peevey said with a proud nod of her head. "He's no moocher. He walks or takes the taxi."

"I'll drive the limo," Julian said decisively. "But there's no time to dress. Just throw on a coat, put on some shoes and let's get out of here. I'll meet you out front in the limo, Tilly."

"I want to go, too," Mrs. Peevey said as she followed them through the living room and down the hall.

"Mrs. Peevey, you're not going to want to see Dunbar in the condition he'll be in," Tilly heard the duke warning her from his bedroom across the hall.

She took off her robe and slipped into her khaki trench coat, belting it tightly at the waist.

"I've seen 'im drunk before," Mrs. Peevey said as she followed the duke into the hall again.

"He might be worse than drunk," the duke responded, walking quickly past Tilly's bedroom wearing bedroom slippers and an open, flapping trench coat that exposed his bare chest. He'd look ludicrous if he didn't look so damned sexy. Tilly sat down on her bed and put on a pair of white tennis shoes.

"If you mean he might be hurt—" Mrs. Peevey's voice faltered. "Well, I've seen him battered before, too. He'll need me to kiss the boo-boos and wipe the blood off 'is broken nose, won't he?"

Tilly hurried into the living room just in time to see the duke open the door and turn back to Mrs. Peevey with a sigh. "Very well, then. But hurry and put on a coat. If you're not standing on the curb when I pull up with the limo, I'll leave you behind."

Tilly ran for the door as Mrs. Peevey sped past to her bedroom. The duke stepped on the elevator, and Tilly slipped between the doors just as they were closing.

"I told you I'd meet you out front," Julian groused, turning to scowl at her.

"You ought to know by now that I'm terrible at obeying orders."

He grunted and faced forward again. "This is a hell of a situation."

"You're worried about Dunbar?"

"Of course. He's been in his share of barroom brawls in the past, but Mrs. Peevey's influence had cured him since they've been together. He's always healed fast enough, but I'm less worried about black eyes and more worried about the repercussions if we don't get there in time and he's arrested.''

''Repercussions?''

''It might delay our trip home.''

Before, during and after the amorous incident, Tilly had known she was an idiot to kiss the duke, but now reality hit her like a slap in the face. He was scheduled to fly home on Saturday, and he wanted nothing to interfere with his plans.

Nothing.

After all, Chesterfield Hall in all its splendor awaited him. What on earth was there in the United States that could tempt him to stay longer? Not that she wanted him to stay longer, of course, but what had she been doing contemplating kitchen-table sex with a man who was going to be out of her life in less than a week?

Tilly leaned against the back of the elevator, humbled to the core. Why had she allowed herself to give in to their mutual physical attraction? It had been a bad idea. A *very* bad idea. Now he probably thought she was promiscuous, a woman who fell into bed— or onto a table—with any man she got the hots for after a two-day acquaintance. And she wasn't at all that kind of girl. At least she didn't used to be.

By the time the elevator doors opened on the ground floor, Tilly had made up her mind to cut short this stupid assignment her editor had forced her into. Julian had only one lecture left, and surely he could get through it without her help. And if Harrison wanted to fire her, so be it. She *was* syndicated, after all. She liked the camaraderie at the office and the extra, interesting little stories she found to do, but she could work on her column just as well from a home office.

The duke continued on the elevator to the parking garage and presently pulled up front of the building in the limo to pick up Tilly and—amazingly enough—a fully dressed, breathless Mrs. Peevey. Tilly noticed that the duke had buttoned up his trench coat…thank God. Like a woman on a diet who'd put a padlock on the fridge, she didn't want to see what she was giving up.

"Hurry," the duke barked as both Tilly and Mrs. Peevey scrambled into the front seat beside him. Tilly had nudged Mrs. Peevey in ahead of her. She was already figuratively and physically distancing herself from the duke.

As Tilly shouted directions, the duke raced through the nearly empty downtown streets. "Don't drive too fast," Tilly cautioned him. "If the police stop us to give you a ticket, you're going to defeat the whole purpose of this rescue mission."

The duke only grunted, but he must have been listening somewhat because he did slow down to just ten miles per hour over the speed limit. Tilly crossed her fingers. An unwieldy limo careening down the road was hard to miss.

In just under fifteen minutes, they pulled in front of the Dime-a-Dance. It was a semirespectable establishment that catered to lonely people who wanted to drink and dance to tapes of Glenn Miller's forties-style band music. Tilly realized that even though Mrs. Peevey hadn't yet gone dancing, Dunbar must have decided to pay her back by finding his own slew of dancing partners.

When they entered the dimly lit and sparsely populated bar, Mrs. Peevey instantly spotted and scurried over to Dunbar, who was sprawled on a booth near the door. "Pooky!" she squealed, plopping down on the red vinyl seat beside him and nearly sliding under the table before she caught herself. "Are you hurt, dearest?" Pooky's only response was a roll of his head and a muffled snort. Tilly did notice, however, that other than a swollen eye, he did not appear injured.

"It's about time you got here," a heavyset man snarled from a bar stool. "I own this joint, and your driver there wanted to bust it up by pickin' fights with every Tom, Dick and Harry. He got the worst of it, though. I gave him the shiner myself."

"*You* gave him the shiner?" Mrs. Peevey repeated indignantly. "Shame on you!"

The guy shrugged. "Had to. He was out of control. Lucky for him I was able to find identification on 'im and tracked you down."

"I'm terribly sorry for the inconvenience," the duke said with cool politeness. He patted his trench-coat pockets and frowned, seeming to suddenly realize he'd left the hotel without a wallet or any identification of his own. "I'd like to pay you for your trouble and thank you for not calling the authorities, but I seem to have left—"

"Here, Your Grace," Mrs. Peevey said, bolting to her feet and digging into her bodice with chubby fingers to pull out a wad of bills. "It shouldn't be your worry, anyhow." She peeled off two one-hundred-dollar bills, but didn't hand them over right away. She glared at the bar owner. "You ought not t' get a thing, seeing as how you roughed 'im up."

"I didn't call the police, did I? He could be spending the night in the city jail."

Mrs. Peevey sniffed and handed him the bills. "Will that do?"

The bar owner took the money, but his eyes gleamed with avarice as he watched Mrs. Peevey restore the remaining wad to its previous nest.

"I'm sure it will," the duke answered for him in a voice that brooked no argument. Tilly had to admit the duke was a handy man to have around when you wanted to intimidate someone.

"Margaret? Margaret Mary? Is that you?"

Tilly turned to see that Dunbar, at least for the moment, had regained consciousness. He stared up, bleary-eyed, at Mrs. Peevey.

"Yes, Pooky, it's me. I came as soon as I heard you were brawlin' again."

Dunbar pouted and said, in a pathetic whine, "I wouldn't brawl if you'd take me back, Margaret." He grabbed her face and squeezed it affectionately between his palms till she had lips like a goldfish. "I *mish* you. I *mish* your *shweet* kisses. I *mish* our bed, Margaret Mary!" he exclaimed with the poetic earnestness of a man under the influence. "Take me home. Take me home and tuck me in, then cuddle up *beshide* me."

Tilly held her breath. This was a real test for Mrs. Peevey and a defining moment in their relationship. It was perfectly natural and understandable that she'd be worried and run to Dunbar's side when she found out he was drunk and disorderly. And since he probably got himself good and soused because of their argument earlier and his frustration over his continued banishment from Mrs. Peevey's bed, she no doubt felt responsible for his current state. But if she gave in to him now, she'd regret it. Things would just go back to the way they were.

Tilly watched and waited for Mrs. Peevey's response. She didn't dare look at Julian. He was probably crossing all his aristocratic fingers and toes hoping Mrs. Peevey and Dunbar reconciled. But Tilly was hoping Mrs. Peevey would hold out for that marriage proposal she so desperately wanted and deserved.

Mrs. Peevey turned to Tilly, her face etched with pain. It was then that Tilly knew she wasn't going to cave in. She was planning on disappointing her precious Pooky, and that made her sad.

Mrs. Peevey turned back to Dunbar with the sort of gentle smile and firm jut of the chin one might see on the face of a mother who is dealing with a beloved but troublesome child. "I'll tuck you in, Pooky, but in your own bed, y' hear? And I won't climb in t' cuddle you. You're in your cups, you are, and are no more a fit companion for a lady like myself than any other common drunk on the street," she scolded him. "Do you think I'm goin' to reward this behavior with kisses and hugs and all that other stuff you like me to do? Not in a million years, Tom Dunbar."

Julian looked over at Tilly. She was beaming…the baggage.

"Margaret, you're a hard woman," Dunbar moaned. "And I'm a broken man. Show me a little pity, won't ya?"

"If anyone's to be pitied, it's me," Julian interrupted grimly. "My employees think they're starring in some silly, romantic melodrama." He bent down and threw Dunbar's limp arm over his shoulder. "Now stand up and walk to the car like a man, Dunbar. And if you upchuck in my limo, I'll put you to work shoveling horse manure back home in Dorset. That'd get the blokes down at the pub laughing themselves sick, wouldn't it?"

This threat seemed to sober Dunbar, at least enough to allow him to put one foot in front of the other till they made it to the car. He tumbled into the back and sprawled across an entire seat, Mrs. Peevey climbed in with her Pooky to pet his head and scold, and Tilly had no choice but to sit in the front.

Soon after Julian pulled the limo away from the curb and started home, Mrs. Peevey began to croon an Irish ditty to her drowsy sweetheart. Two short choruses later, Tilly leaned over and hissed in Julian's ear, "We need to talk, Rothwell, as soon as we get back to the hotel."

Julian was immediately intrigued. Now that there was no threat of having to bail Dunbar out of jail, his thoughts kept returning to those delightful few moments in the kitchen with the bane of his existence, the cause of all his domestic difficulties, the exasperating, the delicious Ms. Mathilda McKinney.

He wasn't sure how he felt about the fact that they'd nearly made love on the chopping table. It certainly had not been his plan. But the best-laid plans of mice and men, and all that rot... Perhaps he should ascertain Tilly's feelings on the subject.

He pressed a button, and the glass barrier between the front and back seats came up with a quiet whir. The barrier was quite effective, completely eliminating any noise from the back and making it impossible for Mrs. Peevey and Dunbar to hear anything said in the front unless he turned on the intercom.

"We can talk now," he said.

He noticed she squirmed in her seat. "Now? But—"

"They can't hear us. And they're not paying us a lick of attention, anyway."

She nodded reluctantly, as if she conceded his point but didn't want to. "All right. We'll talk, then." Her tone was suddenly tough and business-like, as if she wanted to sound more in control than she might actually feel. *Adorable.* "I think we should talk about...well, *you know.* About what happened in the kitchen. And about what might have happened if Mrs. Peevey hadn't interrupted us."

"There's no 'might' about it, Tilly. If Mrs. Peevey hadn't interrupted us, we'd have made love."

In the dark car he couldn't see her face, but he knew she was blushing. "It was a mistake. I don't want it to happen again."

"Nothing will happen if you don't want it to," Julian assured her. "But I thought we were *both* enjoying ourselves."

"That's not the point," she retorted. "Like I said...it was a mistake. And to make sure it doesn't happen again, I'm going home first thing in the morning."

Julian's head snapped in her direction. "What?" He very nearly swerved onto the curb, then righted himself and tried to keep his eye on the road and talk at the same time. "What do you mean you're going home? You *have* to stay and work as my secretary till Wednesday. Harrison Gray mandated it."

"Pooh," she scoffed.

"Pooh?"

"Harrison Gray can go where the sun don't shine—"

"Pardon?"

"He can go to hell, and so can you. *You* won't sue the paper, and *he* won't fire me. But even if he did fire me, my column is syndicated. As long as I have a laptop, I can work out of a cardboard box if I want to."

She was right. But he was unwilling to concede. "Don't underestimate me, McKinney. I can and *will* sue."

She laughed. "So we're back to last names, are we? Give me a break, Rothwell. Your threatening to sue was just a ruse, and Harrison probably knew that from the start. He's got his own angle for forcing me into this cohabitation fiasco with you, although I haven't quite figured it out yet. Maybe you promised him croquet on the royal lawn or a date with Fergie. As for *your* angle…"

"I'm listening," he murmured as he turned right at a stop sign.

"Your angle is an easy one to figure out. You wanted to get back at me for screwing up your happy little household."

"And prevent you from creating even more havoc by keeping close tabs on you."

Her chin climbed two inches. "Which I'm happy to say was a dismal failure."

"Granted."

"And now that we've actually been stupid enough to let our libidos take over…"

They were stopped at a red light. He turned to look at her. The lights of passing cars flickered over her face. Even at one o'clock in the morning, sans makeup and with a scowl marring her brow, she was lovely.

"Why *did* we let our libidos take over, McKinney?" he asked her. "Do you suppose that underneath our hostility we actually like each other?"

She shook her head emphatically. "Oh, heavens no! We couldn't be more different. We come from different parts of the world, different cultures. You're royalty and I'm not."

"Well, not exactly royalty," he demurred.

"Just a notch below, then," she conceded. "But the fact remains that we don't have a *thing* in common. And our personalities clash. You know, like plaids and stripes?"

"I see," Julian drawled as he drove the limo through the intersection. "Our insurmountable and glaring differences notwithstanding, you'll still do as a secretary. We had a deal, McKinney."

"Agreed upon under duress. I don't feel the slightest compunction about bidding you adieu, Rothwell."

"But I *need* a secretary—!"

"No, you don't! You don't need half the people you hire. Goodness, what would you do if you had to fend for yourself for a month or two, or even a day or two?"

"I'd manage."

"Sure, as long as you didn't have to leave your five-star hotel or the ducal stronghold. But what if you really had to work, Rothwell? You know, work *hard*...like on a farm?" She snorted. "I was busting my butt pitching hay and milking cows when I was knee-high to a butter churn. I can't even imagine you doing physical labor.''

Julian was quite certain he ought to be offended. If she only knew what half his hobbies were... It only proved how little she knew about him. But instead of being offended, he saw an opportunity. And playing up his "wounded pride" would work perfectly into his plan.

"McKinney, you've served me a low blow," he said solemnly.

This time her laugh was a bit forced. "Really, Rothwell, don't be so sensitive."

"You've essentially cast aspersions on my manhood."

"No, I haven't! I mean, how could I after—? Well, you know."

"I'm like a gigolo, eh? Good in the sack—you *presume,* but of course will never know—but useless in every other manly endeavor."

"You're taking this much too seriously—"

"I'll make you a deal, McKinney."

"What kind of deal?" she asked suspiciously.

"If you work for me till Wednesday, I'll work on your father's farm Thursday and Friday."

"Don't be ridiculous!" she scoffed, but Julian thought he detected a note of panic under the derisive tone.

"Why not?"

"What for?"

"To prove myself. I'll do whatever needs to be done. I'll bust my butt, as you so colorfully put it, pitching hay, milking cows, towing the line, lifting the barge...whatever. You know, *farm* things."

Her laugh was shaky. "You realize, Rothwell,

you're bound to get dirty doing 'farm' things. I'm sorry, but I just can't picture you in dust-covered jeans picking your way through a field full of cow pies by day, and picking dirt out of your manicured nails by night.''

"But wouldn't you like to?"

They'd pulled up to the curb in front of the Royal Covington. The duke flicked on the intercom that connected him with the back seat and said, "Hold on a minute, Mrs. Peevey. Don't try to get out with Dunbar till I'm done having a word with Ms. McKinney," then clicked it off and turned to Tilly.

It seemed the duke had only granted Tilly a minute to come up with an answer to his challenge. She studied his face in the glow from the hotel's outdoor lights. His expression gave nothing away. She suspected that he wasn't worried about proving his manhood at all, but was simply trying to finagle a way to aggravate her for a few more days. But why?

Surely it couldn't be because he wanted to complete his seduction of her. She'd already made herself clear about that…although perhaps now he considered her a challenge. The idea frightened, thrilled and infuriated all at once. She couldn't imagine that, compared to all the other women he must have dallied with, she was anything special. But maybe another notch in the ducal bedpost was all he wanted.

"You're afraid, McKinney."

"I am not!" Of course she was.

"You're chicken."

"You're wrong." He was right.

"*Bach, bach, bach.*"

"You'd better take that back!"

"You're either afraid of having me around any

longer for fear we'll end up on your parents' kitchen table—''

"Bite your tongue."

"It's already been bitten, thank you. Or you're afraid I'll prove you wrong about being able to hold my own as a farmhand. Which is it, McKinney? Which are you afraid of…or is it both?''

Tilly was furious. She wasn't stupid enough not to know she was being taunted and manipulated, but she wasn't strong enough to resist the temptation to prove him absolutely, one hundred percent dead wrong.

"All right," she said at last, extending her hand to close the deal with a shake. "I'll stay till Wednesday if you agree to work as a farmhand for my father on Thursday and Friday. And you can't bring a single one of your minions with you. For this test you go solo, Rothwell. Agreed?"

"Agreed, McKinney."

He shook hands with her, and the jolt of attraction she felt reminded her to add a contingency clause to their agreement. "And as long as I'm under your roof, there'll be no more kissy-face."

"You drive a hard bargain," the duke murmured.

You have no idea, she thought to herself as she reluctantly slipped her hand out of his.

"Speaking of driving, we'd better get my intoxicated chauffeur inside so he can sleep it off by tonight. We'll disappoint the adoring masses if I don't show up at the lecture in a limo."

Tilly knew he was teasing, but she gave a disapproving "Humph!" anyway, then got out of the limo. She opened the back door as the duke walked around to their side of the car. When Mrs. Peevey emerged, her face glowed, her eyes glistened with happy tears and her lips were curved in a huge smile.

"Why, Mrs. Peevey, you look radiant," Tilly exclaimed. "What's going on?"

Now it was Dunbar's turn to make an appearance. With the duke's assistance, he got out of the limo, teetered for a moment, then stood with his chest out and his head held high beside Mrs. Peevey.

"We're gettin' married, that's what," Dunbar announced.

"Today!" Mrs. Peevey added triumphantly.

"Today?" Tilly and Julian repeated together.

"Today," Dunbar confirmed, his voice a bit quavery but his smile brave and determined. "Today, I'll become—" he gulped "—a married man."

Chapter Ten

After another restless night, Tilly woke up to the smell of freshly brewed coffee. Since such a delicious aroma was not—to say the least—a morning staple in the duke's household, she blinked her eyes open and stared confusedly at the stout shape that hovered over her bed. Eventually she recognized Mrs. Peevey, holding a breakfast tray and smiling to beat the band.

"Good mornin', Ms. McKinney. Rise and shine and have your breakfast. I won't have you helpin' me find a weddin' gown on an empty stomach."

Tilly propped herself on her elbows and scooted to a sitting position, then leaned back against the cushioned headboard. Pushing her hair out of her eyes, she smiled back. Despite her own uncertainty about the day's outcome, it was impossible not to respond to Mrs. Peevey's genuine and heartfelt happiness.

"Breakfast in bed? What's the occasion, Mrs. Peevey? It's not my birthday."

Mrs. Peevey placed the tray over Tilly's lap. "If I could, I'd serve you breakfast in bed for the next ten years, Ms. McKinney," she said. "Because of

you, today's my weddin' day.'' She lifted the cover
on the largest plate, revealing eggs Benedict, bacon
and a croissant. In addition to steaming coffee, there
were glasses of milk and orange juice on the tray, a
bowl of raspberry jam and a crystal vase with a single white rose.

"If I ate a breakfast like this every day for the
next ten years, I'd easily gain fifty pounds," Tilly
joked.

Mrs. Peevey chuckled as she unwrapped Tilly's
silverware from a snowy white napkin. "As active
and busy as you are, Ms. McKinney, I'd say you
don't need to worry about losin' that cute little figure
of yours. Now eat up while it's hot. I'll be back in
a jiff with a whole pot of coffee for you. I sent down
to the kitchen for freshly ground beans and a coffeemaker first thing this morning. But I'd best be off. I
need to call the courthouse as soon as it opens and
find out if there's a specific time when Pooky and I
must come down to exchange our *I do's.*"

"Mrs. Peevey, wait!"

Mrs. Peevey turned at the door. "Yes, Ms. Mc-
Kinney, did I forget something?"

Tilly nervously licked her lips. "No, you didn't
forget a thing." *Just spit it out, Tilly.* "I was…I was
just wondering if you've seen Dunbar yet this morning."

Mrs. Peevey's smile broadened at the mention of
her intended. "Not yet. The poor dear, he's no doubt
sleepin' off the whiskey. I expect his head feels as
big as a watermelon this mornin'." Her cheeks
bloomed like roses. "I hope he's not got a headache
tonight for the honeymoon."

Tilly felt like a heel, but she had to prepare Mrs.

Peevey just in case Dunbar had a morning-after
memory loss. "Do you think he's still intending to
walk down the aisle...er...*today,* Mrs. Peevey? I
mean, after all, he was so drunk last night he might
not remember, or...er...*want* to remember that
he—"

She was interrupted by the sudden appearance of
Fox at her door. He glanced into her room briefly,
saw her in bed, then immediately glanced away.
Looking straight at Mrs. Peevey, he handed her a
large bouquet of yellow flowers of unidentifiable va-
riety.

"These are from Dunbar, Mrs. Peevey," he announced in his usual no-nonsense voice. "He said it
was unlucky for the groom to see the bride before
the wedding, so he sent them with me. Since no flo-
rists were open at dawn—which is when he got up
this morning—he picked them from alongside the
freeway. He says they're probably just weeds, but he
wanted you to have something pretty to look at first
thing on your wedding day."

Mrs. Peevey had buried her nose in the bouquet,
her eyes misting with emotion...or allergies, Tilly
wasn't sure which. She looked up now and said to
Fox, "Thank you, dear boy. That was a lovely
speech and probably embarrassed you considerable.
But it made my day!"

Fox allowed himself a small grin, gave a crisp nod,
then withdrew. Mrs. Peevey then turned to Tilly and
inquired with a coy smile, "What was it you were
sayin' about Dunbar and his maybe not wantin' to
remember somethin'?"

Tilly laughed. "Well, I haven't even lifted my
fork, and I've already got egg on my face." She

sobered and looked apologetically at Mrs. Peevey. "I guess my years as an advice columnist have made me a little cynical. I just didn't want you to be disappointed if Dunbar tried to back out of the proposal. With his history and all, and his condition last night…you understand why I was worried, don't you?"

Mrs. Peevey nodded. "I understand, Ms. McKinney, and I know you were only lookin' out for me, but I knew in my heart he was finally ready to tie the nuptial knot." She looked fondly at the bouquet of wildflowers. "And now to hear he's been up for hours already, walkin' alongside a busy freeway pickin' these flowers, just makes me love 'im more."

Tilly nodded back, smiling. "I can certainly understand why." A picture of the duke picking flowers for *her* floated romantically through her mind, but she immediately banished it.

"Now eat and drink while everything's hot," Mrs. Peevey scolded. "I'd like to get shopping as soon as the stores open." She turned to go, then turned immediately back, a stricken expression on her face. "You *will* go with me, won't you? Shoppin', I mean. You'll know all the places to look for a pretty dress, but foolish me, I just realized I haven't even asked you! I've been makin' plans in my head all night, not even thinkin' of what anyone else might be needin' to do."

Tilly took a sip of the fragrant coffee, then said warmly, "I'd love to go shopping with you." She paused, set down her cup. "But have you okayed all these plans with the duke?"

Mrs. Peevey nodded eagerly. "Yes, he knows my plans and approves them all. He's given you permis-

sion to spend the day helping me with the weddin',
if you will, and only requires your assistance as a
secretary this afternoon just prior to the lecture…and
at the lecture, too, of course.''

'''Permission…require,''' Tilly said grimly. ''*His*
words, I gather.''

Mrs. Peevey chuckled. ''He's a man used to givin'
orders, Ms. McKinney.'' She arched a brow. ''But it
doesn't detract from his considerable charm, I'm
thinkin'.'' Then she quickly turned and left before
Tilly could think of a thing to say in reply.

Tilly sourly admitted to herself that Mrs. Peevey
was right. The duke was dictatorial, but very charming. She took a bite of egg and chewed slowly, her
thoughts transported back to the highly charged moments they'd shared in the kitchen. Just remembering
the way he'd kissed her, caressed her, made her usually sluggish morning blood race through her veins
like liquid mercury.

And now, in the sober light of day, it was easy to
realize that she'd been suckered into sticking around
till Wednesday. As for actually agreeing to take the
duke down to her folks' farm for two and a half more
days of torture in the dratted man's company, it was
sheer lunacy!

''McKinney. You're up.''

Tilly's fork clattered to the plate, and she grabbed
her blanket with both hands, gripping it in a tight
wad against her chest. The duke was standing just
inside the open door, dressed in a blue turtleneck
sweater and a pair of gray slacks. ''What do *you*
want? I'm not dressed and…and I'm eating breakfast.''

The duke's eyes twinkled, as if he was amused by

her modesty. He took a step into the room. "So I see. How do you rate, McKinney? I haven't been served breakfast in bed since I was sick with the flu five years ago."

"I'm sure Mrs. Peevey would deliver your breakfast to the moon if that's where you wanted to eat it," Tilly retorted. "You always get what you want, don't you?"

His gaze strayed over her face, her shoulders, her fingers gripping the blanket so tightly. He pursed his lips consideringly and raised a brow. "Not always."

She felt her cheeks flame with color. "You haven't answered my question. What do you want? And whatever it is, couldn't it have waited till I was dressed?"

The duke lifted his right hand and waved a thin, dun-colored envelope in the air as he crossed the room to stand next to her bed. As he looked down at her with those brilliant baby blues, Tilly couldn't help but make that Victorian analogy again....

He was the noble lord of the manor, and she the lowly chambermaid...or governess—let's say chambermaid, in this case—helpless and trembling in his masterful clutches. He'd come to her small attic room to make her the object of his ardent, unsanctified desire. The sighing, yearning, throbbing recipient of his unquenchable lust...

"McKinney?"

"Hmm?" Tilly shook herself free of the fantasy. She felt disoriented, surprised that the duke was wearing twentieth-century clothing instead of a ruffled shirt and skintight pantaloons. Or any clothes at all, for that matter.

"You look dazed. Not enough caffeine pumping through your system yet?"

Maybe he was on to something there. Tilly flattened the blanket against her chest so it wouldn't fall down and took another gulp of coffee. Then another. Fortified, she faced him.

"Are you going to tell me why you've disturbed the sanctity of my bedroom or not?"

He waved the paper at her, this time right under her nose. "I've been trying to get you to take this ever since I came in. It's a telegram, McKinney. For you."

Tilly snatched the telegram. "People don't send telegrams anymore," she grumbled anxiously. "If something was wrong at home, my mom would have called my apartment...and I've been checking my messages."

"Relax, it's not from your mother. I believe it's from Miss Darling."

"From Emma?" Tilly quickly ripped open the telegram and read the short message inside as the duke waited. When she'd finished it, she couldn't help a whoop of joy.

"Don't tell me," the duke murmured dryly. "She's married. She and Mendenhall got married the minute he set foot on British soil after flying there willy-nilly on the Concorde, and they're off to a honeymoon in Hawaii."

"Close," Tilly answered with an exultant smile. "They're engaged and they're off to the Lake District to visit her parents."

The duke scowled. "Oh. I didn't know her parents lived in the Lake District."

"You wouldn't," Tilly replied with a sniff.

Without an invitation the duke sat down on the edge of Tilly's bed. She eyed him warily as he plucked the rose from her vase and held it to his nose. He eyed her back till Tilly thought her bones would turn to jelly. But she wouldn't be the first to look away. She wouldn't allow herself to show just how much he discomposed her.

"This is a banner day for you, isn't it, McKinney?"

"What do you mean?"

"Miss Darling and Mendenhall have telegraphed to announce their engagement, and Mrs. Peevey and Dunbar will be married by day's end. You have succeeded in joining together two couples that might otherwise have never overcome the obstacles to wedded bliss. You're a regular cupid with arrows flying like machine-gun bullets in every direction."

"You're mocking me."

"I'm praising you. Aren't you pleased with what you've accomplished?"

"Are you?"

"Yes, actually, I'm very happy for both couples. Only—"

"Only what?"

He handed her the rose and stood up, then walked slowly to the door. He turned, and just before closing the door behind him, said, "But who's next, McKinney? Is no one safe from your arrows?"

Tilly stared at the door long after the duke was gone. She had a sneaky and very troubling idea that one of her arrows might have boomeranged.

ON THE WAY DOWNTOWN to the courthouse, Julian had a man-to-man talk with Dunbar. While the ladies had been transported via limo, with Fox at the wheel, they'd taken a taxi.

"You're an old-fashioned chap, Dunbar," Julian began.

"How's that, Your Grace?" Dunbar nervously adjusted his tie.

"You made sure you and Mrs. Peevey didn't cross paths all day."

"Bad luck to see the bride before the weddin'," Dunbar said. "I'm in no mind to start my marriage off on the wrong foot, that's what."

"Your turnaround was rather sudden, wasn't it?"

Dunbar shrugged. "Truth to tell, I don't know why I've been pussyfootin' so long. I've been a blamed fool."

"I think her decision to go dancing without you scared the living daylights out of you."

He looked sheepish. "Maybe so. But I love 'er, that's what. And the more I think on it, the more I like the idea of bein' shackled to Margaret Mary for the rest of my born days."

"What about your...er...other interests?"

Dunbar gave a firm shake of his head. "I'll never look at another woman."

"Dunbar..."

Dunbar grinned. "Well, maybe I'll look, but that's all. I'll never hurt her again, Your Grace—that's a promise."

"See that you keep it."

"Or I'll be mucking out the manure from the horse stalls, right, Your Grace?"

Julian gave Dunbar's shoulder an affectionate squeeze. "Worse than that, Dunbar. You'll find yourself facedown in a pile of the stuff with a sore jaw."

Dunbar laughed. "I'll remember that. But I'm not worried. It's time, Your Grace. I should have married her years ago. When it's right, there's no point in waitin'." Dunbar looked keenly at Julian. "You'll know, too."

"What will I know?"

"When it's right. When it's time."

"Will I?" Julian murmured.

THE WEDDING WENT OFF without a hitch. Mrs. Peevey looked like a more youthful version of the Queen Mum, beaming and regal in a lavender dress and a matching hat tastefully decorated with tiny violets and a white net. Even Tilly wore a dress. Julian had seen her legs the night before in that short nightie she'd been wearing, but it didn't lessen the impact of seeing them again, all sleek and smooth in nude panty hose, her pastel-painted toenails peeking through strappy sandals that matched her short yellow dress.

Julian and Tilly stood up as witnesses while Fox and the others waited outside in the limo. Standing across from her, Julian watched the play of emotions on Tilly's expressive face as she listened to the simple words of the wedding ceremony, clipped out unromantically by the officiating clerk. But he could tell that no flower-decked chapel or lofty cathedral could have made Dunbar and Mrs. Peevey look happier or more in love. Tilly saw it, too. Once or twice he was surprised to see that she even surreptitiously wiped away a tear. Her hard-nosed style as an advice columnist hadn't prepared him for the possibility that she'd cry at weddings.

Julian marveled at the difference in the lives of

four of his employees in less than a week. His life, too. His "family" had diminished by two, and two others would be cooing and cohabitating by day's end. And all because of a petite redhead with a penchant for meddling. He really was happy for the marrying couples, but he was more than a little worried about his own increasing interest in the aforementioned meddler.

In fact Julian was beginning to think he'd made a colossal mistake in issuing the challenge to work on her father's farm. He should have just let her go when she'd announced her plans to abandon her agreement to work for him through Wednesday. But in dealing with Mathilda McKinney, he often found himself acting in direct opposition to common sense.

She was right, after all. They were worlds apart in almost every apparent way. A brief romance was so tempting…but if she was tender-hearted enough to cry at weddings, there was no doubt she'd be hurt by a brief romance that had no possibility of a storybook ending.

THE LECTURE WENT just as Tilly had expected. Although since the wedding the duke had been aloof as all get-out toward her, he was warmer than ever toward his audience and managed to dazzle them as usual. Afterward Tilly received not one, but three petitions from groupies for the privilege of enjoying the duke of Chesterfield's company somewhere…say…*more private* than Seattle's main public library.

Tilly was polite but cool and promptly threw away the papers with phone numbers written on them and the key to room 329 at a local no-tell motel. She wasn't going to bother to tell the duke about them; she had no intention of pandering to his ego. Besides, he was barely speaking to her.

His recent frosty demeanor notwithstanding, there had been signs of a rather large heart beating in the ducal chest earlier that day at a celebratory lunch after the wedding ceremony. During a champagne toast, the duke had handed Dunbar the keys to the honeymoon suite at the Royal Covington. He instructed both Dunbar and Mrs. Peevey not to worry about feeding him or driving him anywhere for the duration of their stay in America. They were official honeymooners from that moment until they left for England Saturday afternoon. And once they got back home to Dorset, further arrangements for honeymooning would be discussed.

Needless to say, Dunbar and Mrs. Peevey were grateful and happy. Tilly was happy for them, too...until later that evening when Fox was driving them home from the lecture and she realized that she'd be sleeping in the duke's suite without even the nominal chaperonage of Mrs. Peevey!

"Fox, drop Ms. McKinney off at the hotel, then I want you to drive me to another address."

"Will you want me to wait for you, Your Grace, or will I pick you up later?"

"I'll take a taxi home, Fox."

"Yes, Your Grace."

This exchange relieved Tilly of the concern about whether or not the duke had plans for her and the kitchen table again, but instead of being happy, she was instantly depressed. Where was he going? To visit Jamie Grisswold? To pay a visit to a groupie who'd had the chutzpah to bypass his secretary and hand a telephone number and a hotel key directly to him?

Tilly didn't want to think about it. She got out of the limo at the hotel without waiting for assistance from Fox, then barely looked back at the duke as she bid him a curt good-night. If he replied, it was lost in the sound of the slamming door.

When Tilly got to her room, she called herself every kind of idiot for about fifteen minutes, then decided to phone her mother. After all, her family ought to be warned that she'd be accompanied by a royal pain in the you-know-what when she came to visit, and she also wanted to make sure some rigorous farmwork was lined up for the overconfident duke.

Her mother answered after the second ring. "Hello?"

"Hi, Mom."

"Tilly, honey. You're still coming tomorrow, aren't you?"

"Sure, Mom. Only I'm bringing a...another person."

"A new boyfriend?" her mother suggested hopefully.

"Nope. A duke."

"A what?"

"Did you watch the ten-o'clock news last night...channel four?"

"Yes. We rarely miss it, you know."

"Did you see the story Gretchen Blaisdell did on the duke of Chesterfield, the one who's doing lectures on Roman artifacts?"

"Did I ever! He's one cute duke." There was a stunned pause. "You don't mean—?"

"Yes, Mom. Get out the good jelly glasses. The duke is coming to dinner."

"You're teasing me."

"No. We've got a bet going. I've been working for him to make up for his secretary quitting—he claims it was *my* fault—but I threatened to bail ship and he conned me into staying if he agreed to work for Dad for a couple of days."

"Tilly, dear, slow down! I don't understand. You work for the *Globe*. How can you work for the duke? How did you two even meet, for heaven's sake?"

"It's a long story, Mom," Tilly warned.

"I've got time," her mother assured her.

At the end of Tilly's explanation, interrupted by a lot of questions and exclamations of surprise, her mother laughed delightedly.

"What's so funny?" Tilly demanded grimly, her own mouth curved in a reluctant smile. "He's been a royal pain."

"Sounds to me like you've met your match, Tilly. Is there the slightest possibility of a romance budding here?"

Tilly had not and never would tell her mother about the close call on the kitchen table. "Not a chance. We bug each other. Besides, I'm just a commoner, not good enough for a duke, I'm sure."

"You're good enough for anyone," her mother briskly informed her. "My only concern would be if he's good enough for you."

"Spoken in true motherly fashion," Tilly said dryly. "But forget the romance stuff, Mom. What I want to know is what Dad has lined up in the fields for the next two days."

"The hay's been cut and drying for a day or two.

Dad plans to bale it on Thursday and get it stored in the barn, hopefully before we get another storm.''

''All in one day?''

''You know your father. He doesn't want to take the chance of leaving the bales in the field any longer than necessary.''

Tilly smiled. ''That's good. And what about Angie? Do you think we could convince her to give up her sow-tending duties and hand them over to the duke for a day?''

There was another pause, then a low chuckle. ''Tilly, you're wicked.''

Tilly grinned into the telephone receiver. ''I know, Mom. Aren't you proud?''

TILLY DIDN'T KNOW when the duke got home that night, and she'd convinced herself she didn't care. She was awakened at seven the following morning by a sharp rap on her door and, after hastily running a comb through her hair and throwing on a robe, she tried to persuade herself that she didn't care that it was Fox instead of the duke standing on her threshold when she opened the door.

''His Grace requires your assistance in the office as soon as possible for the organization and packing up of his materials and files, and to type a few necessary thank-you notes,'' Fox informed her.

Tilly winced at the word *required* again, but only said, ''I'll get there as soon as I can.''

She ordered a bagel and coffee from room service, showered, packed all her clothes and managed to make it to the office by eight. When she entered the room, the duke was standing by the desk, sifting through some mail. When he looked up and their gazes met, Tilly felt the impact to the tips of her toes. How she wished she could get over such a dumb, schoolgirlish reaction to a pair of gorgeous blue eyes!

She had dressed for the drive to Washougal, seeing no sense in changing again in just four hours. She'd put on a pair of jeans and a pale pink T-shirt she'd tucked into her belt. His gaze flickered briefly over her figure, then shifted back to the mail. "Good morning, McKinney. I trust you slept well."

She waited. "What? No dig about my tardiness? No beleaguered comment about my unprofessional attire?"

He didn't bother to look up again. "Why state the obvious? There's a lot to do. Let's start with a little dictation, shall we? I can't leave Seattle without a few fond farewells."

Then, without further ado, he got down to business, issuing orders and efficiently tackling all the necessary last-minute tasks that were a part of finishing up the lecture tour. Tilly just as efficiently did her part in cleaning up the office and typing letters, but frustration was building in her by the minute.

If he was going to be silent as a tomb and about as communicative as a mummy, why was he bothering to go with her to Washougal at all?

"Thank you, McKinney," the duke finally said as she licked her last envelope. "That should do it. Fox can mail the letters when he takes these boxes to the van."

Tilly stood with her hands on her hips. "So, I guess I've been dismissed."

He raised a brow. "Yes, of course. Perhaps you have a few things to do before we leave for Washougal?"

"I'm packed and ready to go."

"Good. I'm not, however."

"You don't have to."

"I don't have to what?"

"You don't have to pack."

Now he raised both brows. "Why not?"

"Because you don't have to come."

"We had a deal—"

"It's off."

The mobile brows lowered. "What do you mean it's off? McKinney, you have the most damnable propensity to try to back out of agreements."

"But I'm offering *you* an out," she protested. "Not *me!*"

"I'm not so sure about that! Besides, *I* don't want an out. *I* don't renege on deals. You upheld your end of it—now it's my turn to do what I'm supposed to do."

"Believe me, I'm not going to demand a duel at dawn if you don't come to Washougal. This whole deal was a bad idea to begin with, and it's obvious you'd rather stick your tongue to a frozen flagpole than work on my father's farm for the next two days."

"My tongue has suffered enough abuse lately, McKinney," the duke drawled sardonically. "Believe me, I'd rather work on the farm."

She blushed, effectively silenced by his allusion to the tongue incident.

"Besides," he continued, "what makes you think I no longer relish the idea of being a farmhand?"

"You've barely spoken to me since the wedding yesterday. You haven't even been as rude and snotty as usual. You're obviously as sick of me as I—" up came her chin "—as I am of you. This is your chance, Rothwell. You don't have to go to Washougal. You can spend the next three days in Seattle without me around to annoy you. Doesn't that sound like paradise?"

To Julian it sounded more like hell. A quiet, rather peaceful hell, but hell nonetheless.

He observed Tilly's flushed face and tried to read her thoughts. He suspected she was as afraid as he was that this whole Washougal trip would blow up in their faces. That a sexual undertow would drag them out into a sea of complicated feelings neither of them wanted to deal with. Hadn't he spent most of last evening walking the streets of Seattle, then stayed in Dunbar's room last night instead of his own as a precaution against giving in to their attraction for each other?

It was madness to continue to tempt fate, but as he stared at her he tried to imagine saying goodbye to her today. Now. The idea was totally unacceptable.

He also tried to imagine spending the next three days in Seattle without going nuts wondering what she was doing down on the farm. He had an earnest desire to meet her family, to see where she grew up, to try to put together, then disassemble, all the elements that made Tilly the irritating, alluring little baggage she was today.

Then maybe he'd get her out of his system, satisfy this strange curiosity about her without bedding her and breaking her heart. And maybe he could go home and eventually find the peace of mind he'd had before barging into her office a few days ago.

"You're chickening out again," he taunted her.

"You just don't want to give me the chance to prove I can work on a farm as hard as any man. Neither of us will enjoy the next couple of days, but the deal's *on*, McKinney. And as far as I'm concerned, that's the last word on the subject."

She said nothing, but her chin climbed another inch before she turned on her heel and stomped out of the room. The view of her shapely derriere as she disappeared down the hall elicited from him a deep sigh and the whispered words, "Rothwell, you're a bloody fool...."

Chapter Eleven

"So now you're giving *me* the silent treatment."

Tilly removed her earphones. "I'm sorry, did you say something?"

"I *said*...so now you're giving *me* the silent treatment."

"I didn't think you'd notice," Tilly commented dryly.

"After the first hundred miles, I got a clue."

"You're a smart man, Rothwell."

"Smart enough to know this isn't getting us anywhere."

Tilly glanced at the speedometer. "Well, if we're going nowhere, why are we trying to get there so fast?"

Julian let up a little on the gas. He was always a little heavy-footed when he was irritable...or randy. Or both, as in this case. "You're being deliberately provoking," he growled.

"You started it."

"Now you're talking like a child."

"Going home always brings out the child in me."

He sighed. "Are we almost there?"

Tilly chuckled. "Now you sound like the child."

She'd spent most of the trip slumped in the seat, earphones on her head and her eyes glued to the passing landscape. Julian wouldn't have minded it so much if he hadn't known it was a deliberate snub. He knew he had it coming, but enough was enough.

"We've passed Vancouver, so it's about twenty more miles." Having offered that much information, Tilly slumped in the seat and put on her earphones again.

Julian heaved another sigh. She'd been like this ever since he'd turned down her offer to scrap the deal that pitted him against the rigors of farmwork. While he'd packed for the trip, digging out of the back of a drawer a pair of well-worn jeans he'd unfortunately had little occasion to wear during his lecture tour, she'd gone back to her apartment to check on Rebound, dropped off the clothes she'd worn while working as his secretary and picked up the more casual clothes she'd wear on the farm.

He'd hoped she'd be in a better, more communicative mood when she returned, but that hadn't been the case. She'd simply thrown him the keys to her forest green Jeep Cherokee, announced that she'd gassed it up already and that he could drive the two hundred miles to Washougal because she just wasn't "in the mood."

"You do realize that in my country we drive on the left side of the road," he'd said. "Do you think you can trust me?"

"If you can't drive a car and keep it on the right side of the road, Rothwell, you might as well throw in the towel now. Operating farm machinery can be tricky and sometimes downright dangerous."

Julian had had no worries about driving the Jeep;

he'd only wanted to rattle her cage. Evidently she was having a rattle-proof day.

Despite Tilly's frustrating noncompany, he'd enjoyed the trip down Interstate 5 through the beautiful forests and rolling hills, with magnificent snow-capped peaks in the background. According to his map and signposts along the way, they'd passed near Mount Olympus, then Mount Rainier, and even the infamous Mount St. Helens.

Too bad he'd had no one to share such beautiful sights with. His traveling companion *was* looking at the sights—sights familiar to her already—and thoroughly enjoying them, too, judging by that appreciative gleam in her eyes. But she was apparently satisfied to keep her delight to herself.

To make matters worse, he was having a devil of a time keeping his hand from straying where it frequently rested on the gearshift to her shapely, jean-clad thigh just inches away. She looked damned sexy in jeans and a T-shirt, and he could remember all too well how good it felt to kiss her, touch her. And the way she'd responded that night in the kitchen had promised the sort of sexual experience a man would have a hard time forgetting.

After that thought, Julian spent the next twenty miles trying to forget what he hadn't even had the pleasure to experience and remember in the first place....

Suddenly Tilly rolled down the window on her side of the vehicle and sniffed. She pulled off her earphones and showed signs of heightened excitement. "Do you smell that awful cabbagelike stink?"

He sniffed, too. "Yes. What is it? A paper mill?"

"Bingo, Rothwell. How'd you know? It's the paper mill. I guess they all smell like that, huh?"

"It's the processing methods they use."

"Well, if we can smell the mill, it means we're almost to Camas. Two minutes outside of Camas, we'll hit Washougal. Blink your eyes and we'll have passed through Washougal and be practically at my parents' front door."

She was right. In less than ten minutes they were driving up the quarter-mile lane to a large, two-story house with a wraparound porch, surrounded by tall trees and various other outbuildings and barns. All the buildings were on the east side of the lane, and on the west side were acres of cultivated land.

"This is quite a farm," Julian remarked.

"Yes, it is," Tilly agreed with pride. "There's 245 acres altogether. My great-great-grandfather, James McKinney, a Scottish immigrant, bought the farm in 1860. In 1910 my great-grandfather, William McKinney, built the house that we live in now."

"What does your father plant? Wait, you told me once...wasn't it hay and wheat?"

She eyed him warily for a moment, as if wondering if he was really interested. "Yes. And corn, too. He also raises some livestock. Mostly pigs and a few cattle. My brother, Dave, is a dairy farmer and he rents a farm just over the hill from us. He and my dad work the land together."

"You've never said how many siblings you have."

"You've never asked."

"I'm asking now, McKinney."

"Well, there's Dave. He's twenty-four, married and about to become a father for the first time. I've also got a little sister, Angie, fourteen, all legs, braces, freckles and long, carrot red hair.'' She chuckled. ''The poor thing is in a constant state of mortification. She hardly ever smiles for fear of showing her braces.''

''Typical teenager,'' Julian commented sympathetically.

''How do you know? You're an only child, aren't you, Rothwell?''

He pulled onto a gravel drive parallel to the house and killed the engine, then he turned to her with a wry smile. ''I may be an only child, but I do have the usual tools for observation. Eyes, ears, etcetera. I even find that despite my repressive upbringing in stuffy old England, I can sometimes relate to other human beings—even, dare I brag, in other parts of the world—with a fair amount of success.''

Tilly had no reply, but simply stared at him with a puzzled wrinkle etched in her brow. She was about to say something, when suddenly her family began to pour out of the front door and converge on the Jeep en masse.

The duke got out of the Jeep and came around to Tilly's side just as she was warmly greeted by each member of the family with a hug and a kiss. Although she'd told him that it had only been three weeks since her last visit, her family seemed as thrilled to see her as if she'd been absent three years.

Julian felt a strange visceral ache as he watched the touching scene, and memories of his own father's indifferent reception of him when he returned home for summer holidays from boarding school flashed painfully through his mind.

On the periphery of the circle surrounding Tilly

was a short white dog with so much long, fluffy hair it looked like it had been tossed in the dryer and left too long. It panted and barked and jumped excitedly, and Tilly finally stooped on one knee and gave the delirious animal a hug and a few well-appreciated scratches behind the ear.

"Juno, you're fatter than ever," Tilly scolded affectionately. "I wonder why Angie doesn't shave you and toss you in with the sows." She looked up just then, laughing, and caught Julian's eye. The flush of happiness on her face made his heart flipflop.

But suddenly it was Julian's turn to be the center of attention. "Hello. You must be our volunteer farmhand for the next two days." A tall, dark-haired, ruggedly handsome man who looked to be in his late forties greeted him with a firm handshake and a friendly smile. "Didn't mean to ignore you, but there's always a fuss when Tilly comes home. I'm her dad, Jim."

Julian returned the handshake just as firmly and smiled back. "Please call me Julian."

Jim nodded. "Julian. Now, let me introduce you to the rest of the family."

Julian immediately liked Tilly's father, and her mother, too, who was just an older version of Tilly. Same height, same red hair with a little gray sprinkled in, same vivacious personality, snapping green eyes and trim figure in jeans and a lightweight blue sweater. And best of all, there was no nervous kowtowing from either of them, as if he were something special simply because he'd been born with a title.

Her brother, Dave, was tall and dark like her father, his wife, Lisa, a petite, smiling blonde, very much pregnant. Her sister, Angie, was exactly the way Tilly had described her. She hovered shyly in the background, probably mortified because she had a small pimple on her chin that no one could see but herself. His compassion roused, Julian smiled at her warmly. She blushed and smiled back, unintentionally revealing her braces, then quickly clamped her mouth shut again and stared at the ground.

Introductions over, the family filed into the house. Dave and Jim insisted on carrying the suitcases up the stairs and Tilly's mother, Carol, showed Julian his room and pointed out the communal bathroom at the end of the hall.

"Tilly says we're not to give you special treatment," she said with a mischievous grin as she leaned against the doorjamb with her arms folded, watching him set his suitcase on a trunk at the foot of the bed. "But I hope that doesn't mean you're banned from dinner and have to eat stale bread and watered-down soup that I'm required to scoot through a trap in the door."

Julian laughed. "I hope not, either. It sounds like I'll need my strength to do all the hard labor Tilly has in mind for me."

"The work will definitely be hard. Jim's planning on square-baling hay all day long tomorrow." Her twinkling gaze took a quick perusal of him, from head to toe. "But I think you're up to it."

"I'm gratified by your confidence, Mrs. McKinney," Julian replied with the same amused air. "Your daughter, on the other hand, hasn't got any confidence in me at all."

"Give her some time," Carol said, still smiling but with a more serious tone in her voice. "Tilly's a skeptic. That's what makes her such a good advice columnist. She refuses to look at the world through rose-colored glasses. She doesn't think anyone should base their happiness on anything but the facts, ma'am.'' Her smile broadened as she pushed off from the doorjamb and headed down the hall. "Dinner's in half an hour," she called over her shoulder. "Just follow your nose."

Left alone to get settled in, Julian sat down on the edge of the antique brass bed, covered in a blue-and-white wedding-ring quilt, to briefly ponder the significance of Carol's words. She'd begun by explaining why Tilly didn't think he could do hard farmwork, then somehow turned it into a revealing allusion to Tilly's requirements for happiness. He had an inkling of what she was hinting at, but he was unwilling at the moment to follow that alarming train of thought. Instead he took stock of his surroundings.

The house was old but well kept, clean as a whistle and full of excellent antiques. It struck Julian that this family had as much respect for tradition and artifacts—albeit artifacts only from a previous century, not a previous millennium—as he did.

Julian stood and walked to the window, looking out over the green landscape, dark and dewy in the long shadows of the late afternoon. He was surprised to see Tilly standing by the gate at the end of the cobbled walkway that led from the porch, across the lawn, to the lane. Juno stood, wagging her tail, beside her. Tilly was simply staring out over the waving sea of wheat in the field opposite the house.

As he continued to watch her, she turned to walk back to the house and he was mesmerized by the dreamy, peaceful expression on her face. Like him, apparently, she loved the beauty of the land. Especially when the land she loved was called home.

That was when Julian really understood how he and Tilly were the same...but so very different. This was home to her, and to Julian there was no other place on earth besides England that he could ever call home. His roots there were as deep and heart binding as possible. And judging by her wistful smile as she took one last look over her shoulder before going inside, she felt the same way about Washougal, Washington, as he did about the shire of Dorset in England.

Julian sighed and turned away from the window. He'd come there to learn about Tilly, and he'd learned enough in the past five minutes to decide his course for the next two days. He intended to enjoy himself, have some fun and make friends, but he knew now that it would be a big mistake to repeat what had happened two nights ago in the kitchen of his suite at the Royal Covington.

But why not? he asked himself. The answer that came from the depths of his soul was this: Tilly was not the sort of girl you only dallied with. He'd been avoiding facing the truth for some time, but he knew now without a doubt that Tilly was only the sort of girl you took *home.*

But home for Tilly could never be England, because what did he have to offer her there? Lots of land, lots of luxuries, certainly, but nothing like what she already had right there in the bosom of her family. Love. Acceptance. Warmth.

Julian shook his head, chuckled derisively at the idea that Tilly might even have the slightest inclination to want anything permanent from him in the

first place—they were stripes and plaid, after all—
collected a change of clothes and headed for the
bathroom down the hall for a nice cold shower.

Cold, because no matter what he told himself, he
still wanted her.

Bloody hell.

"UP AND AT 'EM, Rothwell!" In the dim morning
light that filtered through the hall window, Tilly
pounded for the third time on Julian's bedroom door,
then paused with her fist hovering over the panels
and listened. Nothing. Not even the merest rustle of
sheets could be detected from the other side.

She pounded again. "It's five-thirty, Rothwell.
Breakfast'll be on the table in fifteen minutes, and
it's first come first served. If you're not careful, Angie'll feed your sausage to the dog!" She pressed her
ear to the door. Still nothing.

Tilly couldn't believe he could sleep through all
the commotion she was making! But the sooner he
learned that life on a farm began early...*very*
early...the sooner—

"Looking for me, McKinney?"

Tilly jumped at the sound of Julian's voice, the
words spoken so near her ear she could feel his warm
breath. She twirled around, her hand clutching her
throat. "Rothwell, you scared the living—"

She stopped midscold, her gaze flickering over
him from head to toe. His hair was wet. The hair on
his chest that peeked above the V of his white terry
robe was wet. The hair on his muscular forearms
below the raglan cuffs of his robe was wet. The hair
on his long, sexy legs that showed at the bottom of
the knee-length robe was wet.

Hell, he was wet all over! He had no business looking that sexy mere feet away from her puberty-impaired, hormone-ridden little sister's bedroom. Seeing such a sight—*such a man*—at such an impressionable age might ruin poor Angie for anyone else for the rest of her life!

"What are you doing outside your bedroom—" she fluttered her hand furtively in his general direction "—like that. I have a shy little sister, you know."

He raised his brows, spread his open palms in an innocent gesture. "Like what? I'm decently covered. Besides, I thought Angie told me last night that she gets up before breakfast to feed the pigs."

He was right. Angie was outside feeding the pigs and was in no danger of being scarred for life, but what about *her?* "Why didn't you take a change of clothes with you?" she hissed, trying hard not to stare at his chest.

"I did that last night, and despite the fact that I took a cold shower, it was too sticky in there to put my clothes on right away. Air's humid."

She felt twitchy inside, argumentative. "Well... well, couldn't you have at least dried off before traipsing down the hall?"

He looked amused. "Does my damp state bother you?"

"Why should it?" she snapped.

"Or is there a rule on the farm about how one should dry oneself off? I hope not, because I confess that my favorite way of drying off is to stretch out on the bed and dry au naturel. It's very cooling." He smiled wryly. "And trust me, McKinney, I need cooling."

Tilly felt the heat rush up her neck to flood her cheeks with what she was sure was an all too obvious blush. "What you need is a hard day's work, Rothwell," she croaked, her throat suddenly dry. "That'll cool your jets." She headed for the stairs. "And as for rules about drying off au naturel, there aren't any, but any thinking person would know it's not a very time-effective or efficient way of drying off." She stomped down a couple of steps, then shouted, "By the way, I meant what I said about your sausage."

He chuckled. "What about my sausage?"

He was laughing at her...*the nerve!* "Oh, never mind."

Tilly hurried down the stairs and into the high-ceilinged kitchen, where her mother was busy cooking at the stove and her father was reading the paper at the long oak table by the window.

Her mother turned expectantly. "So, how's he like them? Over easy? Scrambled?"

"I forgot to ask," Tilly said peevishly, plopping into her usual chair next to her father.

Her father peered at her over the paper. "I thought I heard some shouting about a...sausage? Were you two having an argument?"

Tilly crossed her arms. "Arguing is all we ever do."

Her father exchanged a glance with her mother, then remarked casually, "I like him. He has a firm handshake and he looks you straight in the eye when you're talking to him."

"You guys were up late enough last night," Tilly commented sulkily. "You kept me awake till after midnight with all your talking and laughing."

"Goodness, Tilly, you went to bed so early. It was

only nine o'clock, as I recall. You must have been lying in bed for three hours," her mother remarked. "How frustrating for you. If you couldn't sleep, why didn't you come down and join us?"

"I was beat. Besides, I *could* have slept if you guys'd piped down."

"We were having some delightful discussions," her mother continued as she expertly wielded her spatula. "After Julian asked every imaginable question about the farm and our dull little lives, we finally got him to talk a bit about himself, his artifacts, his children's books and so on. Heavens, he does so *many* different things! He's what I would call a Renaissance man."

"He plays a mean game of Chinese checkers, too," her father added from behind his paper. "Angie only beat him twice out of six times, and she's the hands-down champ in this family."

Tilly leaned back in her chair as her mother poured her a steaming mug of coffee. "I can't believe you let Angie stay up that late on a school night."

"Well, it isn't every day we have a duke as a houseguest," her mother replied.

"I told you not to give him special treatment," Tilly reminded her, then gulped some coffee and burned her tongue. *"Damn."*

Her mother and father both looked at her.

"Sorry," she muttered. "Burned my tongue."

"I hate it when I do that," came the duke's voice from behind her. She jumped again, just as she'd picked up her cup, splashing coffee over the side and onto one of her mother's nicer cotton tablecloths. She cursed under her breath again, grabbed a paper napkin and started blotting.

"But then, any injury to the tongue is painful," the duke continued, pulling out a chair on the opposite side of the table. He smiled genially. "Good morning, everyone."

The duke's arrival was immediately followed by a bustle of talk and activity. Her mother poured him a cup of just-steeped Earl Grey, then couldn't wait to find out how he liked his eggs, whether or not he'd slept well and whether or not he'd had plenty of hot water for his shower that morning.

"He takes cold showers," Tilly muttered into her coffee cup. "And plenty of them. At least he has ever since *I've* known him."

This statement was followed by silence, during which Tilly became aware of the possible interpretation that could be put on her perfectly innocent words. Her blush returned with the force of a heatstroke.

"Have you ever baled hay before, Julian?" her father adroitly inquired at this juncture.

"No, but I've seen it done. I've never driven a tractor, either, for any reason. Are you square-baling or round-baling?"

"Square. That's why I'll need at least four hands today."

"The machine does the actual baling, but hands are needed to drive the tractor, stack the bales on a flat wagon, then transport them to barns for storage, right?"

"Right." Jim grinned. "Sounds like you've got it down pretty well."

Julian grinned back. "But as I said, I've only watched it being done. I've never actually done it.

Do you do much round-baling, or are most of your stock inside in the winter?''

Tilly was incredulous. She had no idea Julian knew so much about hay and the livestock that ate it.

Soon the two men were deep in a discussion about livestock, crops, harvesting, then on to the differences between farming in the Australian outback and farming in the wetter, more fertile soil of southwestern Washington State.

Tilly's amazement grew. She listened as long as she could, then couldn't help interrupting. "You own a farm in Australia?"

Julian nodded. "Well, it's primarily a sheep ranch, but we do a little farming on the side."

Tilly gave a huff of disbelief. "Don't tell me...you've worked on this Aussie farm, haven't you?"

Julian's eyes twinkled, but he didn't allow even a ghost of a smile to curve his lips. "Yes, I have. In fact I frequently spend a few days each year on the ranch, usually around Christmastime. The seasons are reversed there, you know."

"I know," Tilly said grimly.

"I like to do a little hands-on management now and then, get my manicured nails dirty." He grinned, and Tilly wanted to slap him. "But don't worry, today will still be a challenge."

Angie entered the kitchen just then, slamming the back door behind her, with a panting Juno hot on her heels. Juno headed straight for a bowl of water in the corner of the room and began to lap noisily.

"Mornin', Julian!" Angie chirped, racing past him to the kitchen sink to wash her hands. She smiled over her shoulder, her braces on full display. "Think you'll be up for another game of Chinese checkers tonight?"

Tilly was flabbergasted. This was not the way her self-conscious little sister usually behaved. The dratted man had charmed her entire family.

"Let's see how I feel after I've slaved all day," Julian replied with a wink. "Your dad's got big plans for me."

Tilly's eyes narrowed as her father passed Julian the jar of homemade peach jam—her father's favorite and one that he rarely liked to share—and her mother heaped steaming mounds of scrambled eggs onto Julian's plate. It was as plain as the nose on her face that if Julian was going to work as hard as she wanted him to work, she'd have to be the enforcer. Her father certainly couldn't be trusted to crack the whip.

She had had other plans for the day, but now she decided that she would bale hay, too, just to keep an eye on the duke. If she didn't, there was a chance that as soon as Julian broke a sweat on his regal brow, her father would send him off to lounge on the hammock under the big maple tree in the backyard, and her mother would serve him cookies and iced tea. She might even stand over him with a waving palm frond and drop grapes in his mouth. But that wasn't going to happen. Not as long as *Tilly* had anything to say about it!

"I'll help out with the baling, too, Dad," she suddenly blurted, in complete disregard of the conversation going on between the two men.

Her father looked at her for a moment, smiled,

patted her hand and replied, "I thought you might, honey."

As it turned out, Tilly would have been asked to help bale hay even if it hadn't been her idea. Fred, a farmhand her father hired and paid by the hour as the work dictated, called at six-fifteen to announce that he'd been summoned that morning to his sick mother's bedside in Goldendale. Tilly's dad said he understood and sent his well-wishes to Fred's mother, then finished his breakfast and went into the closed-in back porch to put on his boots.

Right on time, Dave showed up at 6:20, and the four of them set out for the hay fields in her father's truck. Her mother had packed them a lunch, and each of them carried a gallon-sized bottle of drinking water. Julian jumped immediately into the back of the truck, and while Tilly had tried to get into the cab with her dad and Dave, she'd been grinned at and elbowed out by her mischief-making brother. She was forced to sit in the back with Julian.

On the way to their destination, Julian just sat there, saying nothing, one long arm resting along the rim of the truck bed, looking out over the land with a relaxed expression on his handsome face. The cool morning air ruffled his hair as the truck sailed over the smooth dirt road that connected one end of the McKinney farm to the other.

One long, jean-clad leg was stretched out in front of him, and the other was bent at the knee, over which he rested his other arm. Tilly had to admit he looked mighty fine in a pair of jeans, and that the faded black T-shirt her dad had loaned him stretched nicely over his taut chest muscles.

It took about five minutes to get to the hay fields, where the mixture of alfalfa, clover and pasture grass had already been cut and raked by tractor into neat windrows. Two tractors, two flatbed wagons and a square-baler already attached to one of the tractors were assembled and ready to go.

Tilly jumped out of the truck as soon as they arrived and looked out over the acres of mowed pastureland. The sun had come up just minutes before, and the fields were bathed in a golden glow. There was still a springlike nip in the air and Tilly had worn a Levi's jacket over her old white T-shirt and faded jeans. She knew that an hour from then she'd be shucking that jacket and every other piece of clothing she could within the bounds of decency, but at the moment it felt pretty good.

"Dave, you start out driving the tractor with the square-baler," her dad directed. "Julian and I will stack the bales till we've got a full flatbed, then Tilly and Julian can take the first load back to the barn, unload them and come back for more. We'll have another wagon full of bales by then. Later we can switch jobs, but that's how I think we oughta start out."

No one argued, but Tilly wondered how she managed to be immediately coupled with Julian. She didn't mind the arrangement, though, because that way she could keep an eye on him and make sure he worked up a good sweat.

They all put on heavy gloves to protect their hands from the coarse hay, which easily cut bare skin, and went to work. Dave drove, the square-baler swept up the raked hay, packed it into bales, tied it twice lengthwise with twine, then spit it out the back. Her dad took the bale from there, stacked it or heaved it to Julian, who stacked it at the other end of the wagon. All Tilly did was scoot bales a few inches now and then to even the load.

Shreds of hay flew every time a bale was moved. The work was scratchy, dusty and dirty. It didn't take long to fill the first wagon, but even with her dad helping, Julian's brow dripped with moisture and the front of his T-shirt showed a V-shaped patch of perspiration.

When Dave had to stop the tractor for a minute and the bales quit coming, Julian took a drink out of his water bottle, then stood with his hands on his lean hips with his head arched, his back stretched, his eyes closed against the glare of the sun. His Adam's apple was prominent.

Tilly just stared. What would the groupies that lusted after the erudite, charming duke of Chesterfield think if they saw him now? All dusty and sweaty, his upper lip gleaming with shiny little drops of water mixed with salty perspiration...

Tilly involuntarily licked her own upper lip. She had a feeling she knew exactly what those groupies would think. They'd think he looked sexier than ever. They'd hope and plan that sometime in the very near future they'd find themselves alone with him in a private spot. Maybe in the middle of a wheat field, where a couple of entangled bodies could sink to the ground without being detected.

Ah, yes, a wheat field would be a perfect spot to have her wicked way with him. First she'd rip away his ruffled shirt, then undo his tight pantaloons, slowly, one button after the other....

Tilly smiled. Now who was the aggressor in her

fantasy? The meek little chambermaid or the lusty duke?

"Good God, McKinney, what *are* you thinking about?"

Chapter Twelve

Tilly's smile faded guiltily away. "I'm not thinking about anything, Rothwell."

His eyes narrowed. "You've claimed that before, McKinney, and I don't believe you. You were thinking something, all right, and judging by the smile on your face, it was quite pleasurable."

Tilly bit her lip and cocked her head to see past Julian to where her father had been standing. He was gone. He'd jumped off the wagon and he was fiddling with some mechanism on the square-baler.

Julian followed her gaze and suggested teasingly, "Were you thinking something that would surprise and horrify your father?"

Surprise him? Maybe a little. Horrify him? She doubted it...although *she* was rather horrified.

"You *wish*. For the last time, Rothwell, I wasn't thinking anything."

Julian was obviously unconvinced. He seemed to challenge her with a frank appraisal that started with her face and traveled ever so slowly, ever so boldly over every inch of her body. She'd stripped off her jacket long ago, and when his gaze paused on her breasts, to her horror she felt her nipples harden. But maybe he wouldn't notice....

He noticed. His gaze flicked back to hers for a heated moment as they both recognized their mutual arousal. By the time he finally looked away, Tilly felt naked before him, as if every thought, every desire, was exposed.

Her father finally returned to the wagon, and the tractor started moving again. Tilly concentrated on the work and tried not to look at Julian for more than a second, and only when it was absolutely necessary.

When the hay was stacked the length of the wagon and as high as Julian's head, Tilly's father called to Dave to stop the tractor. They all jumped off, unhitched the full wagon from the square-baler and hitched up the empty one. Then they hitched the full wagon to the second tractor.

Tilly climbed onto the seat of the second tractor and drove in the direction of the barn, with the duke riding behind in the wagon. She enjoyed this brief respite from Julian's company because she was finding it harder and harder to ignore her desire to tackle the sexy duke to the hay-strewed ground and do what came naturally. After all, what better place than on a farm? she thought with grim humor.

Since the tractor could only go twenty miles per hour full throttle, it took nearly ten minutes to drive to the barn. When they got there, Tilly jumped off the tractor and nearly into the arms of Julian, who happened at that moment to walk directly into her path. They both stepped quickly back and eyed each other with uncertain intent.

"We'd better get busy, McKinney," the duke warned her.

"Right," she answered. She swallowed hard, then pointed toward the barn. "See that mechanical arm?"

He continued to stare at her, then finally tore his gaze away and looked distractedly in the direction she indicated. "You mean that conveyer belt?"

"Right. Actually we call it an elevator. I'm going to connect the tractor gear to it to make it move. We'll stack the bales, one at a time, on the belt, and it'll carry them up to that window in the hayloft. We've got to work fast because Dad and Dave will need this wagon back very soon so they can fill it up again without breaking their flow. There's nothing my dad hates more than standing around in the field with work to be done and no way to do it."

"I understand completely," Julian answered. Then, with a sort of fierce determination, added, "And there's nothing I'd like more at the moment than to work till I'm ready to drop from exhaustion. Which position do you want, Tilly. Top or bottom?"

Tilly knew darned well that he was asking her if she wanted to put the bales on at the bottom of the elevator, or take them off at the top, *but*... She stared at him, at his brilliant eyes, his flushed skin and the perspiration-soaked front of his shirt that was plastered against his hard chest. Had he intended the double entendre?

And did she intend the double entendre when she replied, "I don't care which position I'm in. I manage to do them both pretty well."

Julian took a sharp breath and briefly closed his eyes. "All right," he said, his voice faint and tightly controlled. "I'll put the bales onto the belt. It looks a bit more difficult on this end of it."

Tilly nodded, but didn't move.

Julian raised a brow. "You'd better get going, my dear, off to the hayloft before I change my mind."

That comment could have a double meaning, too!

Tilly hurried away to the hayloft. Julian loaded the conveyer belt and kept the bales coming at a grueling rate, throwing one on about every five seconds. But Tilly was glad to be working, glad to be using all her muscles to capacity. Glad to be so busy she could barely think or feel.

After they finished, Tilly drove the tractor back to the field and Julian again rode in the wagon. On the return trip with another full wagon, Julian drove the tractor after receiving a quick tutorial from her father on the basic controls. He was a quick study and had no trouble at all.

As the day wore on, the sky clouded over and the humidity increased. It was hot and sticky, and the hay dust coated their faces and arms and every exposed surface of their skin. It sifted down the backs of their shirts, into their gloves to cake between their fingers, and dusted their eyebrows and lashes.

By midafternoon they'd put up eight loads of hay and had thrown bales that weighed an accumulated sixteen tons. Tilly would never admit it, but despite the fact that she'd baled many times before, her back was killing her.

On the return trip to the house in the back of the truck, it started sprinkling, and by the time they rolled onto the gravel driveway, the sky opened up and the rain fell in huge, cool drops that promised to soothe away all the gritty dust and grime.

"You can have the first shower, Tilly," Tilly's father called as he and her brother ran to the house.

"No, you go ahead. I'm already getting a shower," Tilly called back, standing under the streaming sky. Julian joined her and they both stood on the lawn, getting soaking wet, their arms raised to the heavens, their hair plastered to their foolishly smiling faces. Suddenly a flash of lightning lit up the sky, and a boom of thunder exploded out of the thick cover of gray clouds.

Tilly should have been afraid, but she wasn't. She continued to stand, her arms outstretched, her eyes closed, till she felt Julian's fingers slide down her wet arm to clasp her hand. She opened her eyes. He stood beside her, looking so wet, so sexy, so damned kissable she was seriously thinking of scandalizing her parents—and any neighbors who might be spying on them with binoculars—by attacking the duke then and there.

"It's dangerous out here, Tilly. Come inside," he said softly.

For once she said nothing, and obeyed.

AFTER A DELICIOUS, filling dinner of lasagna, salad, rolls and chocolate cake, none of them had enough energy left to do anything but sit on the porch, sip lemonade and listen to the constant drum of rain on the tin roof of the porch. It was a soothing sound that managed to comfort and relax Julian despite his continued fierce physical hunger for a certain redhead.

Yes, exhaustion was the friend that got him through the night...well, at least most of it. The minute his head hit the pillow he slept like a stone till four-thirty, opened his eyes to observe the time on the bedside alarm clock, then plunged into an erotic dream the likes of which he hadn't enjoyed—or endured, depending on how you looked at it—since adolescence.

At five-thirty he was jolted from his dream of *unfulfilled* sexual yearning by the sound of someone knocking on the bedroom door.

"Julian? Julian, are you awake? It's time to feed the pigs."

It was Angie. Ah, yes, now he remembered. Today he was to take over Angie's responsibilities as overseer of the farm's 350 or so swine.

Julian sat up and groggily rubbed his eyes. "Do I have time for a shower?" he called. Judging by the still aroused state of his mind and body, it would have to be another cold one.

He heard a low chuckle coming from the other side of the door that reminded him only too well of Angie's older sister. "I think you're going to want to save your shower for later. Besides, there's no time. Can't you hear the sows squealing for their breakfast?"

Julian couldn't differentiate among the assorted animal noises he heard coming from the general direction of the barnyard. But Angie was used to listening for the pigs, and he took her word for it that they were hungry.

He got up and dressed—gingerly, because muscles in places where he hadn't even known he had muscles were crying out in agony—made a painful dash to the bathroom to brush his teeth and run a comb through his hair, then met Angie and Juno at the back porch.

Sometime during the night the rain had ceased. The sun had not yet climbed above the surrounding hills, but a gray light filled the humid air. It was early. So early, in fact, Carol wasn't even up yet and in the kitchen clattering pots and preparing breakfast.

"Here, put this on." Angie handed him an oversize hooded sweatshirt. "It'll be chilly till the sun's up. And you'd better borrow Dad's rubber boots. The mud'll be deep in the barnyard."

Julian sat down on the bench and pulled on the boots, wincing as he bent over, then looked up at Angie to ask, "Do you do this every morning before school?"

"Yep."

"And every Saturday and Sunday, and all summer long?"

"Yep. But I get to sleep in on weekends till seven-thirty."

"Seven-thirty, eh?"

"Well, the pigs've got to eat."

"Can't they be fed at some other, more civilized time of the day?"

"Sure, but this is the only free time I have till late afternoon, and they're used to being fed early."

"I thought feeder pigs ate all day, so they'll get fat for market?"

"The feeder pigs *do* eat all day, and I make sure their bins are always full. But the sows live in the old hay field by the barn most of the year and graze on grass and clover and alfalfa. If they ate corn all day like the feeder pigs, they'd get too fat to deliver babies."

"I see."

"But every morning I feed them corn to supplement their diets. That's why they're squealing now. They want their corn."

He stood up and gave her an admiring smile.

"You know so much about the animals. You're a remarkable young lady."

Angie shrugged, her cheeks pinkening prettily. "Everyone does their part on a farm. And taking care of the pigs is an important job. We make fifty thousand dollars a year just on the pigs."

Julian raised his brows. "Is that right?"

Angie shrugged again. "Dad says it's good for the farm and good for me, too. It teaches me responsibility, he says."

"Did Tilly used to take care of the pigs?"

"Yep. She taught me just about everything I know about them. She got up every single morning, just like I do, till she went away to college."

Julian's eyes crinkled with amusement. "And when you go off to college, I suppose that's the first break you'll get, too?"

Angie smiled back, her braces glinting in the porch light. "I get a break sometimes when Tilly comes home for a visit. She'll feed the pigs and I'll sleep in."

"How self-sacrificing of her," he observed with mild sarcasm. "I would think that Tilly would rather sleep in when she's away from her job and the bustle of the city."

"Oh, Tilly actually *enjoys* feeding the pigs," Angie said with a laugh. "She says it keeps her honest and down-to-earth."

"Talking about me, Ange?" came Tilly's voice from behind them. Julian turned to observe the starring figure in last night's dream. Well, at least the *other* starring figure in the dream.

"What are you doing up, McKinney?" he inquired, not sure if he was more happy or alarmed.

Either way, his heart had begun to jump around frantically like a frog in a bucket. She was wearing a T-shirt and jeans again, a combination lethal to his peace of mind.

Tilly reached for the Levi's jacket hanging on a hook on the wall and slipped into it. "I'm here to crack the whip, Rothwell. If I know Angie, she'll do all the work and let you just watch."

"Well, why not?" Angie said in a defensive tone that clearly implicated her. "I think he worked hard enough yesterday. He's not used to baling hay, and I'll bet his muscles hurt like the dickens."

"Do they, Rothwell?" Tilly asked him, her green eyes daring him to lie.

"Like the dickens," Julian admitted ruefully.

She smiled, seeming pleased by his honesty...and probably, too, by the fact that he was in exquisite pain. "Then it's a good thing you're up and around. Lying in bed would only make you stiff."

"Er...yes." Remembering his dream, he decided that was probably a most appropriate term.

"I'll make sure you work the kinks out."

"If only you could," he murmured.

She peered at him suspiciously, so he put on his blandest expression.

"I guess *I'm* not needed," Angie said with a pout, looking from her sister to him as they continued to stare at each other.

Tilly collected herself. "Oh, you're still welcome to come, Angie," she assured her. In fact Julian thought she sounded hopeful that Angie would stick around. Was she as nervous around him as he was around her? There was certainly reason to be.

Angie pondered for a minute, probably weighing

the novelty of seeing a duke feed pigs against the luxury of going back to bed for an hour or having a long bubble bath before school. In the end the duke didn't have a chance.

"Nah. If I'm not needed, I've got better things to do. See you guys later," Angie said cheerfully, her pique at having her authority usurped immediately forgotten. "Have fun!" Then she tossed off her coat and boots and headed inside without a backward glance, with Juno in close pursuit. Apparently the dog had better things to do, too.

"Ready, Rothwell?" Tilly asked him, tucking her hands in her pockets.

"As I'll ever be," he said with a sigh.

They crossed the damp lawn to an outbuilding by one of the barns that evidently served as a sort of garage for various farm vehicles and machines. Out of this, Tilly drove a tractor, instructing Julian to stand to the side.

He obeyed, but secretly wondered if being flattened by a tractor might be preferable to enduring another day with a woman with whom he continually argued, but for whom he still had "the hots," as the Americans liked to say.

Once Tilly had the tractor outside, they filled the bucket on the front with ground corn from a large mixer and dumped it over the side of the fence surrounding the pasture. Most of the sows were already waiting by the fence, and the rest came running on their stubby legs as soon as they heard the approaching tractor. The chorus of grunts and snorts as they enjoyed their breakfast reminded him of the dining hall at Eton when he was a student there.

"Count them, Rothwell. There should be thirty-five."

"Why?"

"Because if one's missing, she's probably somewhere in the pasture giving birth...or about to."

He grimaced. "You mean I might have to assist in delivering piglets?"

"If you're lucky."

They counted and they both came up with thirty-five sows. Julian couldn't have been more pleased. Delivering piglets was not a goal he strived for, especially so early in the day and just prior to eating bacon for breakfast.

Next they fed the swine that lived in a large barn that had one side open to a fenced-in dirt lot. Two groups of pigs of different sizes and weights shared the same barn and lot, the barn partitioned by a wooden wall and the lot partitioned by a fence. In the lot were self-feeding bins, and into the bins Tilly and Julian dumped more cornmeal.

"Angie never lets the bins get empty."

"Yes, so she said. And they're full to the brim again, so we're done...right?" Julian prompted, brushing his hands together. He was thinking the only really bad part about feeding the pigs was getting up so early. He was also thinking about the breakfast Carol was probably getting ready to put on the table about then, back at the house.

Tilly eyed him. He suspected she was trying to come up with a reason to keep him standing out there in the muddy barnyard, hungry and horny. He was right.

"Angie usually grinds the feed in the afternoon, or after dinner, but we probably ought to do it now."

"Now? Before breakfast? Why?"

"Because Dad wants to take you up to Dave's dairy farm to do a few chores later and plans to keep you there till dinner. After dinner, as you know, we're driving you back to Seattle to catch a plane in the morning. And I just can't bear the thought of you leaving our beautiful country without learning how to run a mixer mill."

Julian had hoped the flash of emotions he'd detected in her eyes earlier was regret that their time together was almost over, but now he suspected it was a gleam of vengeful anticipation.

"Won't your mother be waiting breakfast on us?"

"No. She'll just stick it in the oven to keep warm." She grinned. "Why, Rothwell? Has your zeal for proving your manhood as a superman on the farm front waned?"

"Of course not," he drawled, suppressing the urge to yank her into his arms and kiss that smart-alecky little smile off her face. "Lead on, slave driver."

She led and he followed to the mixer mill, which towered over them by several feet. By now the sun was up in a clear blue sky and beating down on his back and shoulders. By all indications, it was going to be a very warm day.

Julian took off his sweatshirt and tossed it into a nearby wheelbarrow. He was wearing a clean but faded blue T-shirt underneath, another loan from Jim, who seemed to have an endless supply. He was surprised but gratified when Tilly's gaze lingered on his chest. He would have been happy to return the compliment, but she was still wearing her Levi's jacket.

She caught him looking at her looking at him, and she immediately barked out like a drill sergeant, "All right, Rothwell, listen up. If you don't run this machine right, you could lose an arm.''

Rothwell listened, but it was hard. Tilly was standing close enough that he could smell her hair. It got easier to pay attention when she turned on the machine, and the loud grinding sound made his teeth rattle.

She showed him how to feed corn into the hopper and stand by to make sure the ears flowed freely. Julian stood by as he was told to, and was rewarded for his obedience by having his face frequently stung by flying bits of corn, while fine particles, like dust, began to stick to his perspiring brow. The whole tedious endeavor was about as pleasant as snapping oneself repeatedly with a rubber band.

By the time they were through, Julian was really famished. The only thing he might have enjoyed more than breakfast at that point was a shower to wash away the ground corn that had stuck to his face and powdered his hair.

But when he picked up his sweatshirt and started for the house, Tilly lagged behind. He turned around and found her still standing by the barn, looking flushed and indecisive.

''Aren't you coming?''

''No, you go ahead. I have one more thing to do.''

''All right.'' He wasn't going to argue with her. If he did, she might try to get him to help her with that ''one more thing.''

When he arrived at the house, the kitchen was empty but breakfast was warm and waiting in the oven. Next to his plate on the table, there was a folded note addressed to him from Tilly's father.

Julian,
Gone to town with Carol. Will return at noon
for lunch, then we'll head to Dave's. If Tilly's
let up on you for a few minutes, take a breather
and hike over to the swimming hole for a cool
dip or fishing. Poles on the porch. Ask Tilly for
directions, or if you don't dare for fear she'll
put you to work again, follow mine.

                                            Jim

Julian chuckled at Jim's humor. At the bottom of
the note, he'd drawn a simple map directing him to
the swimming hole, which was apparently fed by a
small stream that branched off the nearby Columbia
River. It was just over the hill behind the cow pasture
in what looked like a woodsy area. As a child in
Cornwall, he'd loved to swim in the tide pools that
collected in the sheltered coves near their cottage.
This promised to be just as novel and refreshing. And
a cool dip was never a bad idea these days.

He gulped down his breakfast in hopes of beating
it out of there before Tilly came in, grabbed the map
for reference if necessary and headed for the hills
behind the cow pasture.

TILLY WAS FLOATING on her back, minding her own
business, when a splash at the other end of the swimming hole alerted her to the fact that she was not
alone. Since she wasn't wearing a stitch of clothing,
this could prove to be problematic. She'd seen her
parents drive off in the truck an hour earlier, so who
was disturbing her peaceful swim? Who, besides her
family, would dare to use their private swimming
hole?

Making as little noise as possible, Tilly moved along the shore of the kidney-shaped pond, keeping close to vegetation to hide herself from view. In a place where the land jutted slightly out and the water was shallow enough for her feet to touch bottom, she peeked around some tall grass for a view of the other end of the pond where the intruder must have jumped in. She saw nothing. Nothing and no one who could have caused those ripples in the water...

Suddenly something surged out of the pond right in front of her...Julian. He opened his eyes, his lashes heavy with moisture and with water streaming down his face, shoulders and chest, seeming as startled to see her as she was to see him!

"You!" she exclaimed, bending her knees till the water came to just below her shoulders, and crossing her arms over her chest where miniwaves crested against her bare breasts. "Did you follow me?"

Julian stood erect, the water hitting him just above the waist to lap against his taut stomach muscles. He ran his fingers through his hair, slicking it back and away from his forehead. "I didn't follow you, McKinney," he growled. "I went back to the house and ate my breakfast."

"Then...then how did you know about—?"

"Your father left me a note, kindly advising me to take a breather from your whip cracking by visiting the family swimming hole. He even left me a map."

"That's my dad," Tilly mumbled. "Mr. Hospitality."

Julian chuckled, but Tilly thought he sounded as nervous as she felt. "What's the matter, Mathilda?

Not feeling as hospitable as your dad? Don't want to share your swimming hole?''

"Not with you," she snapped. "And if you'll let me by, I'll go get my clothes and towel and leave you alone to enjoy it by yourself."

His eyes flickered over her wet hair and bare shoulders. She saw his Adam's apple bob up and down as he swallowed. "You're completely naked, aren't you?" he croaked.

"I...I won't be for long," she assured him in a quavery voice. "Don't get your shorts in a knot over it."

"That's not a concern. I'm not wearing any shorts."

Tilly had suspected as much, but to know the bare truth—no pun intended—was more than a little disconcerting. Oh, lordy, why did he have to be so handsome, so sexy, so...so...*irresistible?*

"Tilly, I—" He reached out, his hand stopping just before his fingers touched her face. How she yearned for the feel of those fingers against her skin....

They stared at each other. Julian's gaze was a mixture of desire and apology. Hers probably was, too. They both knew what was going to happen and they had absolutely no control over it.

If a female reader had written a letter to Aunt Tilly and described how she'd found herself naked in a swimming hole with a man with whom she had no future—a man, moreover, with whom she traded barbs with the same regularity and fervor that a Wall Street wizard traded commodities—but had decided to remain in the pool with him and tempt fate, Aunt Tilly would have tagged her "a weak-willed ninny."

Okay, Tilly freely admitted it. She was weak-willed. She was a ninny. She didn't want to just tempt fate; she was begging for it to take over completely so she could finally do what she'd been wanting to do since the minute Julian Rothwell had walked into her office a week ago and dictated his first imperious order. And it would start now...with a touch.

He touched her. His fingers traced the curve of her cheek. She closed her eyes to savor the sensation, then reached up impulsively to draw his hand to her lips, kissing each of the curved knuckles with methodical reverence.

He took her gently by the shoulders and drew her out of the water till she was standing upright, her breasts cooled by the air, the nipples drawn up tightly and as hard as pebbles. She opened her eyes and saw him staring down at her. His lips were parted, his chest rising and falling with each quick breath.

His hands traveled up her shoulders, then cupped her skull at the nape of her neck, his thumbs caressing her cheeks and mouth. Her head lolled in his palms. She was enjoying the moment, enjoying the anticipation of what was coming.

"Tilly, you're so beautiful," he whispered. "I thought so that first day. You were on your knees, your head under your desk, searching for some silly Mickey Mouse pen."

"Goofy," she corrected breathlessly.

He raised one of those wicked brows of his. "You think I'm goofy?"

"No. The pen. It was—" She chuckled, her hands reaching up to circle his strong wrists. "Oh, never mind. Just tell me more about—" she smiled shyly

"—what you thought and how you felt when you first saw me."

He smiled down at her tenderly, his hands sliding down to her shoulders again to knead and caress. "Actions speak louder than words. Why don't I show you how I feel about you, Mathilda Jean?"

Chapter Thirteen

There were no more words.

He pulled her against his water-slick body and kissed her deeply and hard. She returned his kisses with equal fervor, the two of them clinging and caressing like desperate lovers who had been separated too long. It was as if a dam had broken and all the pent-up power released. They seemed to be drowning in their desire for each other. Overwhelmed. Overjoyed.

After they greedily plundered each other's mouths, Julian lifted her, dipped his head and took turns at each breast, teasing, nipping, sucking. Ah, the feel of him... The feel of his lips, his tongue. The feel of his hard, hot body against her skin. Tilly thought she might die from the sheer pleasure of it.

Then, when she was almost too weak to support herself, Julian cradled her in his arms and carried her to the nearest bank of the swimming hole, lifted her out and laid her gently down on the cool, green grass.

The hot sun warmed her till he covered her in the shadow of his long, beautiful body. Then *he* warmed her....

There was no leisurely foreplay, no murmured intimate questions and endearments. Somehow they each knew what the other wanted and couldn't wait to give and receive. Once, just after he entered her, he paused and they stared into each other's eyes, panting, straining, holding back for a single precious moment to convey feelings they didn't dare express out loud...or perhaps didn't even understand well enough to put into words.

He smiled at her. It was a small, crooked smile...almost a wince. She smiled back. A tear formed in the corner of her eye, then trickled down her cheek. She felt foolish. It was embarrassing to get so emotional, but she couldn't help it.

He kissed the track that single tear made down her cheek, then began to move inside her. She moved with him, meeting his rhythm perfectly, the tempo increasing, the tension building.

Their climaxes came quickly and together. She clutched his hair and cried out. He buried his face against her neck and whispered her name.

WITH HER HEAD NESTLED against his shoulder, her breath spilling over his chest, Tilly had fallen asleep like a trusting child. Julian lay on his back, one arm stretched above his head and bent at the elbow to serve as a pillow. The other arm was wrapped around Tilly's back.

Her arm rested on his chest, an open palm spread like a starfish over his flat nipple. Her legs were tangled with his, slim and smooth and quite simply made to be shown off in short skirts.

He smiled down at her, marveling that she could have dozed off so easily. He, too, had been content enough at first to fall asleep, but as each moment passed he'd felt more and more anxious.

What had he done? He had been so determined not to make love to her, but he had underestimated the strength of his desire. Hers, too. But the fact remained that he *had* made love to her...and she'd cried. It was a single tear, but there was revelation in that small salty drop. What exactly did it mean? Would he ever know?

Making love to Tilly had shattered all his previous theories about romance. With other women, the chase was the thing. Then once he'd captured and bedded the charming object of his pursuit, his interest ebbed. He'd had fairly long-term relationships before, of course, but none of them seemed to ring true or to satisfy after a while.

It was different with Tilly. Her responses were so pure, so honest, so open. And as soon it was over, he'd wanted to start again immediately. His desire for her wasn't curbed, but was made stronger by their lovemaking. So strong it scared him.

Good Lord...could he be in love with her?

Generally Julian used the good sense God gave him. But not with Tilly. He'd had plenty of warning that something like this might happen. He'd suspected early on that she was fully capable of leaving a lasting impact on his jaded heart. But instead of running away as he should have, he'd stayed and tortured them both.

It was torture because a relationship with Tilly quite simply couldn't work. Hadn't she said so herself? They were stripes and plaid, she'd said. They clashed.

But did they really clash, or had they simply gotten

off on a wrong foot and then kept up the sparring to fend off their mutual attraction? Were they just too stubborn to admit the truth…that they actually cared for each other?

But how could he ever ask her to leave her country, her family, her *home?* She was a woman of strong attachments. Was there anything in England that could possibly make up for what she'd lose by trading her small, cozy apartment for a huge mansion full of heirlooms but no family and no nearby neighbors?

Suddenly Julian heard Jim's truck coming up the lane, the gears shifting down as the vehicle approached the house. Tilly must have heard it, too, because she woke up abruptly.

"It's my parents," she whispered, instantly alert and in panic mode. "Oh, my gosh, we'd better get dressed. It's not like they think I've never had sex, but I certainly don't want to confirm their suspicions!"

Julian laughed, grateful for a reprieve from his serious thoughts. They rushed to find their clothes and put them on as quickly as possible. Watching Tilly's beautiful body disappear from view was maddening, frustrating. He had a horrible feeling he'd never see her again as he'd seen her that day. Gloriously naked, passionate and his. *All his.*

When they were completely dressed and had assured each other about the decency of their appearances, they walked back to the house. Their plan was for Julian to enter the house first to enthuse over his dip in the family swimming hole, and Tilly would come in a few minutes later, claiming to have been exploring favorite haunts around the farm.

Julian wasn't sure what Jim and Carol suspected about their relationship, but he was just as eager as Tilly to keep speculation at a minimum. Hell, *he* wasn't even sure what was going on! And Tilly had been so anxious to keep her parents in the dark about their tryst at the swimming hole, they hadn't had a chance to talk and he couldn't even guess what she was thinking or feeling about what had happened between them. Possibly she was as confused as he was.

If Jim and Carol suspected something, they pretended not to. The day continued as planned, with Julian spending most of the afternoon at Dave's dairy farm and Tilly remaining behind at the house. He'd enjoyed Dave's enthusiastic tour of the farm and Lisa's quiet contentment as she waited for the "blessed event." Her rhubarb pie wasn't half-bad, either. All in all, though, he certainly didn't do much work, which left him more time to think.

Before Julian knew it, it was time to return to Seattle. As he and Tilly prepared for departure, Julian suspected he felt as sad as she did about saying good-bye. Or maybe even more sad. The thing was, she'd be coming back. He wouldn't.

"I don't care what Tilly says about you," Angie informed him as she gave him a big hug on the porch where they'd all congregated, "I *like* you."

Julian laughed and slid an amused look toward Tilly, but she averted her eyes. She'd been doing that ever since his return from Dave's. She hadn't even quizzed him about how hard he'd worked, and had acted distant throughout dinner. Was she embarrassed that they'd made love? Angry? Distressed? Ashamed?

"I like you, too, Julian," Carol assured him. She

hugged him, then whispered in his ear so low no one else could possibly hear, "Remember what I told you about Tilly. She's a skeptic. She needs time to assimilate things. Time to *believe*."

Julian didn't have a chance to respond to Carol's advice, and he wasn't sure how to apply it, either. His emotions were as new to him and as befuddled as Tilly's probably were. The only solution to his confused state would be to have a long talk with the source of his confusion, one Mathilda Jean McKinney. He looked forward to getting her alone in the car. As the sun set over the beautiful mountain ranges they'd pass, hopefully they'd work things out.

After a firm handshake and a hearty slap on the back from Jim, Julian finally climbed into the driver's seat of the Jeep, Tilly got in on the passenger's side and they headed down the lane, then over to the highway and to the nearest freeway on-ramp. Once they were zipping along Interstate 5 toward Seattle, Julian turned to Tilly and said, "We need to talk."

But she didn't reply. She was asleep.

Or pretending to be.

TILLY WASN'T SURE if she could pull it off, but she was determined to try. She knew that her alter ego, Aunt Tilly, would disapprove highly of faking sleep to avoid a necessary confrontation. She'd say she was "showing the backbone of a jellyfish" and simply delaying the inevitable. But Tilly couldn't bear the thought of Julian giving her the "it was just something that happened, it was nice, you're a great girl and I'll always remember you" speech, then having to be imprisoned in the car with him for two hours.

Oh, sure, he'd be kind. She'd learned that Julian was, at heart, a kind man. But there was no getting around the fact that he was a duke and she was a nobody. Some things hadn't changed all that much since the Victorian age. In the nineteenth century chambermaids and governesses didn't marry peers of the realm, and in the twentieth century dukes— whose rank was only one notch below royalty—simply didn't embark on lasting relationships with nobodies.

So she pretended to be asleep, even though sleeping was the last thing she was capable of doing at the moment. Her mind was a jumble of thoughts. Her heart was a jumble of feelings.

And there was no use in denying it any longer. She was in love with Julian.

If Tilly weren't pretending to be asleep, she'd have laughed hysterically. She'd never been in love in her life, and when she finally succumbed to the malady, it had to be with a duke, for crying out loud! Why couldn't she have fallen in love with a farmer, a veterinarian or even a sports writer? Why couldn't she have fallen in love with a man where there was a chance he might actually love her back?

Ah, but at least she had memories, wonderful memories of arguing and laughing and making love. She'd told him once that they were stripes and plaid, incompatible. Although *he* probably still believed they were incompatible, she didn't anymore. As a man and a woman, she thought they suited each other to a tee. They complemented each other like two disparate spices that, when mixed together, made one mouthwatering dish.

The trouble wasn't between them or inside them. The trouble was *outside* them, in the circumstances of their stations in life, in the way they'd lived their lives so far and in the way they expected to continue to live their lives.

For a relationship between them to work, they'd each have to make adjustments and compromises. Julian knew it, and so did Tilly. But it was a fact much easier for Julian to accept than Tilly...because Julian wasn't in love with her. After all, if he had those sorts of feelings for her, wouldn't he have said so by now?

All things considered, it was probably a good thing that he wasn't in love with her, Tilly reasoned, trying to see the practical side even while she fought back tears. If he loved her as much as she loved him, they'd have to find a way to make things work. They'd have to be together, no matter what. In Tilly's estimation it would be well worth the trouble and actually kind of exciting to embark on such an adventure together, but she could only assume that Julian thought differently.

Tilly turned her head toward the window to hide a bittersweet smile. It was startling to realize the strength of her feelings. She was a smart and savvy advice columnist who'd spent years counseling her readers to do the practical thing, but she was willing to do absolutely anything, to make any sacrifice, for love.

TILLY KEPT her eyes closed till they were a block from the hotel. Stretching and yawning, she made a halfway convincing show of waking up from a sound sleep. But Julian wasn't deceived, and by now he was damned mad.

Why didn't she have the courage to talk to him, to give him the brush-off speech to his face? *You're a royal pain in the rear, Rothwell,* she'd have said, *but not too bad in the sack. That thing that happened at the swimming hole between us was nice, but it was something that just…well…happened. You know how it is. Have a great life. Bye now.*

Didn't he deserve at least that much? he fumed to himself.

"We're already here?" Tilly said in a groggy voice. "Goodness, time goes by fast when you're down for the count."

Julian pulled up in front of the Royal Covington, but waved away the approaching bellman. He was going to have his talk with Tilly whether she was willing or not.

"Will you come in for a few minutes, Tilly? We need to talk." He faced forward and waited for the expected response.

"I don't know, Julian. It's kind of late."

He turned to face her, his expression grim. "I was sure you'd chicken out."

She stiffened. "What do you mean?"

"It's only eight o'clock."

"Can't a girl just want to go home and curl up with a good book? Jeez, men are so egotistical!"

"Is that your professional opinion, Aunt Tilly?" Julian inquired sarcastically. "Or are you talking specifically about me? I wasn't planning on seducing you, if that's what you're afraid of."

"I'm not afraid of anything," Tilly lied. "I don't

want to fight, Julian. And I don't want to talk. What's the point? You're going home to England tomorrow."

"That I'm going home tomorrow precisely *is* the point. This is goodbye, Tilly! This is it! This might be the last time we ever see each other. We made love. How do you feel about that? What do you think? Hell, don't you have *anything* to say to me?"

Tilly remained silent. What could she say without revealing how very much she loved him? All she'd accomplish would be to make him feel guilty about "lovin' her and leavin' her," as the cliché went. There was no point in making him as miserable as she was. If she only knew what he wanted her to say, she'd say it in a heartbeat.

Tilly thought for a minute, then decided that maybe he already felt a little guilty and was hoping she'd say something to get him off the hook. Something to reassure him that she wasn't going to pine away for him after he was gone, ruined for all other men. Okay, she could do that. It would be a stretch, but Tilly was willing to do and say whatever made him happy.

"Julian..."

"I'm listening."

She braced herself and met his eyes. Those lovely, brilliant blue eyes. How she would miss them, and the man who went with them! She sighed, then began, "We've had an interesting few days together."

"To say the least," he murmured.

"And you acquitted yourself well at my dad's farm."

His beautiful mouth quirked in a coy smile. "Are you talking about my work in the hay fields or...?"

She felt herself blushing. She didn't want to think about their lovemaking, because it only made her ache to hold him again. She could barely resist touching him now, and all day long, whenever he'd been near, it had been a struggle to keep her hands to herself. That's why she'd kept her distance. Touching could lead to something more, and making love again would only make the final parting even more painful.

"Let's just say you acquitted yourself on *all* counts," she admitted with a shy, rueful smile in return.

His smile fell away. He searched her eyes. "But...?"

"There are no *but*s about it. It was great, Julian. I'll always remember our...our time together. But now we have to go on with our lives. Our *separate* lives."

Julian gazed at her, sick at heart. She'd said exactly what he was afraid she'd say, the words almost verbatim.

"So...no letters, no phone calls?" he said dully.

"Right," she answered with a shrug. "I mean...what's the point?"

Julian felt as though he'd been punched in the stomach. Her disinterest in continuing their relationship somehow drove home stronger than ever the fact that he loved her. And there lay the greatest irony of all. He'd finally found someone to love, and she didn't love him back. He guessed it was one of those little jokes life played on you now and then.

Hell, maybe there was something to the way his father had conducted his life, after all—aloof, his heart locked away and protected against pain. If only

Julian had conducted himself the same way, he wouldn't be hurting like hell now. But at least there was pride left. Thank God he hadn't revealed his own feelings.

"Well, I'm glad we cleared the air," Julian said briskly. "I would have felt like a heel if you'd somehow read something more into our lovemaking than I did."

"Yes, I'm glad we talked," Tilly agreed in the same brisk tone. "You were right. It's better to be up front about our feelings so there's no misunderstandings."

"And now we understand each other perfectly...right?"

"Perfectly," she agreed with a smile that seemed to strain every muscle in her face.

He stared at her. "Then I guess this is goodbye."

She nodded, her throat aching so hard she could barely speak above a whisper. "Yes, goodbye, Julian. Take care. And do say hello to Emma and Brian when you see them. Wish them the best for me."

Julian nodded, opened the door and stepped out. While Tilly moved over to the driver's seat, Julian retrieved his suitcase from the back of the Jeep and handed it to the hovering bellman. Julian walked to the revolving doors, then turned to wave. Tilly waved back, forced another smile as she choked back tears, then started the engine and drove off.

But in the rearview mirror she saw Julian again. For some reason he'd walked back to the curb to see her off, one hand raised high above his head in a final farewell. She swiped away the tears and kept her eyes glued to that mirror as his image got smaller and smaller, then finally disappeared.

Chapter Fourteen

"Here's your tea, Tilly. Just the way you like it. Earl Grey, two sugars, no cream. Can I get you anything else?"

Tilly lifted her eyes from the letter she was reading, one of the many requests for advice that had come in the mail that afternoon. She smiled. "No, thanks, Amy. But stand at alert, will ya? I might need another cup in a few minutes. I've got to stay late tonight to finish up some work."

Amy set the large foam cup on a tiny, uncluttered corner of Tilly's desk and stood with her hands folded demurely in front of her. "Why don't you just drink coffee like you used to?" she asked. "It'd give you a better buzz and help you through a bushel of paperwork."

"I still drink coffee in the mornings," Tilly replied a little defensively, returning her gaze to the letter she held. "It's just that in the afternoon I've found tea to be more refreshing."

"I'll bet the duke converted you," Amy suggested saucily. "Have you heard from him since he went back to England a couple of weeks ago?"

"Amy, I thought you said John was waiting for you to pick up some stuff he needs to have faxed right away?" Tilly said without lifting her head.

"Oh, yeah. Right. See you later, Tilly. Holler when you want that tea."

After Amy left the room and closed the door behind her, Tilly dropped the letter to the pile in front of her and rubbed her weary eyes with the heels of her hands.

Three weeks. He'd been gone three weeks, not just a couple. And Tilly was still dreaming about him, still missing him. Her life seemed to have lost its spark since he'd gone. Oh, she still did things with her friends, had been on a couple of dates, had even been down to see her folks again. But it had been a struggle to appear happy all the time. Her parents hadn't asked any questions about her sometimes listless behavior, though, so maybe she'd pulled it off without tipping her hand.

She knew the old adage "Time heals all wounds" applied to her and to this situation just as well as it did to other people and other situations. Hadn't she quoted those very words to her readers over and over again? But what were you supposed to do to help you through the pain while you were healing?

Since losing her heart to Julian, Tilly commiserated more with her readers. It took longer to do a column, to dish out advice with the same cheerful confidence. Because now she knew firsthand how hard it was to do the right thing, the smart thing, when your heart was telling you to do something else entirely.

Many times she'd considered calling him, writing

him a note. But they'd agreed not to do that. And it would be foolish to do so, anyway. The fact still remained that he didn't have the same feelings for her that she had for him. As Aunt Tilly herself once advised her readers, "There's no use chasing a man who doesn't want to get caught. All you'll end up with are blisters and corns, a bruised ego and a broken heart."

Tilly truly believed that advice and she was going to stick by it come hell or high water. Someday she'd feel normal again. Someday she'd be over the duke. Someday—

"Tilly? Sorry to interrupt again."

Tilly had been staring into space and was startled to see Amy's head poking around the door. "Oh, Amy. What is it? It's too soon for more tea. I haven't even—"

"I know. I just thought I'd better drop this by." She came in and handed Tilly another letter. "It's certified."

"Certified?"

"Yep. That means it's important, right? Hadn't you better open it?"

Tilly looked at the letter—addressed in her mother's handwriting to "Aunt Tilly"—and at the return address. Sure enough, it was from Washougal. She grabbed her letter opener and slit the envelope. "Thanks, Amy," she said with a smile, but in a politely dismissive tone. Amy nodded, obviously still curious, and reluctantly left the room.

Tilly was more intrigued than alarmed by what the contents of the letter might be. She knew her folks could easily get hold of her at work or at home if there was an emergency in the family. And why was her mother writing to Aunt Tilly? Curiouser and curiouser. Maybe it was just a joke. Left alone, she unfolded the letter and began to read.

Dear Aunt Tilly,

I've never allowed myself to be a meddling mother, but sometimes you just can't keep quiet any longer. You see, I've got a beautiful, smart, talented daughter who's acting like she hasn't got a brain cell to spare. Three weeks ago she brought a good-looking man to the house to work with her father on the farm. There was some deal between them about him proving he could work hard without the help of his ever present staff. Well, he could work, all right, and he proved it. And since the man is probably richer than JFK Jr. and twice as handsome, he could easily have been the high-and-mighty type who felt no need to prove himself to anyone.

During the two days he spent with the family, he was a pleasure to be around, as undemanding, polite and down-to-earth as he could be. He fit right in with the family, having the same values we do of love of land, of tradition, of family, of learning, and love of a good plateful of plain and simple country cooking. I could see from the moment they arrived that he and my daughter had eyes for each other, but neither of them wanted to believe it or admit it. They scrapped constantly, but neither of them would let the other out of sight. It was clearly a case of love. Sometimes the way he'd look at her made me want to cry...you know, like mothers do. But by the last day, it was plain they'd fought or maybe got a little too close and were scared.

Next thing I knew, the guy had gone back to his home clear across the Atlantic Ocean and my daughter was sulking around like she'd lost her best friend. In my opinion she had. Pride or stubbornness or a misunderstanding had played a part in this split between them, but what's really aggravating about this whole thing is that they're still apart! Maybe my daughter thinks he doesn't love her—he does—maybe she thinks they're too different—they're as alike as two peas in a pod—or maybe she's just too scared to take a chance. Whatever the reason, it isn't good enough to justify the continued suffering I know they're both enduring.

What do you think I should do, Aunt Tilly? I kind of think they both need a good swift kick in the behind, but my daughter's the only one close enough to reach with my boot. Maybe if they just communicated... It's a novel idea, I know, but the results are sometimes as magical as a pumpkin turning into a coach. I just want my daughter to be as happy as I am. I don't think guys like this one come along more than once in a lifetime.

Please advise, Aunt Tilly. And remember...
I love you, Mathilda Jean.
Put on your rose-colored

glasses, because this time
the fairy tale's for real.

Mom

Tilly pressed the letter to her chest, tears welling in her eyes, her lips curved in a tentative smile. Could it be possible? Could her mother be right? Did Julian love her? Or was her mother just seeing things like a mother would, all wishful and dewy eyed and prejudiced?

"Tilly?"

Tilly startled and blinked back the embarrassing tears. Through a blur she saw Amy standing at the door again. "Amy? What now?"

Amy came in. "I've got another certified letter for you."

Tilly sat up straighter and immediately dropped her mother's letter to reach for the one Amy held out with a coy, sort of knowing smile on her face. "Another one?"

"And this one's from England."

Tilly's heart started beating like a jackhammer. She took the letter and stared at it till her blurry vision cleared. It was addressed to Aunt Tilly just like her mother's was. It was a bit of a disappointment when the return address didn't read "Chesterfield Hall, Dorset" but instead was from somewhere in Derbyshire, but she quickly recovered and split the envelope with her letter opener.

Tilly looked up and was grateful that Amy had slipped out this time without having to resort to hints to get rid of her. She unfolded the letter and began to read. The letter was from Emma!

Dear Aunt Tilly,

I'm writing to thank you for the good advice you gave both me and Brian. We couldn't be happier! I can't believe we wasted so much time by keeping feelings to ourselves. I'm also writing to ask your advice about a friend. Actually it's the man I once thought I was in love with before I understood my true feelings for Brian. It's easy to see how I could have been confused, of course, because this other man I thought I was in love with is the very best sort of person you'd ever want to meet. The trouble is, most people get a wrong impression of him at first. Sometimes he comes across proud and haughty, but inside he's anything but. It takes him a while to get close to people, but once he's taken a liking to someone, he's as steadfast in his affections as can be.

Lately, however, he's been very glum. Since his return to England, Brian and I have seen him on several occasions, and while to most people he appears unchanged, we've noted a marked difference. And we ought to know, because we spent years actually living in the same house with him. I think I know what's wrong, but I'm not sure how to handle it. I don't want to offend him, but I do want to help him. And you taught me, Aunt Tilly, to be brave when it's so very important to fix something.

You see, I believe this man is in love with someone, but has decided it's a hopeless case. From what Brian and I have been able to observe, we don't think the case is at all hopeless.

We think she loves him as much as he loves her.

What do you suggest we do, Aunt Tilly? Would it be awfully interfering of us to write this woman a letter and tell her what we think? Please advise.

And do plan on attending our wedding in August.

Love,

Emma

Tilly stood up and began to pace the floor, full of energy, full of hope, a smile splitting her face from ear to ear. Oh, joyful day, Julian was *glum!* Could it be possible, could he truly love her?

"Tilly?"

This time Tilly wasn't surprised to see Amy at her door. She strode quickly across the room, held out her hand and cheerfully demanded, "Okay, where's my next letter? By the way, Amy, is this some sort of a conspiracy and you're the double agent? Who are you working for, anyway?"

Amy giggled and slapped the sealed, certified envelope into Tilly's palm. "Happy reading," she chirped as she ducked out, shutting the door behind her.

Tilly eagerly looked for the return address, and this time it was the one she'd been hoping for—Chesterfield Hall, Dorset. But she made herself sit down and take a deep breath before opening it. She also told herself that the letter might be from Mrs. Peevey, not Julian. Thus having reasoned with and prepared herself, she opened the letter with fingers that trembled just as violently as before.

The address on the outer envelope had been typed, but inside the writing was done in longhand. She recognized Julian's elegant script immediately.

Dear Aunt Tilly,

I never thought I'd find myself writing to an advice column for guidance. But then, life sometimes throws curves. I've heard you're very good. In fact it seems at least four of my friends owe their present happiness to your meddling...er...I mean advice. But seeing my friends happy makes me all the more miserable myself.

You see, Aunt Tilly, three weeks ago I met and fell in love with the most wonderful, the most irritating, the most beautiful, the most maddening female in the world. Trouble is, I didn't tell her. I was under the impression that she didn't return my tender feelings, but that shouldn't have stopped me from expressing my own. I didn't want to hurt my "pride." Because of this sniveling bit of cowardice, I've wondered ever since if there might have been a chance for us. My friends, and even this female's mother— who is as charming as the woman I love, and not nearly as prickly—have threatened to interfere if I don't do something right away.

But you see, Aunt Tilly, I had decided to write to you long before my friends and my future mother-in-law—I hope—demanded action. It's just that I've written and rewritten so many versions of this letter, I've filled several trash bins at Chesterfield Hall to overflowing and have incurred the wrath of my fastidious butler, Henchpenny, so that he no longer brings me my evening glass of brandy without being asked.

Mentioning Henchpenny brings me to another point of concern I have. My life is quite different from the life the woman I love enjoys in an American city. She is surrounded by friends and family, and I've wondered if—in the happy event that I can convince her to marry me—I have any right to ask her to leave it all behind. But not being without sufficient funds, I am in a position to fly her home frequently for visits, and to fly her entire family out here for holidays whenever I can lure them away from their delightful home in a quaintly named farming community of Washougal. And God willing, I hope we'll be able to begin our own family soon enough....

What do you think, Aunt Tilly? Should I lay my stuffy old English pride on the line and tell this woman how much I adore her? Please advise, and do it soon because I can't wait much longer. I miss her.

Sincerely,

Julian Rothwell,
Duke of Chesterfield

By the way, will you marry me? If you have an answer I might like, please meet me in the downstairs foyer. I'll be the one with the stiff upper lip—that is, till I see you. Then I'll be smiling my fool head off.

Tilly wasted no time. She threw the letter on the desk and flew out of the room, leaving her office door flung open behind her like a gaping mouth.

Speaking of gaping mouths, there were plenty of those scattered among the office staff as she weaved in and out of cubicles in a mad dash for the stairs. There was no way she was going to wait for some poky elevator!

As she sprinted down the steps two at a time, she looked down at her bare knees showing below a recently purchased denim miniskirt and laughed out loud. Wouldn't he be smug when he found out he'd converted her to skirts *and* Earl Grey tea!

After running down twelve flights of stairs, she reached ground zero considerably out of breath. She leaned against the wall just outside the door to the stairwell, waiting for her breathing to return to normal and wondering for the first time if she'd combed her hair recently or applied lipstick. She hadn't given a single thought to her appearance and was considering a detour to a nearby ladies' room when…she saw him.

Dressed in a heather gray suit, he leaned against the opposite wall with his arms folded over his chest, facing the elevator. Tilly's heart filled with joy as she feasted her eyes on that beautiful patrician profile again, that glorious golden hair. Oh, how she'd missed him! He'd been right about the stiff upper lip. He wasn't smiling, and his expression was so intense, so expectant, so *worried* as he searched every group that stepped off the elevator.

Suddenly Tilly didn't care about how she looked. All she wanted to do was erase that worried look from his face and watch him "smile his fool head off."

She began to cross the lobby, slowly, tentatively. Halfway there he turned and saw her. She stopped in her tracks, suddenly shy. But then he smiled. He unfolded his arms and held them out to her, and Tilly ran to him like some heroine in a corny forties flick.

"Tilly," he groaned into her hair as he held her fiercely against him, her feet dangling inches above the floor. "Oh, Lord, girl, I've missed you so much."

Tilly was laughing and crying at the same time. She kissed his face a dozen times before he set her down on the ground again, then they kissed for real.

Tilly was in heaven. The kiss was everything she remembered and more, because now she knew how he felt about her. Now she knew he loved her as much as she loved him. It gave the kiss—which was as sexy as ever—an added emotional dimension.

How could such a wonderful thing be happening? she wondered as he continued to hold her and kiss her despite the busy comings and goings of crowds in the lobby. She was Cinderella at the ball. She was Michael Jordan at the NBA playoffs. She was Meryl Streep at the Oscars. She wasn't a nobody. She was a *somebody*. And Julian Rothwell loved her just for herself.

They drew slightly apart—her hands locked behind his neck, his hands locked and resting in the small of her back—and simply basked in each other's smiles.

"Are you taking me to dinner, Rothwell? I'm suddenly starved."

"If I feed you, will you marry me?"

She gave a coy roll of her shoulder. "Is Dunbar outside in the limo, waiting to whisk us off to some elegant restaurant?"

"Dunbar's in the limo, yes, and eager to see you. But I'll have hell to pay with Mrs. Peevey—or rather, Mrs. Dunbar, I can't get used to that—if I don't bring you back willy-nilly to my suite in the Royal Covington to partake of the gourmet meal she's presently preparing for you. I'll have to take you to an elegant restaurant tomorrow night. Then, the day after and no later—on orders from your father—I'm to bring you down to Washougal for an engagement party."

"Was I the only one left out of this conspiracy?" Tilly demanded with a chuckle.

"You had to be. We were all plotting against you."

"And you've done a marvelous job of it. I had no idea what I was up against."

Julian lifted an imperious brow. "You haven't answered my question yet, Mathilda. You keep skirting the issue, but—"

"Oh, did you notice my skirt, Julian?"

"Of course I did," he growled, pulling her closer. "Your legs are as luscious as ever. But, Tilly, I want an answer. My great-grandmother's wedding ring is burning a hole in my pocket!"

Tilly's eyes widened. "Your great-grandmother's ring! Oh, Julian, let me see—"

"You won't see it till you give me an answer,

Tilly. Or must I coax you with another kiss?'' He nuzzled her neck.

Tilly giggled with delight. "Well, I had to confer with wise old Aunt Tilly, of course—"

"And just what did Aunt Tilly say, you exasperating little brat?" Julian demanded, his brilliant blue eyes gleaming like jewels. Tilly could tell he was about out of patience, which proved it was still as fun as ever teasing him.

She stroked his lapel and grinned up at him. "Well, she said I'd be a 'blamed fool' to pass up a great guy like you. Not to mention being rich and titled and too handsome for his own good."

He slapped her lightly on the bottom. "So, you're marrying me for my money, eh, baggage?"

She cuddled closer. "No, Julian Rothwell. I'm marrying you because I love you. Now shut up and kiss me."

Disregarding the setting of a precedent he might regret at a later date, he did exactly as she ordered. He kissed her.

Take 2 bestselling love stories FREE

Plus get a FREE surprise gift!

*For a limited time, Harlequin and Silhouette
have an offer you just can't refuse.*

In November and December 1998:

BUY **ANY** TWO HARLEQUIN
OR SILHOUETTE BOOKS and
SAVE $10.00
off future purchases

OR BUY ANY THREE HARLEQUIN OR SILHOUETTE BOOKS
AND **SAVE $20.00** OFF FUTURE PURCHASES!

(each coupon is good for $1.00 off the purchase of two
Harlequin or Silhouette books)

JUST BUY 2 HARLEQUIN OR SILHOUETTE BOOKS, SEND US YOUR
NAME, ADDRESS AND 2 PROOFS OF PURCHASE (CASH REGISTER
RECEIPTS) AND HARLEQUIN WILL SEND YOU A COUPON BOOKLET
WORTH **$10.00 OFF** FUTURE PURCHASES OF HARLEQUIN OR
SILHOUETTE BOOKS IN 1999. SEND US 3 PROOFS OF PURCHASE AND
WE WILL SEND YOU 2 COUPON BOOKLETS WITH A TOTAL **SAVING OF
$20.00.** (ALLOW 4-6 WEEKS DELIVERY) OFFER EXPIRES
DECEMBER 31, 1998.

I accept your offer! Please send me a coupon booklet(s), to:

NAME: _____

ADDRESS: _____

CITY: _____ STATE/PROV.: _____ POSTAL/ZIP CODE: _____

Send your name and address, along with your cash register
receipts for proofs of purchase, to:

In the U.S.	**In Canada**
Harlequin Books	**Harlequin Books**
P.O. Box 9057	**P.O. Box 622**
Buffalo, NY	**Fort Erie, Ontario**
14269	**L2A 5X3**

PHQ4982

COMING NEXT MONTH
Christmas Is For Kids

#753 SMOOCHIN' SANTA by Jule McBride
The Little Matchmaker
Little Christy Holt was the wiliest seven-year-old to hit Mistletoe Mountain in years. Within minutes of having pregnant cabbie Nikki Ryder drive her to Jon Sleet's mountain retreat, she'd created a crazy story that Jon was her father...and just by looking at her, Nikki could tell that the child wanted to create a ready-made family by Christmas.

#754 BABY'S FIRST CHRISTMAS by Cathy Gillen Thacker
The ordinarily calm ER doctor Michael Sloane broke a sweat when he met Kate Montgomery...and saw her belly full of his baby. He'd never expected the frisson of longing to be a father that zinged through his heart, nor the instant attraction to the very pregnant Kate. Darned if he didn't want to be a daddy and a husband to her by Christmas.

#755 COWBOY SANTA by Judy Christenberry
When cowboy Sam Crawford played Santa for the kids of Saddle, Wyoming, he thought it his duty to be sure the kids got their wishes. Most especially when the son of that knockout newcomer Joni Evans asked Santa for a horse, a train...and a daddy!

#756 GIFT-WRAPPED DAD by Muriel Jensen
Janie Cummings and her baby brother knew the moment Joe Carpenter walked into their mother's bed-and-breakfast that he was Santa's "gift" to them. Now if they could just convince their mother, Maribeth, that she needed him....

AVAILABLE THIS MONTH:

#749 IF WISHES WERE... DADDIES
Jo Leigh

#750 SIGN ME, SPEECHLESS IN SEATTLE
Emily Dalton

#751 SHE'S HAVING HIS BABY
Linda Randall Wisdom

#752 DOORSTEP DADDY
Linda Cajio

Look us up on-line at: http://www.romance.net